He was regarding her with a look she could not begin to decipher.

Before she guessed what he was about, she was in his arms and he was kissing her. Kissing her! And thoroughly, too, in ways she'd never imagined that kisses could be. Time stopped, moons and planets ground to a halt, and her mind spun away, leaving the rest of her to revel in her first taste of bliss.

When he finally let her go and stepped away, she could only gaze blankly at him. Bewildered, bedazzled, she saw him swing onto his horse and look back at her with a smile on the lips she wished were still pressed to hers. . . .

By Lynn Kerstan
Published by Fawcett Books:

FRANCESCA'S RAKE
A MIDNIGHT CLEAR
CELIA'S GRAND PASSION
LUCY IN DISGUISE

LUCY IN DISGUISE

Lynn Kerstan

FAWCETT CREST • NEW YORK

A Fawcett Crest Book
Published by The Ballantine Publishing Group
Copyright © 1998 by Lynn Kerstan Horobetz

http://www.randomhouse.com

Library of Congress Catalog Card Number: 98-92820

ISBN 0-449-00184-9

Manufactured in the United States of America

First Edition: August 1998

10 9 8 7 6 5 4 3 2 1

For Diane Hayward,
in celebration of friendship,
good times, and her excellent advice:
"Lynn, you should write a romance novel!"

Chapter 1

Late on a moonless night, a luminous figure walked the high cliff overlooking Morecambe Bay.

Below, the tide was out. Starlight glittered on the rivulets of water left on the beach, silver ribbons across dark sand, soon obscured as clouds scudded overhead.

In the far distance, Lucy Jennet Preston saw faint golden lights.

Cocklers, perhaps, or mussel diggers. But she doubted it.

She dropped to her belly and slithered to the edge of the cliff. The lights, four of them, moved steadily inland, and she guessed them to be half-shuttered lanterns. For a time she thought they were headed directly toward her, and then she decided they were angled slightly south. It was impossible to be sure.

Ought she to stand again and hope to frighten them away? That was, after all, the whole point of being an apparition. But she held in place, watching the dim lights come ever closer, debating her next move. If they had some other destination in mind, the last thing she wanted to do was call attention to this one.

Suddenly there were more lights, six or seven brighter ones, surrounding the four she had been tracking. Lanterns snapped open—at a signal, most likely—to reveal the silhouettes of a horse and wagon, two more animals laden with wide panniers, and nearly a dozen men.

What in blazes was going on? She could see only shadowy figures illuminated by flickering red-gold light. For a minute or two no one moved. Then the donkeys were led away in a northerly direction.

Three men stood near the horse and wagon, which was piled high with what she supposed to be boxes. One man reached out, and for a moment he seemed to be struggling with the horse. She heard a sharp sound, like a crack of distant thunder, and three men broke into a run. All were carrying the shuttered lanterns, and they aimed themselves south toward Jenny Brown's Point.

Meanwhile the bright lanterns went quickly in the direction in which the donkeys had been taken. One lantern lay abandoned on the sand near the wagon.

Whatever had transpired down there appeared to be over. The men were soon out of sight, but she waited and watched for a long time in case they returned for the horse and cargo they had left behind.

The horse!

By now the wagon wheels were probably sinking into the muddy sand. The few times she had wandered any distance from the shore, Lucy had found that it didn't do to stand in one place for very long. Should the stranded animal fail to pull the wagon free very soon, it was surely doomed.

Lucy scrambled to her feet, sighing. However diligently one planned, something always came along to throw a spanner in the works. She didn't even *like* horses.

Grumbling, she stripped off her costume and rolled it into a tight bundle. If she had to go out on the sands, she would do better wearing only her shirt and trousers.

How she would unhook the horse from the wagon she had no idea. With any luck, not that she ever had much of it, there would be only a few buckles to unloose. Otherwise she could only hope that the wagon had settled on a patch of hard sand, making it possible to lead the horse and wagon to safety.

She ran the short distance to Cow's Mouth Inlet, where a steep path wound down from the cliff to the beach. A flat rock jutting from the limestone headland marked the place to start.

Stashing her costume on a ledge beneath the rock, Lucy began the precipitous descent.

In the dark she had to go by feel alone, but she'd made the trip any number of times in the past few days. She always told herself it was like climbing a tree and tried not to notice when pebbles dislodged by her boots clattered down the cliffside and landed with a hollow thud.

Grasping for handholds, she lowered herself bit by bit until her feet touched the ground of the inlet. From there, the sands were invisible. She followed the narrow break in the cliff around a curve to the shoreline and aimed herself toward the lantern. At ground level, she could barely make it out.

The air was charged with electricity. It caused the hair at her nape to spring out, as it always did just before a storm. Overhead, the clouds were rolling in, sometimes releasing fat drops of rain. Only now and again could she glimpse a few stars winking in the black night, and soon they disappeared altogether.

Once her boot sank ankle-deep in a gully of soft sand, and for several terrifying moments she was not at all sure she would be able to wrench it out. But it finally popped free and from then on she moved more slowly, taking care to avoid any spot where water had pooled.

Robbie had warned her that the sands were treacherous. When the tide turned, a high wave would sweep into the bay with the speed of a galloping horse. Perhaps she ought to have paid more attention to the schedule he provided her, but until now there was no reason to venture onto the bay. Already she was much farther out than she had ever been.

As she drew closer to the fallen lantern she saw more clearly the outlines of the horse, which wore a saddle, and of the flatbed wagon. It was indeed piled with wooden boxes. An exceptionally large box had apparently fallen off and lay on the sand directly behind it.

The horse nickered and tossed its head restively. No docile wagon puller, it was an enormous beast, eyes glowing like fiery coals in the lantern light. She approached it gingerly.

"Please stay still," she said in the most soothing tone she could produce from a constricted throat. "Truly, I won't hurt you."

"I am relieved to hear it."

Lucy stopped dead in her tracks, her heart pounding. Surely not! Horses couldn't talk.

"Hullo," said the voice. "I'm back here."

She could see nothing beyond the wagon except the outline of the fallen box. "Come out then. Slowly. And hold up your hands. I have a pistol."

"You, too? Is everyone but me carrying a weapon tonight?" There was a rumble of male laughter. "I would oblige you, to be sure, but at the moment I'm unable to move. M'foot is trapped under a box."

"So you say." She advanced one cautious step in his direction. "How can I be sure?"

"I suppose you could take my word for it. Or you could come and see for yourself. Do hurry, though. Time and tide wait for no man, or so I am told, and we will both be underwater fairly soon. *I* certainly will, if you cannot help me to extricate myself. You, of course, are free to leave whenever you like."

He sounded harmless. Even amused. And he could have jumped on her long before now if he'd a mind to, or if he were able to. She picked up the lantern and moved alongside the wagon, stopping when she reached the oversize back wheel. Sure enough, a black-clad figure was stretched out behind the box. As she looked at him he sat forward, propping himself up on one elbow. His right leg was buried under the sand from the knee down, and the box was planted where his foot would likely be.

She raised the lantern for a better look at him. There wasn't much to see. His hair was covered by a knit cap and his face had been blackened. White teeth flashed at her, though, when he smiled.

"Well? Do you mean to help me or not?"

Gazing at him, she sensed disaster. Alarm prickled at her

spine. He was a large man, and powerful, if one was to judge by a set of wide shoulders and a broad chest. "Can you not kick away the box with your other foot?"

"Believe me, I've been trying. Thing is, my buried foot hit a patch of wet sand and sank in. Then the box fell off the wagon and landed right atop it. Not to mention that someone shot me along the way. My left arm is fairly useless at the moment, and I can't seem to get the leverage for a good hard push."

"Oh." She moved from behind the dubious protection of the wagon. "Who are you?"

"A smuggler, retired as of a few minutes ago. And a few minutes from now the bore tide will be upon us. Much as I hate to say this, m'dear, you really ought to head back to shore while you can."

She wanted to do exactly that, but of course she could not. After placing the lantern on the back of the wagon, she went behind the fallen box, knelt, and gave a mighty pull. It moved a fraction of an inch and dropped back again. Three more tries were equally futile. The box was heavy and it had sunk very deep.

"Try putting your foot against the top," she directed. "Shove as best you can when I give the sign." Curling her fingers around the edge of the box near the corner, she planted herself firmly and took a deep breath. "Now!"

He pushed, she pulled, and except for a sucking noise, nothing happened. They gave it several more attempts, but if anything, the box sank lower still into the quagmire.

Still kneeling, Lucy wiped sweat from her forehead with her sleeve.

"There's a knife in the scabbard on my belt," the man said quietly. "Use it to cut the horse loose and lead him to shore. His name is Jason. Take care of him, and I'll put in a good word for you at the Pearly Gates."

"Don't be stupid." She jumped onto the wagon, looking for something to stuff underneath the box. There were only more heavy boxes, nailed shut, and a battered umbrella. Taking it with her, she dropped back to the ground, opened the umbrella, and proceeded to stomp on it until all the spines had broken and it lay flat. Then she knelt and used her hands like a pair of trowels to scoop sand from the base of the wooden box. Almost as fast as she dug, the heavy wet sand settled back again.

She redoubled her efforts, frantically plowing the ground. Her nails broke down to the quick, but at last she was able to dig her fingers under the box and hold it up. It must be full of rocks, she thought, panting heavily. With her teeth, she tugged the remains of the umbrella to the very edge of the box and used her chin to push it forward, never letting go her hold on the box although her hands were aching like the very devil. She'd got the fabric of the umbrella scrunched up about two inches underneath when she absolutely had to give it up.

Not at all sure the box wouldn't crush her fingers in the process, she gave a quick mental count to three and snatched her hands away.

The edge of the box collapsed onto the umbrella, free of the boggy sand for no more than a few seconds. She crawled rapidly to the man's side and sat with her elbows on the ground and her feet planted near the top of the box. "Get ready, sir. Put your foot at the corner. When I give the word, push up and forward with all your strength."

"I'm set."

"Go!"

Groaning with effort, they shoved and shoved. The box almost came loose, but then it fell back again.

"You must leave now," he said urgently. "I mean it."

"Go!"

They pushed again until she thought her skin would burst. Slowly the box rose. This was it, she knew. Should it fall back, they would never be able to pry it up again. Together, they fought the pull of the sand, working side by side in what had to be their final effort.

And all of a sudden, as if it were lighter than a rubber ball, the box rolled over and away.

Dear Lord. For a few moments she lay flat and stared dizzily into space. Then she was up again, tunneling into the sand that imprisoned his foot. Soon his boot was exposed, and in another minute he raised his leg and made cautious circles with his ankle.

"No harm done. I'll thank you some other time, but for God's sake, get out of here." He pulled a formidable-looking knife from its sheath and passed it to her. "Cut the horse free and ride him to shore. I'll follow."

"We'll go together." She went to the harnesses and began sawing through them. "Can you get on your feet?"

He scrambled to the box that had trapped him and used it to lever himself upright. From there he tottered to the wagon wheel and clung to it.

Watching him from the corners of her eyes, she could tell he would be unable to walk more than a few yards, if that far. "Could you possibly get yourself up on the wagon, sir? From there, you'll find it easier to slide onto the saddle."

"There isn't time."

"Do it! And how can you be sure the tide is on its way in?"

"We were cutting it close as it was. Delays before we started." He heaved himself onto the back of the wagon and knelt with his shoulder propped against a box.

When the horse was free, she led him to where the man waited to climb aboard. "There is no time for niceties, sir. Unless you can mount in one try, please settle for draping yourself over the saddle."

After restoring the knife to its sheath, he did precisely that. She took up the lantern and set out for the shore.

"This is humiliating," the man grumbled.

"As if that signifies. Take care not to fall off, because we'll never get you back on." He had her so convinced that the tide would wash over them at any moment that she jumped when a drop of rainwater hit her nose. Oh, excellent, she thought. Rain was precisely what they needed right now.

The man was ominously silent. "How are you feeling, sir?"

"Merry as a grig," he assured her. "What exactly *is* a grig?" he asked after a while. "I've always wondered."

"Grigs are young eels."

"Oh. But why are they merry? How do we *know* they are merry?"

Clearly she was risking her life to save a lunatic. "I've no idea, sir. Perhaps because they don't have to deal with the likes of you." The sand was firmer there and she sensed they were on an upward slope. Raising the lantern, she was able to see the cliff looming directly ahead.

Now what was she to do?

The horse would have to stay the night in the cave, of course. The nearest way onto land for him was more than a mile away. But she dared not reveal the cave's location to the smuggler, not while there was any chance he could climb up the same way she had come down.

She was fairly sure he could not. And why bring him this far only to have him die on solid land? But to take him through the cave would put Diana at risk. Oh, damn.

With little hope, she decided to gamble he could make the ascent up the cliff. If he faltered, they would simply have to go around the other way. At least they were well beyond reach of the bore tide. She led the horse to the inlet and came to a halt beside a large boulder. "Will he stand if I let go his bridle?"

"He'll stand. Jason, old lad, behave yourself."

Lucy helped the man slip off the horse, bearing much of his weight when his feet hit the ground. She assisted him to the boulder and gestured for him to sit. "I'm going to leave you here for a short time, sir. The horse cannot go up this way, so I'll secure him a little distance down the beach, where he will be perfectly safe until I can do better for him."

"Where *is* the way up?"

"About a dozen yards behind you. It's not an easy climb. I'll be back within five minutes."

The horse was soon tethered to a rock deep inside the cave and away from the coming storm. But the man was nowhere in sight when she returned to where she'd left him. Blessedly, the rain was falling only in occasional brief sputters. Lantern in hand, she entered Cow's Mouth Inlet and discovered the man crawling on hands and knees up the path. He was nearly half-way to the top.

"If I'm going the wrong way," he called over his shoulder, "don't tell me."

"You are doing fine," she said bracingly. On her own, she'd have extinguished the lantern and left it behind, but she greatly feared he would require its light when he came to the sharp vertical climb near the top and the jutting rock directly above. "Slow a bit! Let me catch up with you." She maneuvered herself along the rocky track with the lantern handle clasped between her teeth.

He waited until she was at his heels before moving again, inches at a time. She could hear the breath rasping in his throat and almost feel in her bones what every inch of progress was costing him. He crept steadily ahead, though, without complaint.

At one point her hand fell on a wet rock. She thought nothing of it, assuming the moisture to be rainwater. But when she used the hand to wipe perspiration from her forehead, she smelled the coppery tang of blood. Nausea rose to her throat as she scrubbed her hand against her trouser leg. What if he bled himself dry there on the cliffside?

"Who are you?" he asked, pausing for a few seconds before continuing on.

She removed the lantern from her mouth. "L-Luke."

"Glad to know you, Luke. More than I can say. My name is Kit. I should advise you that I'm a trifle muzzy and am like to tumble off the edge at any moment. But I won't be any less grateful for your help as I plunge to my doom."

"Might I suggest you save your strength for the climb?" she shot back at him. "The hardest part is at the top."

He chuckled. "I should have guessed."

When he reached the last, almost perpendicular few yards of

the cliff, she tugged at his foot. "Huddle to one side, please. I shall try to go around you."

"Is that a good idea?"

"No. But you'll need me to pull you up. Take the lantern, will you?"

He did, and she slithered past him with half her body hanging over the side of the cliff. Should they both survive this ordeal, she thought, she would kill him for putting her through it. With a final burst of maniacal strength, she clambered over the jutting rock and flattened herself atop it.

"You're almost done, sir. Put down the lantern and grab hold of my hands."

"Make that one hand. I've only the one to grab with."

Knitting her fingers together, she made a sort of sling for him to hang on to as he thrust himself up and over to safety. He must have kicked the lantern on his final push. It tumbled off the cliff and fell like a shooting star, the light flaming out when it crashed against the ground below. That could have been either one of them, she realized, suddenly icy cold from scalp to toes.

He flopped onto his back, breathing heavily. "Well, that was a treat. I'll try it again about fifty years from now. Are we there yet? Or do you have another mountain for us to play on?"

If she had ever doubted it before, she was now convinced the man was daft. "It's perhaps a hundred yards from here to our destination. Can you walk if I support you, or would you prefer to crawl?"

"Walk, thank you." He lurched to his feet and seized hold of her waist.

As they teetered in the direction of the cottage, Lucy began to realize that her problems had only just begun. She could not take him immediately inside, not without warning Diana and making preparations. Somehow there must be a way to get through this debacle without ruining everything, but she had no idea what that way could be. A dark corner of her soul wished the smuggler had been shot through the heart instead of the arm. Or that he'd tumbled off the cliff.

But he was alive, drat him, a heavy weight against her now and an impossible burden to carry from here on out.

To one side, she spotted the large flat tree stump that rose from the ground a short way from the cottage. Some previous resident had smoothed the top and now it provided a nice bench to sit on, with a view of the woodlands in daylight. She detoured over to it and let go of the smuggler's waist. "You'll have to wait here a few moments, sir. Let me help you sit."

"Again?" He lowered himself onto the stump with a low groan. "We're making more stops than a London post deliverer."

"Yes. It's unfortunate. I'll be back directly." He would simply have to remain befuddled, Lucy thought as she dashed to the cottage and slipped inside.

Diana, seated at a small table beside the hearth, looked up with alarm. "What happened? Where is your witch's—"

"Never mind that. There's a man waiting outside. He's been shot." She waved a hand when Diana tried to speak again. "I can't tend to him alone, so you must be Mrs. Preston. Wear the veil and pretend to be mute."

"Is he badly hurt?"

"I don't know. He's not right in the head, and he's lost a good deal of blood. We'll need bandages, scissors, perhaps needle and thread. Any medicines you have that might be useful. Is there laudanum?"

"Yes. I'll bring everything I can think of." Taking her book, Diana went to the door that led to the cottage's only other room. "Hadn't you better fetch him inside?"

"In a moment." Lucy darted around the sparsely furnished room, grabbing up anything that might provide a clue to their identities and concealing the items in her portmanteau. Finally, taking along a sturdy walking stick, she went outside to collect the smuggler.

Chapter 2

Kit watched Luke vanish into the dark cottage, abandoning him to his tree stump.

An odd development, to be sure, but unexpected things had been happening all night. At least he was apt to be among the living come tomorrow. For a few thorny minutes there, his foot embedded in wet sand under that wretched box, he had been fairly sure he was about to cock up his toes. One set of toes, anyway.

By now, the bore tide was driving up the bay. It might already have swamped the wagon, and he would currently be making the acquaintance of the local fish had Luke not pulled him free. Only to leave him, it seemed, to pour out his life's blood on a tree stump.

With his rescuer in no apparent hurry to come back for him, he turned his thoughts from his near demise to the mystery of her identity. *Her,* for if Luke was of the male persuasion, Christopher Etheridge Valliant was the Queen of Sheba.

He certainly knew a female body when he felt one, and he'd had several opportunities to detect the swell of breasts under that heavy homespun shirt and makeshift binding. While leaning against her for support, his hand had encountered the flare of feminine hips and a sweetly rounded derriere.

He wouldn't object in the least to encountering them again. When he'd recovered his strength, perhaps she would permit him to reward her for saving his life.

The door opened again, and this time a narrow slice of light fell onto the ground. Luke strode swiftly to the tree stump, a blackthorn walking stick in her hand. "Well, come along, then," she said. "Lean on this."

One hand clutching the knobby tip, Kit lurched to his good foot and reeled precariously, struggling to regain his balance.

Luke anchored him with one arm wrapped around his waist. "Steady on. It's only a few steps more."

They tottered slowly toward the door, the sudden exertion having sucked what remained of Kit's blood to his legs. They felt like overcooked noodles, and it required iron concentration to compel them to move.

Luke towed him inside and maneuvered him to an object he could not quite make out. A large spider? he wondered dizzily as she turned him around.

"There is a chair directly behind you," she told him. "Sit."

The walking stick slipped from his hand when he tried to lower himself. Luke seized his belt with both hands and helped him settle on the chair. Then he felt a pressure against the back of his neck.

"Bend forward, sir." She pushed his head down between his knees. "Stay in this position until I tell you otherwise."

Sit. Stay. What the devil did she think he was—a bloody spaniel?

But he obeyed, and soon his head began to clear. Marginally, anyway. He became aware of a packed-dirt floor, two boots caked with wet sand, and the god-awful pain in his shoulder.

Lifting his gaze, he saw a narrow cot set in the corner, a small, rough-hewn square table beside him, and another primitive wooden chair. There was a fire at his back, he could tell, and Luke was at the hearth, pouring something liquid into a metal pot. Then he heard wood against wood as she added logs to the fire, and the crackle of sparks shooting up the chimney.

"Are you still alive?" she asked briskly.

"I believe so."

"Try to remain so a bit longer, then. When we have got things organized, we'll tend to your shoulder as best we can."

We? He wrenched his head from between his legs and looked around the small room. Luke was poking at the fire, but there was no sign of anyone else. He did see two doors, both closed. One would have to be the one he'd just come through, so the other probably led to a second room.

His brain felt as if it were marinating in molasses. "Where the deuce am I?"

"Not at a proper surgery where you belong, I'm afraid. The locals call this outpost Cow's Mouth Cottage, and Mrs. Preston is currently in residence here. She is gathering bandages and implements, but we've little to work with and shall be forced to improvise."

That sounded ominous. Carefully, Kit rotated his shoulder. It moved well enough, so he experimented with his arm. Everything responded as it ought, but the pain sent sweat to his forehead and from there down into his eyes, carrying with it particles of gritty charcoal dust. They filtered through his lashes and burned under his lids.

"C-could you possibly wash my face?" he asked hesitantly.

"Good heavens!" She sounded contemptuous. "We'll attend to that later. You may be sure your appearance is not of the slightest concern to anyone here."

"I'm quite serious. Grains of coal dust have set themselves to blind me."

"Oh. I beg your pardon. Yes, I shall certainly scrub you up a bit."

He heard metal again, and water being poured. Soon she set something on the table beside him and pulled off his black knit hat.

After a barely discernible pause, she plastered one hand over his eyes and set to work on his forehead with what felt like a sponge dipped in warm water. After a few dabs, she rinsed the sponge and began again.

When his lids had been cleaned, he opened his eyes and watched her work on the rest of his face. Her hair, what he could see of it, fascinated him. It was the color of pearls, a sleek, silky cap tapering to her neck with an uneven fringe across her forehead.

She attended fiercely to what she was doing, never meeting his gaze, her slim pert nose slightly crinkled in concentration. Although her lips were set in a narrow line, he could tell they were naturally soft and full. Firelight was reflected in her eyes, making it impossible to determine their color. Her lashes were long but pale, best appreciated from the closeness of an embrace.

It was altogether an elegant face, perfectly sculpted, the lines clean and distinct. Her fine-grained complexion put him in mind of the most exquisite porcelain, or of fresh cream with a touch of apricot on her high cheekbones. A chap could look at this face for an infinite time, and he was in no hurry for her to finish what she was doing.

Twice she rose gracefully, emptied the fouled water outside, and returned with a refilled basin. Head swimming, Kit sagged against the chair back, allowing himself to enjoy her attentions while he could.

She had just gotten to his lips when something appeared to overset her. "*Must* you sit there grinning like the village idiot?" she demanded.

"I must," he replied amiably. "I cannot help myself. You are preposterously lovely."

Color flamed in her cheeks. "Did that box bounce off your head before landing on your foot, sir? Men are not considered to be lovely."

"Nevertheless, *you* most assuredly are."

She scrubbed at his neck with a vengeance, her lips carved in a rigid line.

"If you mean to separate my skin from the rest of me, may I suggest that sandpaper would be more efficacious?"

"Oh." She rinsed the sponge and dabbed more gently at his raw flesh. "I apologize, sir. You were talking nonsense, and I feared you were about to swoon. We must see to your wound."

"No more than a scratch, I'm fairly certain. Nothing seems

15

to be broken." He lifted his left arm and stroked his forefinger down her cheek. "See?"

Her eyes widened with shock. A beat later she jerked her head away. "Don't *do* that, you . . . you *dolt*."

He already regretted the move excessively but could not resist crossing swords with her. It distracted him from the pain. "Ah, moonbeam, I do love it when you talk sweet to me."

With an exasperated oath, she rose, grabbed up the basin, and stomped to the door, slamming it behind her when she returned. The basin hit the stone hearth with a resounding clang. "Keep in mind, sir, that I will soon be probing at your shoulder with something excessively sharp." She came around in front of him, hands planted on her hips. "Have you anything else objectionable to say to me?"

"Only a question, Mistress Luke. Why are you masquerading—ineptly, I might add—as a male?"

She closed her eyes. "I should have left you out there," she muttered grimly. "You would have been drowned and out of everybody's hair by now."

Before he could respond, there came a thudding sound from the back door, as if someone was kicking at it.

"That will be Mrs. Preston," Luke said in a hiss. "Be kind to her. She doesn't speak."

"*Doesn't* as in can't, or won't?"

"Oh, do shut up." She went to the door and raised the latch.

Kit watched with slightly befuddled fascination as a female clad all in black entered the room, carrying a large wooden tray heaped high with bandages, small vials and jars, and other items he couldn't identify. She wore a felt bonnet from which a heavy veil descended, thoroughly concealing her face. Without acknowledging him, she set the tray on the table.

"Bring every lamp and candle we've got," Luke instructed, "and fill the basin with hot water from the kettle." She was all business as she took up a pair of scissors and turned to Kit. "I'm going to cut your shirt away now. Are you able to remain upright and hold yourself still? Be honest. It will be easier to work if you are sitting in the chair, but you can take to the bed if you must."

Although the door and windows were closed, he'd have sworn the room was beginning to fill with fog. Kit took hold of the wooden chair seat under his right hip and held tight. "Have your way with me, Luke. I'll let you know if I'm about to slide to the floor."

Nodding, she unbuckled his belt and tossed it into a corner. "Were you shot from the front or the back?"

"Front."

She moved behind the chair. "Bend forward, please. I'll start here."

He felt the cool metal of the scissors against his back as she clipped steadily from the tail of the black woolen shirt to the neck. Then, gingerly, she lifted a flap of material from his shoulder.

"The bullet must have passed straight through," she said, relief in her voice. "I feared that I would be compelled to dig it out."

"I would not have enjoyed that." Suddenly feeling ghastly cold, he buried his head between his knees.

A cool hand pressed against his forehead, and a soft voice whispered at his ear. "Take your time," it said. "Tell me how I can help you."

He sensed confidence in her tone, and an edge to it that challenged him to rally his spirits. But he gave himself another long minute before pulling upright again. "Time for the front, I expect. Go to it."

The scissors sliced through his shirt, and when she had severed it in two, she pulled the right half down his good arm and let it drop to the ground.

That was easy enough, he was thinking just before she began to separate the fabric from the bloody mess at his left shoulder. Pain washed over him in fiery waves.

"It's stuck," she murmured, putting the scissors to work again.

17

Soon only a fragment of cloth remained directly over the wound. "This is going to hurt, I'm afraid." Slowly, strand by strand, she pulled woolen threads free of the congealed blood.

He took a deep breath, and then another. "Would you mind getting this over with in a hurry?"

"It will be better," Luke agreed. "Di—Mrs. Preston, will you put your arms around his chest and hold him in the chair?"

Two surprisingly strong, black-sheathed arms secured him in place from behind as Luke took hold of the piece of cotton and snapped it loose.

Kit heard a sharp cry of pain and hoped it hadn't come from him. A damp towel was pressed against his forehead and a slim-fingered hand rested on his neck.

"Well done, sir. I wish I could tell you it was over, but we've only just begun."

His head slowly cleared, although black spots danced in front of his eyes when he opened them again. "S-sorry to make so much trouble." Was he *whimpering*, for pity's sake?

There was a swirl of activity around him then. Luke murmured instructions to the silent Mrs. Preston, and after a few moments a length of fabric was tied around his chest, holding him against the back of the chair. Then something cold and burning was pressed against his shoulder.

"I shall tell you what we are doing. The bullet appears to have passed cleanly through a fleshy part of your shoulder, but it may have pushed bits of your shirt inside the wound. They will create problems later if not removed, so I mean to see to them as best I can. If I am forced to probe deeply, you will most definitely feel it."

She had already begun as she spoke, and he could feel it sure enough. He rather wanted to scream, and tears stung his eyes, but he held himself immobile as she worked. It was the least he could do.

Some part of his ragged mind detached itself and remained almost coherent. He decided that for his sins he probably deserved all this. He hoped the measure of pain did not reflect the seriousness of his injury. He loathed feeling so damnably helpless, and above all, he feared it.

After several years she stopped digging into his shoulder with some sort of metallic instrument of torture. He sagged against the bonds holding him to the chair, letting his head drop forward.

"We're nearly done," she said in a calm voice. "I will clean the wound now and apply a paste of Saint-John's-wort. It's all we have tonight, but we shall send for better help and medications when the storm has passed."

Kit became aware of wind whistling over the chimney and window glass rattling in the panes. Rain pelted the slate roof of the cottage. He listened with all his attention, forcing himself to ignore what Luke was doing to his shredded shoulder. Fingers, soothing fingers, stroked through his hair. Mrs. Preston, he thought, trying to help.

Disaster and miracles, both at once. He had tumbled into hell and, contrarily, fallen into the hands of angels.

He heard mumbled words from Luke, and Mrs. Preston moved away from him. Scissors cut through the band of cotton holding him upright on the chair. With effort, he kept himself erect.

"This is water," Luke said, putting a cup against his lips.

He drank greedily, welcoming the cool liquid against his parched mouth and throat. Then another vessel, a thin glass, was held to his mouth.

"This is a bit of cider laced with laudanum. It will help you sleep."

He turned his head away. "I don't want it."

"That is unfortunate. Drink it anyway."

"Dammit, I'll not be drugged." Determination scattered the tendrils of mist in his head. "I want to know what is happening."

Luke patted his good shoulder. "Nothing whatever will be happening after we get you into bed, not until the storm clears. Well, one or the other of us will watch for fever and stand ready to be of help, but the best thing for you right now is sleep. And without the laudanum—very little of it, I assure you—the pain will keep you awake."

"No, it won't," Kit assured her. "I can fall asleep within a minute, at will. I have the habit of it."

She took the glass from Mrs. Preston, who had been holding it, and poked a finger at his chest. "I saved your life tonight, sir. You owe me a favor in return. And what I want is for you to drink this down to the very last drop without further protest. Agreed?"

"What a fierce creature you are," he murmured with genuine admiration. "But I'm wet all over, you know. You won't want me soiling that bed. I shall sleep on the floor by the hearth."

"Rubbish. It will be easier for me to deal with your wound if I can reach you. And I don't care if the bedding gets wet."

"Of course not, since I'll be the one sleeping there. At the least, can we do something about these boots? The right one feels like a sausage casing."

She frowned. "I'd forgot about your foot. But it will hurt dreadfully if I try to pull off the boot."

"Then cut it off. You'll do better with the knife, I expect."

She removed it from the sheath and knelt by his right leg, frowning as she considered the best approach. Finally she slipped the blade between the fabric of his trousers and the top of the boot. "I don't believe this is going to work, sir. I am bound to cut you."

"I'll squawk if you do. Give it a try, anyway."

She gripped the hilt, angled the sharp blade against the rim of the boot, and began to saw through the fold of leather and heavy stitching. Finally she succeeded in breaking through and was able to slice quickly to the sole. Carefully, she removed the boot and used the scissors to cut away his wet, sandy stocking.

His foot and ankle were swollen, but he reckoned the injury was no more serious than a sprain. He would be limping for a few days, but he'd be able to get around.

He glanced up to see Luke holding out the glass of drugged

cider. He'd hoped she had forgot, but no such luck. "I'll make you a deal," he offered. "Permit me to remove these wet trousers and get into bed. Then I'll swallow your bloody witch's brew."

Her eyes widened.

Was she alarmed? he wondered. It wasn't as though he intended to strip directly in front of her.

Not this time, at any rate.

"Agreed," she snapped. "We'll wait in the back room. Call when you are safely under the blanket, or if you encounter any difficulties."

To his annoyance, Luke took the laudanum with her. So much for his plan to dump it somewhere and maintain he'd drunk it like a good lad. Luke wouldn't have believed him, of course, but neither would she have risked giving him a second dose. Well, she had outwitted him, so he would have to swallow his medicine like a good loser.

He unbuttoned his trousers and peeled them down his legs, using the one good arm remaining to him. It took an amazingly long time, and he was sweating profusely when they were finally heaped on the floor. Lacking the strength to pick them up, he left them where they lay and limped to the narrow cot. After a considerable struggle, he got himself settled with the blanket covering him and lowered his head to the thin, bumpy pillow. He wondered which one of them slept here, Mrs. Preston or Luke. "I'm snug in bed," he called.

When Luke came into the room, he produced a wide yawn. "I c'n scarcely keep my eyes open," he said weakly.

"Humbug." She put a hand behind his head, raised it up, and held the glass to his lips.

Casting her a scorching look, he obediently swallowed the cider. "The least you can do is tell me your real name."

"I have done all I intend to do on your behalf this night," she advised him sternly. "Now do me one single kindness, sir, and go directly to sleep."

He regarded her hazily. She was wavering in and out of his

rapidly clouding vision. "I believe that I shall call you Lucy then."

"You cannot!" She shook her head. "That is Mrs. Preston's name."

"Ah. Unfortunate." This time his yawn was real. "G'night, moonbeam. I plan to dream about you."

Chapter 3

Lucy put a finger to her lips, warning Diana to remain silent. Although Kit had begun to snore lightly, she wouldn't have put it past him to be dissembling.

Standing side by side, they watched him closely for several minutes. He never moved, and the rhythm of his breathing remained steady, but still she could not be absolutely certain.

"I think he's well asleep," she said in a booming tone. "And the poker will be heated through by now. Go ahead and secure his wrists with the rope, Mrs. Preston. We mustn't have him thrashing about while I cauterize the wound."

There was no reaction from the man on the cot.

Releasing a sigh, Lucy crossed to the fireplace. "I think we can safely speak, Diana. The laudanum appears to have sent him off, and may the devil take him up and fly away with him."

"Don't *say* such things, I beg you. What if he were to die?"

"Oh, he'll do no such thing." That would make life far too easy, Lucy thought irritably. "The blackguard will live to make us a great deal of trouble caring for him, and a great deal more trying to rid ourselves of him."

Diana removed the veiled hat and worked at the pins attaching the brown wig to her hair. "How do you conclude that he's a blackguard?"

"It's perfectly obvious. He was smuggling contraband of some sort when he got himself shot. And even if he'd chanced to be delivering a sermon at Westminster Abbey when the bullet hit him, the man is patently a scoundrel."

Diana had not left her position beside the cot. "He looks like a lamb."

"Pah!"

"Well, *lamb* is not the correct word, I know. But he doesn't strike me as the least bit dangerous."

"Don't be deceived by his looks. Males often appear innocent, even vulnerable, when they are asleep. I recall gazing down at Henry Turnbridge, the devil's spawn if ever there was one, all snug in his bed, with his sweet face so wonderfully peaceful that I imagined I had misjudged his capacity for evil. The very next day he set fire to the stable."

"You cannot compare a child with a grown man," Diana protested. "I fear you have been a governess too long to maintain any perspective. At the least you must grant that he is exceedingly handsome."

"And he is well aware of it, too." Lucy added water to the teakettle and hung it over the fire. "He is also aware that I am a female."

"Oh, dear."

"I'm not in the least surprised. This disguise was never meant to be seen at close range, and in all the turmoil, I didn't think to alter my voice."

Diana finished detaching the wig and shook out her heavy auburn hair. "You haven't told me what happened. Where did you come upon him?"

"Make the tea, will you? Yours always tastes so much better than mine. And to be honest, I believe I must sit for a few minutes."

While Diana set out the crockery and measured the tea leaves, Lucy gave her a carefully censored description of the events on Morecambe Bay. She omitted the long struggle to dig Kit's leg from under the box and skimmed over the arduous return to shore. Diana need not know they had escaped just ahead of the incoming tide.

"That's perfectly awful," Diana said when she was finished. "The others simply left him there? Who were they?"

"I've no idea, except that there were two separate groups of men—Kit's band of smugglers and the ones who robbed them. He was in no condition to explain what occurred before my arrival."

"His name is Kit? What else do you know about him?"

"Nothing whatever." Lucy had placed herself where she could see his face in case he showed signs of distress. Or of eavesdropping. "Nor have I the slightest notion what we are to *do* with him. If he takes a fever, I suppose we'll have to find a doctor."

"Shouldn't we do that in any case?" Diana poured hot water into the teapot. "Is there one in Silverdale?"

"Not likely. I imagine we'll have to send to Beetham, or even farther. Robbie will know. He's promised to bring a load of firewood and provisions tomorrow, although he'll not arrive until the storm has passed."

"Kit speaks well, I noticed. He cannot be a common smuggler."

Not common in any way, Lucy agreed silently. He was certainly a most *uncommon* nuisance. Because of him, her plan was unraveling, and she could not think how to weave it together again. Clearly a whole new scheme had to be devised, one that allowed for Kit and weeded him away before he could do any more damage.

She combed her fingers through her hair, a habit she had acquired soon after it was shorn. She could not seem to help making sure the rest was still there. "We must revise our scheme immediately, Diana. It's true we've no idea if our unwelcome patient will recover swiftly or take a turn for the worse, or what to do in either circumstance. But we have to begin somewhere."

Diana strained tea into the chipped ceramic mugs. "You are forever telling me that everything will work out for the best. Shall we assume that Robbie will arrive in good time, and that Kit will have slept peacefully through the night?"

Her own feigned optimism was coming back to bite her, Lucy thought sourly. But until now she had truly believed they had a reasonable chance of bringing this off. It had not been so easy a matter to persuade Diana, though. She was fragile as a butterfly's wing.

Nonetheless, she had been a rock of support this evening. Lucy considered that wonder as she watched Diana sit in the chair across from her. How lovely she was. But already, so soon, she had learned to keep the right side of her face turned away.

"You didn't answer my question, Lucy."

"I beg your pardon, but it is difficult to imagine *the best*. For now, let us consider the immediate future. I shall keep watch on him tonight, of course, but since he is in your bed, where are you to sleep? If you take my pallet by the hearth, you'll be forced to wear the wig and veil in case he wakes up."

"I'd rather not. The wig scratches and the pins give me the headache. I shall stay in the other room."

"Unthinkable. There is no heat in there."

"We'll leave the door open, then, and I'll wrap myself up in layers of clothes. Where I spend the rest of the night is the least of our problems, Lucy. What of the morning? Shall I be Mrs. Preston again, or will you?"

Lucy sipped at the strong hot tea. "And now poor Mrs. Preston is mute. What an incredibly stupid idea that was! When I thought of it, I reckoned that later I could take over the role without him recognizing the change of voices. It failed to dawn on me that whichever of us played the part thereafter would be compelled to remain silent."

"He was weak and in pain. He's had a draft of laudanum. Perhaps he won't remember that Mrs. Preston is unable to speak."

"Oh, he'll remember. Nothing escapes him, I'm sorry to say." He had even *flirted* with her, for heaven's sake, although it was only to demonstrate that he'd seen through her disguise. And, she suspected, to show her how clever he was. "I'll be Luke tomorrow, unless Robbie fails to arrive and I am forced to go into Silverdale. Kit can go on wondering why I am dressed in trousers until I come up with a plausible explanation."

Lucy rubbed the back of her neck, which ached with tension.

"There's another problem. I fear that Kit's smugglers were heading for our cave to stash their booty. We must relocate ourselves as soon as possible."

"But why? Didn't you say the robbers made off with—with the booty?"

"Some of it. The rest was loaded on a wagon, which must be several feet underwater by now. *Drat!* I forgot about the horse. We unhooked him from the wagon and brought him ashore. He's in the cave. There's nothing to feed him with, but I should take him some water and remove his saddle."

"I'll do it. But why are you so worried about the smugglers? They might have been going somewhere else entirely."

"Perhaps. I suppose the question is irrelevant now. Kit is here, he knows about us, and we must depart as soon as may be."

Diana looked alarmed. "For where? We have no place to go."

"Of course we do," Lucy lied smoothly. "There are thousands of places, and we have only to make a selection. But leave that to me. I shall think on it later. At the moment I cannot seem to put two coherent thoughts together in a row." She swallowed the last of her tea. "We'll be guessing from here on out, but you mustn't worry. If all else fails, we shall simply make a run for it."

Diana rose and went to fill a battered metal bucket from the oak barrel that held their supply of water. "We ought to set the barrel outside to catch the rainwater," she said over her shoulder. "It's nearly empty."

"I'll see to it." Lucy was relieved to hear a return of spirit in Diana's voice. When there was something of use for her to do, she invariably shook off her mopes and set to work. But most times she was left on her own, with nothing to distract her from her unhappy thoughts. "I'd much rather drag a barrel out into a storm, you know, than tend to a large unpredictable animal."

"Nonsense. One day I shall teach you to ride, and I promise that you'll come to love horses as much as I do. May I take the carrots we were saving for tomorrow's soup?"

"By all means. Give him anything you can find that he

will eat. And bring up the saddle pack, if it is not too heavy to carry."

When Diana had ignited a lantern and departed with the carrots, Lucy rose with a groan and went to examine the bandage on Kit's shoulder. Blood had seeped through, but not terribly much of it, and the rust-colored stain was already dry to the touch. Perhaps he would live after all, the wretch.

Not wanting to think about him right now, she began to order things for the long hours ahead. First she carried her straw pallet into the other room for Diana to sleep on and rummaged through their box of supplies for towels, which she folded into a makeshift pillow. Diana's clothes were stored in the cave, and she could use cloaks and pelisses for blankets.

There was enough firewood to see them through the night, and if the storm persisted, they could always break up the chairs for fuel.

Her brain felt mired in quicksand. She stared at the wig and bonnet for a long time before realizing they could not be left out in plain view. Gathering them up, she stowed them in her portmanteau. What else? She spotted Kit's discarded trousers on the floor and draped them over a chair by the hearth to dry. The remains of his shirt were put into the fire to burn. She ought to prepare a broth for him to drink when he awoke, but she didn't feel up to it at the moment. There would be plenty of time for that later. She'd no intention of sleeping. Should he develop a fever, she would have to do something about it. Cold compresses, she supposed. Which reminded her about the water barrel.

Rain pelted into the cottage and onto her hair and clothes when she opened the door to thrust the barrel outside. Shivering, she rushed back to the fireplace and stood facing it, spreading out her arms and legs to catch the heat. I could fall asleep right here, standing up, she thought as the warmth stole over her body. However am I to keep watch on the smuggler when I can scarcely keep my eyes open?

"What a magnificent horse!" Diana said, snapping Lucy to

attention. "Kit must have paid a small fortune for him. And he's so well mannered. He ate the carrots from my hand and stood still while I removed his saddle."

Lucy turned to see her drop the leather saddle pack on the table. She eyed it curiously. Perhaps there was some clue in there to Kit's identity, not that it mattered a great deal who he was. But information, however irrelevant it might seem at first start, had a way of becoming useful sooner or later. That was her experience, in any case, and she meant to have a look inside. But first she must send Diana, who was too well-bred to approve of riffling through a man's personal effects, off on another errand. "You had better fetch warm clothes from your luggage, I expect. And since I left my cloak outside under a rock, will you bring something for me?"

"Gladly. But it's awfully cold and dark down there. May I leave one or two of our lanterns near to the horse? He is probably frightened to be alone in such a strange place."

"He has all my sympathy," Lucy said crossly. "But we dare not light up the cave at night. You know that."

"I'd leave them well back," Diana protested, "and they cast very little light. Besides, who could possibly be out in this storm to see?"

"No lanterns," Lucy ruled. "We've enough problems as it is without drawing more attention to ourselves, however remote the chance anyone else is lurking about. Please, Diana. I'm frightfully out of temper just now. Bring up what you need for the night and get settled. It's the best thing you can do for me."

Diana fled.

Lucy knew she would feel guilty later, but she had spoken the truth. She was so on edge that she would have torn into the Archbishop of Canterbury if he materialized in front of her.

She went to the table, unbuckled the saddle pack, and sifted through its contents. There were two soft woolen shirts, of good quality but well-worn, and half a dozen cambric handkerchiefs. A pair of heavy wool stockings. A small drawstring bag filled with coins, a few banknotes, and a plain pocket watch. A razor, shaving soap, and cracked mirror all wrapped up in a piece of toweling. A copper-sheathed spyglass. Another drawstring bag, this one larger, holding pencils, a small folding knife, and pieces of charcoal. A sketchbook.

She pulled it out and flipped through the pages. Most were blank, but the first few sheets were covered with drawings. They had no particular significance that she could ascertain. He had sketched whatever caught his fancy—a yew tree, a dinghy tied up to a rustic dock, three or four faces of country folk, a clump of bracken, an ox pulling a plow.

Only one picture, of a little girl sitting on a fallen log with a doll cradled in her arms, was finished in any detail. If ever she saw that child, Lucy knew that she would recognize her immediately. Indeed, from the drawing alone, she felt as if she knew her.

She glanced over at Kit, thinking that she didn't know him at all. Oh, she stuck by everything she had already decided about him, but there was clearly more to the man than she was ready to admit. All the same, a talent for sketching was scarcely a point in his favor. Even criminals had hobbies, she supposed.

Carefully, she restored everything to its place in the saddle pack and took it into the back room. Diana was still in the cave, probably sealing her friendship with the horse. Any company was better than Lucy Preston's, what with her black mood casting shadows over every place she went.

Her real shadow, created by the fire behind her, fell over Kit as she stood with her hands clenched, staring down at him without pleasure. A lamb, indeed! A black sheep, more like, the despair of his family and a blight on decent society. He would probably hang one day, and good riddance to him.

Such a waste of a beautiful man, though. He was nothing like the pale-skinned overdressed dandies that Lady Turnbridge welcomed to her house parties, and more often than not to her bedchamber. His bronzed face and the taut musculature of his tall, lanky body gave evidence of an athletic life spent much in the out-of-doors. His hair, a sun-streaked tangle of light brown and blond, waved slightly and reached to where his collar would be if . . . if he were wearing any clothes.

His bare flesh under that thin blanket did not bear thinking of. She crossed to the hearth and jabbed at the burning logs with the poker, wondering if the fire could be any hotter than she felt. She gazed into the flames, seeing nothing and having vague, irreverent thoughts about large, unpredictable male animals.

After some time Diana came into the room and placed a bundle at her feet before departing in silence. Belatedly, Lucy murmured words of thanks that probably went unheard. Well, she would apologize in the morning for being such a bear. Anger was the only thing that fueled her now, anger at Kit and at Diana's uncle and, shamefully, at every person who had treated her unfairly when she had tried so very hard to do the right thing. Without her anger, she would probably be curled up in a bundle the size of the one Diana had brought, crying her heart out like a frightened child. And what good would *that* do?

If it took rage to keep her going, she would nurture it for however long she must. Diana would simply have to put up with her, and the smuggler deserved whatever he got.

She poured the last of the cold tea into her mug and drank it, hoping it would help to keep her awake for the rest of the night. Rain pounded against the roof and a blast of icy wind made its way down the chimney, causing the fire to sputter and shoot sparks and ashes onto the floor. She set another log on the grate and kept watch until it was blazing, aware all the while of the man who lay asleep only a short distance away.

He was such a vital presence in the room that he might as well have been standing in the middle of it, juggling lit torches.

Lucy dragged a chair closer to the hearth and straddled it with her arms folded over the top rung of the laddered back. Propping her chin on her forearm, she gazed at Kit the Demon Smuggler who had stolen what little remained of her peace.

Go away, she thought. Take the rain with you. Give us what scant chance we may yet have to escape.

Chapter 4

Kit was enjoying his decidedly erotic dream. On the sands, beneath a starry sky, he was making rapturous love with Miss Luke.

Suddenly they were both underwater.

She didn't seem to mind. Still holding him, her hands on his bare shoulders, she smiled into his eyes. But his movements slowed, and he felt himself struggling for breath. Then he began to float, rising up and looking back at her, at her soft, creamy flesh and the cap of pearls on her head. She stretched her arms to him, but try as he might, he could not reach her.

He became aware of his own body then, and a throbbing pain in his shoulder, and more pain at his ankle. He ought to do something, he supposed, but it was as if heavy coins were pressed against his eyelids. Most likely he had put them there himself, for assuredly he had no wish to wake up. He wanted only to return to his dream and reshape the ending.

But his body had its own urgency and was demanding attention. And, too, he had the eerie sensation that someone was staring at him.

Bloody laudanum. He loathed the stuff. It left a man weak and noodle-witted. Forcing himself fully awake, Kit wrenched open his eyes and looked around the cottage.

No one was there. He saw only bare stone walls, a table and two chairs, and a small fire in the hearth. He couldn't guess the time of day. Heavy black curtains hung over what he supposed to be windows, and both doors were closed. He listened, hearing only silence, and reckoned that the storm must have passed.

The odd sensation that he was being watched grew more intense. Sitting up, he scanned the room again, this time noticing the dishes, jars, and cheesecloth-wrapped packets that were set on a shelf running all along the opposite wall. Finally he glanced in the direction of the low, smoke-stained ceiling.

Two round, glossy eyes gazed steadily at him from a white heart-shaped face. The small owl, about the size of his forearm, was perched on a coat peg jutting from the wall.

"Well, hullo there," Kit said. "I don't suppose you could direct me to the nearest chamber pot?"

The owl blinked.

Kit leaned over and peered under the cot. Nothing there. "Luke?" he called. "Mrs. Preston?" No one emerged from the back room.

"It appears the ladies have deserted us, old lad." Swinging his legs over the side, he gently planted both feet on the dirt floor and examined his wrenched ankle. It was red, swollen, and somewhat painful, but it moved easily enough when he made circles with his foot. He was fairly sure he could hobble about with the help of the blackthorn cane, which was perniciously propped against the wall clear on the other side of the room.

Levering himself up, he hopped gracelessly as far as the table and braced himself against the back of a chair to catch his breath. The bouncing had jarred his shoulder, and there was no denying it hurt like the devil. He used the chair's support to cross the rest of the way and finally managed to grab hold of the walking stick.

The owl made a throaty, wheezing sound.

Kit looked up and the owl stared back, its buff-colored head turned ninety degrees in his direction to get a better look. It made the snoring noise again.

Kit suddenly realized that he was bare-arsed naked. He located his trousers, which were draped over a chair near the fire, but he wasn't about to wrestle with them now. Leaning heavily on the cane, he returned to the cot and stripped off the thin blanket, securing it around his waist.

The exertion helped clear his mind of the laudanum, which he was resolved never to touch again. Good clean pain he could deal with, but anytime he decided to get muzzy-headed, he would bloody well do so with a bottle or two of vintage wine.

By the time he crossed the room again, he'd gotten the hang of balancing on the walking stick and limping in a relatively smooth manner. Fog billowed into the room when he opened the door, and the owl swooped past his shoulder.

He could see precious little when he stepped outside—the outline of the roof when he looked back, and what might be a tree near the corner of the cottage. He aimed himself for the concealment of its trunk, although the fog would hide him well enough from anyone who might be in the vicinity.

The owl joined him and perched on a branch directly overhead, still making that throaty sound and gazing at him with keen intensity. Kit decided that he must resemble some exceptionally large form of prey.

What a stroke of luck to have stumbled into this unlikely ménage—a mute woman clad all in black, a glorious female masquerading as a boy, and a singularly demented owl. For adventure, ever his ruling passion, he had assuredly come to the right place.

Gaze focused on his bare feet, he made his way carefully back to the door and was about to step inside when he heard the sound of voices from the other side of the cottage. He crept to the corner and risked a look around.

Two figures, one slim and the other large and burly, swam in and out of the fog. Their voices were muffled, but he recognized Luke's clear alto and the gruff rasp of a Scottish accent.

"I c'n take him with me now," the man said. "Better I do."

"No. If he dies in Silverdale, the authorities will have questions. If he dies here, we can lug his body—oh, I don't know—somewhere miles away and leave it there."

"That bad off, is he?"

"In fact, I've no idea. He slept quietly and has no fever, but he lost a great deal of blood. We shall do our best for him, but once he leaves, he'll doubtless tell someone what he saw at the cottage. We must hold him here until we are gone. Bring Giles back with you, and should he rule that the man requires a doctor, we'll scarper in a hurry."

"If you say so, lass, but I mislike leaving the two of you alone with a stranger."

They moved away then, disappearing into the heavy fog. He heard the Scot ask if she wanted him to bring a pistol but couldn't make out her reply.

He limped as fast as he could into the cottage. When Luke returned he must be flat on his back, just as she'd left him. The owl swooped in as he was closing the door, took up its perch on the coat peg, and followed his every move with those bright black eyes. Kit quickly peeled off the blanket, spread it over the cot, and slid into place. He had barely lowered his head to the pillow and closed his eyes when the door swung open again.

Listening acutely, he heard Luke drop something on the table and cross to him. He felt the warmth of her body as she leaned over him and sensed her gaze probing him like a lancet.

The owl was snoring again. Excellent notion. He faked a snore of his own.

"Don't pretend you are asleep," she said sharply. "The blanket is damp and so is your hair. You've been outside."

Not easily fooled, Lady Luke. He liked her all the more for it. "So I have," he affirmed, opening his eyes. "And it wasn't easy to get myself there, I assure you. But when nature is calling, a man has little choice but to answer."

Red flags blazed on her cheeks. "Yes. I hadn't thought of that. You can walk then?"

"Only if I must. Indeed, I expected that you would eventually find me in a heap somewhere between this spot and a friendly tree. You may be certain that I'm in no hurry to try another excursion."

She tugged the blanket down his chest and examined the bandage. "Fresh blood," she said irritably. "Not much of it, but you've done yourself no good. In future, pray ask for assistance."

"I'd have done, were there anyone of use to ask. The bird was no help at all."

Her gaze shot to the coat peg. "Fidgets! However did you get in here?"

The owl shuffled on its perch, ruffling its feathers.

"I used to smuggle lizards and frogs and snakes into my room," Kit said, "but I've never known anyone to take an owl for a pet."

"He took me." Luke held out her arm and the owl immediately flew to her wrist. "And he isn't a pet. Mostly he's a nuisance. He thinks I am his mother, I expect. The nest he was in got abandoned, and I came upon it just as he was pecking his way from his egg. From then on, of course, I had to feed him— minced meat when he was a chick and whatever I could beg from the kitchen as he grew. He has rewarded me with loyalty, which I could well do without, and of late he sometimes catches a meal for himself. I keep hoping he'll fly off to live the way an owl ought to live, but he shows no inclination to do so."

"Why does he make that growly sound?"

Luke raised a pair of beautifully shaped brows. "I've never heard it. But an ostler to whom I applied for advice about food and the like told me that barn owls make odd noises when they are attempting to woo a mate." She looked at the bird. "Are you in love, Fidgets?"

The owl snorted.

"Well, I cannot applaud your taste," she said, stroking the feathered head. "But perhaps this means that you are a female."

"I certainly hope so," Kit declared. "Cannot you tell?"

"No. It isn't . . . easily apparent. And in either case, the two of you would not suit. Off with you, Fidgets."

The owl flew back to its peg and resumed staring at Kit.

Returning to the table, Lucy began to unpack a large basket. "There is fresh bread, and I made up a pot of soup this morning. Are you hungry?"

"Ravenous." It was true, he realized, hearing his stomach rumble. "Where did you come by the basket?"

"A traveling blacksmith is kind enough to deliver provisions whenever he is passing by."

"On the way to where? This cottage is scarcely on a main road. I doubt it's on *any* road."

"Then he is *very* kind to detour so far out of his way. And kinder still because he has gone to fetch his nephew, who is an apothecary, and a wagon to carry you to a physician if Giles believes that you require one."

"Will he bring along a constable?" Kit asked wryly.

She dropped an apple, which rolled into the corner. "Certainly not. What you were doing last night is none of my concern. If the authorities are searching for you, I'd as soon they find you elsewhere."

"Why is that, I wonder? Because you don't want them to find *you*?"

"Nonsense." She retrieved the apple, providing him with a delectable view of her shapely derriere when she bent to pick it up. "You, sir, are the only felon on the premises. And the sooner you are gone, the better. Mrs. Preston is deeply in mourning for her late husband and requires solitude. It would be most unworthy of you to mention our presence here to anyone."

He could not resist prodding her. "Most particularly the authorities, should they manage to nab me."

"Precisely. We will have harbored a criminal and helped him to escape. Would you punish us for this kindness by subjecting us to an inquisition? I did save your life, you may recall."

"I do, and you've nothing to fear. My word on it."

"The word of a smuggler fails to reassure me," she informed him briskly. "But should you be tempted to speak out of turn, keep in mind that I was witness to what happened last night and can testify against you in a court of law."

She had an answer for everything, he thought, abandoning his efforts to pry information from her by means of direct confrontation. This matter required subtlety, if not downright sneakiness. As she went about her work he contented himself with watching her, slim and vibrant in loose homespun brown trousers and a tan shirt worn outside the pants to conceal her shape. But whenever she passed in front of the fire, he saw the outline of her lovely backside and two small, perfectly shaped breasts.

He had always been especially partial to the company of females, but this one engaged him more than any other in his experience, which was, not to put too fine a point on it, extensive. She fascinated him, with her razor tongue and keen intelligence. She was beautiful, to be sure, and naturally he desired her, but with such ferocity that it rendered him breathless—also wildly uncomfortable in the relevant sectors of his anatomy, which he knew would be forced to wait a considerable time for satisfaction. Miss Luke would not fall easily into his embrace.

She was at the table again, slicing a chunk of bread from a crusty loaf. She tossed it onto a plate beside a mug of steaming liquid, and the aroma of chicken broth caused his belly to rumble again.

He was disappointed when she disappeared into the back room, but she soon emerged with a thin straw-filled pallet. Folding it in half, she propped it against the wall at the head of the cot and helped him to sit up. He had to wriggle backward to prop himself against the pallet, and when he did so, the blanket failed to follow him. Nor did he make the slightest effort to help it along. Well, he thought, what man would?

She blushed to a bright crimson, fixing her gaze well north of where the blanket finally settled. "Pray cover yourself, sir," she murmured, spinning away from the cot as if it had caught fire.

"Sorry." He tugged the blanket to his waist, no farther, enjoying himself immensely.

He was less pleased when she came back and tossed a towel over his chest. Then she pulled a chair to the cot and sat beside him with the plate on her lap and the mug in her hand. "If I hold the cup, can you feed yourself?"

He could, of course, but that wouldn't be nearly as much fun. "I'll try, if you wish. But I'm somewhat shaky." He held out a hand and forced it to tremble. "The aftereffects of laudanum, I expect."

She regarded him suspiciously.

He gave her a look meant to appear earnest, cooperative, and helpless.

She wasn't convinced, he knew, but with a grumble she began to spoon up the soup. It was unexpectedly delicious, a hearty barley broth containing a few bits of stringy chicken, potato, and turnip. She concentrated fixedly on what she was doing, never meeting his gaze, and each time he tried to speak, she stuffed a wad of bread into his mouth.

With little left for him to do except to chew and swallow, he focused on her transparent gray eyes and wonderfully shaped lips, the finely carved cheekbones, the slope of her graceful jaw, and her long, glorious neck. Her startling complexion was pure cream whenever she wasn't blushing, and the sleek, pearly hair outlined the perfect shape of her head.

Why the devil was such a beauty as this hiding out in the back of beyond, shabbily clothed in male garb and keeping company with a veiled widow? She wasn't about to tell him, that was certain, but he suspected that she was as curious about him as he was about her. If she asked questions, though, that would give him an opening to do the same. So she pretended indifference, and he pretended helplessness, and the air between them grew overheated.

When the mug was empty she erupted from the chair, apparently forgetting about the plate on her lap because it tumbled to the floor. She left it there and went over to the owl. "Let's take a walk, Fidgets."

The owl fluttered down to her shoulder and they left the cottage.

Kit erupted in laughter. Oh, she was stubborn, that one. But he could outstubborn her and pare his toenails at the same time. Obstinacy ran in his family.

* * *

Lucy stomped a good long way before she realized that she couldn't see where she was going. Dense fog covered her body like a lover's embrace—

Oh, my. Wherever had such an image come from?

She halted, stunned by the path her wild thoughts had taken. With a sharp pull, she reined them in. Fog was fog. Fog had nothing whatever to do with lovers. And for that matter, neither did she.

Kit had gotten on her already inflamed nerves, that was all. She was snapping at dust balls these days. And really, he was the *most* annoying man on the face of the earth. He had deliberately set himself to rile her up, and she had given him the satisfaction of seeing her thoroughly riled.

"I am a complete idiot," she said.

Fidgets made a sympathetic noise.

"You will do well to stay clear of him," she advised. "Mind you, I am speaking as an idiot, and I know your kind are reputed to be wise. Nevertheless, take a lesson from my own sorry behavior, Fidgets, and direct your affections to a creature who is capable of returning them. Which like does *not*, by the way, include a certain smuggler of our acquaintance."

The owl nuzzled her scalp with its beak.

And now I am talking to a bird, she thought, wholly disgusted with herself.

But what else was there to do? A good healthy walk to dispel her churning energy was out of the question in this weather. She dared not risk the precipitous descent to the cave, where Diana was isolated with the horse and her own thoughts, and she couldn't use the stairs while Kit was awake.

Above all, she must not return to the cottage. Not yet.

So she stood in place for a long time and told Fidgets stories about the five recalcitrant boys in her charge, never mind that the owl had heard them all before.

Until now she hadn't realized how often she confided in the stubby assemblage of feathers and claws. Except for Diana, with whom she had exchanged only a few letters before the last of them begged for her help and brought her north, she had no other friends. Most times she was kept too busy to notice, of course. How came it that her loneliness, her longing for things she could never have, so forcibly struck her at a time when she had more responsibilities than ever to distract her?

Before he sent her wits begging, she had firmly intended to ask Kit for an explanation of what she had muddled into last night. She must discover if he and the other smugglers had been aiming for her cave before they were accosted on the sands. Instead she had staggered out into the fog, weak-kneed and vibrating with absurd, wholly inappropriate female vapors—she didn't know what else to call them—and now here she was. Accomplishing nothing.

Well, she *was* getting wet and cold.

That was something, she decided, and enough of an accomplishment for her to order her feet to start moving again. For several minutes she stumbled about in the fog, but eventually she ran directly into the tree stump where she had parked Kit fewer than eight hours before.

How very odd. She felt as if she had known him for a lifetime. When the plain fact was, she didn't even know his full name.

At least she knew her way from here to the cottage. Fidgets took French leave when she arrived at the door, off on important owl business, she supposed, inconsiderately abandoning her to face Kit all by herself.

Where was an owl when a person really needed one?

Stiffening her spine, she raised the latch and entered the cottage.

Kit was sitting where she'd left him, but he hadn't been there the entire time she was gone. At the very least he'd made his way to the table and back, because he was greedily gnawing his way through the heel end of the bread loaf. The towel she had placed over his bare chest lay in a heap on the floor.

She jabbed a finger in his direction. "You are devouring Mrs. Preston's breakfast, sir."

"Where *is* Mrs. Preston?" he inquired with a full mouth.

"That's none of your business. But when she returns, she'll have nothing to eat."

His face looked contrite, but his eyes were dancing. "In that case, I am truly sorry. She has no taste, I gather, for what is contained in those jars on the shelf?"

Insufferable man! Lucy couldn't imagine why she had a sudden urge to laugh. "You must be feeling better if you can wolf an entire loaf of bread."

"To the contrary." He sank an inch or two on the folded pallet. "I was feeling frailer than a lightskirt's virtue, so I rolled off the cot and crawled to the table and forced myself to take some nourishment. You are meant to be awed by my courage and impressed by my initiative."

"How unfortunate for you, then, that I am only vexed by your effrontery." She mustered the courage to approach the chair beside his cot but lacked the resolve to seat herself. Propping one hand on the chair back for support, she focused her gaze on the wall directly above his head. "If you have no objections, sir, I wish to discuss the events of last night."

"Certainly." He popped the last nugget of bread in his mouth. "Anything to oblige. What do you wish to know?"

She decided that she trusted him least of all when he was being cooperative. "That is perfectly clear, sir. What you were doing, and where you were going, and why you were shot."

"Well, that's simple enough then. My companions and I were, shall we say, *importing* a few bottles of wine and spirits when we were rudely interrupted by a pack of thugs. Being gentlemen, and also because they were pointing guns at us, we graciously offered them our cargo." He gave her a speculative look. "You cannot have been far away, Miss Luke. Did you not see all this for yourself?"

"I was on the cliff, and it was exceedingly dark. Mostly I saw lanterns and shadows. Some of them began running in one direction and some went more slowly in the other, leading what I assume were pack animals. But I'd no idea what was transpiring, I assure you."

42

"Ah." He folded his uninjured arm behind his head. "So long as you are still on your feet, would it be too much trouble to fetch me something to drink?"

"Not at all." It was a relief to escape across the room, truth be told. Looking at him made it infernally difficult to pay attention to anything else. "But do proceed with your story, sir. What was your destination before the thugs appeared?"

"What's that to the point? We never got there, did we?"

"Indulge me." In fact, this was the only piece of information she required of him, but it wouldn't do to say so.

"If you must know," he said amiably, "we were headed to a spot just north of the Keer Channel. We'd have taken a more direct route, but with the tide due to turn, we elected to move closer to shore and follow the coastline."

"I see." Her hands were trembling as she filled a tankard with ale. "You understand my concern, sir. If criminals are operating in this vicinity, it will not be safe for Mrs. Preston to remain here in the cottage."

"She is in no danger from the general run of smugglers, you may be sure. Since the war embargoes ended, most are common folk who mean only to stock their cellars without paying import tariffs. The real criminals have moved on to more profitable ventures."

"Those were not *real criminals* firing bullets last night?"

"I've no idea who they were," he admitted, all trace of amusement in his voice gone. "Come sit beside me, Luke. I'll give you a plain tale, and a truthful one. You are entitled to that much, after placing your own life in danger by coming to my rescue."

Reserving judgment on how much truth she was likely to hear, she gave him the tankard and sat on the chair with her hands folded in her lap.

He took a long swallow of ale. "I pretty much abandoned the midnight trade at war's end, and was a mere dabbler before that. But I'm always ripe for a bit of excitement and chanced to meet up with three Lancashire lads in a pub house several nights ago. After a few togs of ale, they confided their plans to transport a load of goods across the sands, if only they could locate a carter willing to mark the way without betraying them to the constable. It happens I am friendly with one such, so we all joined forces."

"What precisely is a carter?"

"You are not a local then? Well, it's a dangerous business, crossing the sands. Morecambe Bay is much like a saucer, enormous but shallow. You have seen how it empties when the tide goes out. But four rivers and four smaller streams drain into the bay, and the courses of their channels are continually changing. The push and pull of the tide also creates sandbanks and areas of virtual quicksand, never at the same places from one day to the next. A carter is a guide, someone who has made it his profession to ride out when the tide has ebbed and mark a safe crossing with birch branches. Folks have been using the sands as a shortcut for centuries, and I understand the first guides were all from a family by the name of Carter." He grinned. "Well, that was a long answer to a short question. Where was I in my story before I wandered off?"

"You were drinking in a pub," she said tartly. "And plotting with smugglers."

"Nice chaps," he corrected, "and farmers by trade. This was their first venture into the business, and they'd little idea what they were about. They had gotten so far as to take delivery of the shipment but feared to use the land route to carry it from Furness to their destination. That was what caught my attention. No one patrols the roads these days, for smuggling is no longer of real concern to the authorities. Indeed, that is precisely why I lost interest in the profession—no challenge to it anymore."

"Good heavens. You broke the law because it *amused* you to do so?"

"That would be a fair assessment. But we digress. My new confederates told me they had heard of several caravans being ambushed by a band of armed hooligans. I made further inquiries among the suppliers—the fellows who transport the contraband across the Channel—and learned the attacks had begun only a few months ago. They are none too pleased, since the amateurs who have been buying their shipments are losing heart and reneging on their contracts."

"I believe, sir, that I am learning more about smuggling than I really need to know."

He laughed. "Don't forget that you were the one who insisted on this topic to begin with. I'd much rather talk about you, and where you come from, and what you are doing—"

"Never mind that!" she snapped, heat searing her cheeks. "I presume that the thugs who accosted you were the same ones who have been making trouble elsewhere. But how did they know when and where you would be crossing the sands?"

"Does it matter? I was in this for a lark, moonbeam. If thugs are robbing smugglers, someone else will have to get to the bottom of it. To be sure, I hope one day to meet up again with the rascal who shot me. There will be a reckoning then, I promise you. But otherwise, I care nothing for the hows and whys of last night's misadventure. It is done with."

She couldn't decide what she thought of his indifference to an attack during which he might well have died. In his place, she'd not have rested until she solved the mystery and saw the perpetrators hauled off to prison. Bad people should be made to pay for their crimes, or so she had always believed.

"Would you rather I were a bloodthirsty sort of fellow?" Kit inquired amiably. "I'm sorry to disappoint you. But revenge, you know, is a great waste of time. No one gains from it, the avenger least of all. And besides, why would anyone choose to dwell in the past when the future is ever so much more promising?"

"Is it?" Lucy no sooner spoke than she wished the words unsaid. They came out of their own accord, and now she could only hope that Kit did not take their meaning. She hurried to change the subject. "How came the man to shoot you, sir? Did you provoke him?"

When an entire minute passed without a reply, she dragged her gaze to his face.

It was expressionless, but he regarded her steadily from those disconcerting blue eyes. "I wondered if you ever meant to look at me again, moonbeam."

"C-certainly. Whenever there is any need to do so." She ordered her hands to stop clawing at each other. "But you have not answered my questions."

"I'll start with the first one then," he said. "Yes, it is."

He was holding her gaze so firmly that she could not tear it away, however hard she tried. She understood well enough which question he was answering, of course. "If you say so," she said lightly. "On to number two."

Kit shook his head. "Have it your way, my dear. For now. We shall speak again on the subject another day. As for why the scoundrel shot me, I can tell you only what happened. The robbers have never done violence before, so far as I know. In any case, this chap seemed to be in charge of the others. After directing them to make off with the donkeys, he took hold of Jason's bridle and tried to lead him to shore. Jason was out of temper already, mind you. He's not accustomed to being put to haul a wagon and he don't like it worth a fig. So he bit the impertinent fellow."

"Oh."

"*Oh,* indeed. That earned him a swat across the muzzle. Naturally I went after the man who had just hit my horse, but my foot hit a patch of wet sand and sank in directly as he pulled the trigger. The bullet propelled me backward, Jason jolted at the blast of gunfire, a box fell off the wagon and landed atop m'foot; everyone who was still there and able to run, ran off, and there you have it. At the conclusion Jason was still hitched to the wagon and I was trapped under the box, which was how you found us when you came to my rescue."

"A botched job all around," she said, regarding him with a distinct lack of pleasure. "No one involved in this idiotic enterprise can be pleased with the outcome. I certainly am not. And you are under a misapprehension, sir. I did not come to *your* rescue. I came out on the sands to rescue the horse."

He bent over with laughter. "B-bloody hell, woman, what won't you say? Next you'll be telling me you regret picking me up along the way."

"I've had that thought on more than one occasion," she informed him honestly. "In fact, I'm having it right now." Standing, she plucked the empty tankard from his hand and carried it to the table. "I should tell you, I suppose, that Mrs. Preston has grown inordinately fond of your horse and is taking excellent care of him. Unfortunately, it falls to me to take care of *you*."

"You drew the short straw then. But I'll be a good lad, moonbeam, and leave you in peace for a time. Fact is, there is probably more ale inside me than blood at the moment. I'm devilish near to falling asleep."

Sweeter words he could not have spoken. Lucy returned to the cot, lifted away the straw pallet, and helped him settle flat again with his head on the pillow. That required her to wrap her arms around him and lower him down, or so he insisted. He could not move without her help, he said, and she was too relieved that he meant to take a nap to argue with him.

But her palms and fingers were burning from the touch of his skin and the provocative feel of a well-muscled male back when she was done. She rounded up her straying wits. "The blacksmith and the apothecary will be here as soon as the fog lifts, sir. Until then, sleep well."

"We're expecting guests? Lucifer! I had forgot. Wouldn't want to meet 'em in the altogether, would I?" He turned angelic blue eyes to her face. "This is not what I usually say to a female, Miss Luke, but could you possibly help me get into my pants?"

"What a thing to ask!" she declared, her very bones on fire to imagine it. "Certainly not. Robbie will soon be here, and you can beg his assistance."

"Rather have yours," Kit mumbled as his lashes drifted shut.

Chapter 5

Lucy kept her fingers crossed as Giles Handa removed the bandage and examined Kit's wound through his thick round spectacles.

"Ummm," he said, poking at the swollen flesh around the bullet hole, which had already begun to seal itself.

Kit yelped when Giles bent over to check the back of his shoulder.

The apothecary took his time about it. He was an earnest young man, Lucy had discovered when first she met him at his small shop in Silverdale. Tall and gaunt, he had a self-effacing manner that belied his keen intelligence.

At long last he straightened. "The injury is healing cleanly and with remarkable speed, but it should be closely watched. Should there be signs of a high fever, or red streaks radiating from the wound, a physician must be summoned immediately. For now, I should like to clean the area thoroughly and apply basilicum ointment. I also suggest the gentleman keep his arm in a sling until the opening has fully knitted."

Kit made a face.

"Do whatever is necessary," Lucy said before he could object. "Is he well enough to return with you to Silverdale?"

"No," Kit said.

"Yes," Giles said at the same moment. "In my judgment only," he added. "The patient knows best how he feels, of course."

"Weak as a newborn kitten," the patient clarified dolefully.

"Nevertheless, it is certainly best that I go with you. My presence here is a great inconvenience to Luke and Mrs. Preston."

Indeed it is, Lucy thought, clamping her lips together. She'd wager he was feigning both the weakness and the offer to depart, which he'd rendered in a frail, resigned voice. The slight moan at the end had been a nice touch. Giles looked troubled, and even Robbie cast her a questioning glance.

"The track is rough all the way to Silverdale," Giles said hesitantly. "There is some danger that his wound will reopen."

"Oh, very well," she said, glaring at Kit. He gave her back a tremulous, grateful smile.

Giles opened his case of medicines. "Have you a length of fabric with which I can devise a sling?"

"I'll find something," Lucy replied, glad for an excuse to leave the room and Kit's mocking gaze. She rummaged through her portmanteau and found nothing suitable, unless she were to rip apart one of her two plain traveling dresses or demolish her flannel night rail. It seemed that only her shawl—her precious Norwich shawl—would do. She sighed. It was quite the nicest thing she had ever owned, and the colors, primarily deep red and rich purple, were her favorites. She draped it around her shoulders one last time before refolding it and returning to the main room.

She was wickedly gratified to see Kit wince as Giles dabbed his shoulder with ointment. But when he saw her and caught her eye, he winked incorrigibly.

Teeth clenched, she placed the shawl on the table before she used it to strangle him, which she was sorely tempted to do. "Robbie, shall we finish unloading the wagon?"

She marched out the door and headed speedily for the cliff, muttering all the while. The foggy morning had given way to a warm, cloudless afternoon, but she took no pleasure in it. The crystal-blue sky put her too much in mind of a certain gentleman's eyes.

Robbie's long stride soon brought him even with her and

they ascended the grassy slope side by side. "A bit of a lad, he is. I dinna think he's so puny as he makes himself out to be."

"He's a thumping great menace, Robbie, not to mention insufferable. But Giles is correct. Being jostled in the wagon could undo everything, and I am still hoping to avoid summoning a doctor. Some physicians feel obliged to report shootings to the authorities, I am informed."

When the grass began to thin near the top of the hill, Lucy halted. "Wait here a moment." She moved ahead cautiously, pausing again when she caught sight of Morecambe Bay. The tide was out, and miles of brown sand stretched to the horizon. Wishing she had thought to bring Kit's spyglass, she scanned for human figures, found none, and beckoned Robbie to join her at cliff's edge.

"See there?" She pointed to the wagon, still piled with boxes, clearly visible in the bright sunshine. "That's where I found him. I rather thought someone would have retrieved the other boxes by now."

"If they mean to come back, most likely they'll do so after dark. Lowest tide will be 'round about three o'clock, which means they could be on the sands anytime between one and five of the morning."

"The witch must walk, I fear. Did Giles remember to bring the ointment? After a night in the rain, my cape has been washed quite clean."

"He brought it, but that don't mean you should be usin' it." Robbie scoured his chin with an enormous hand. "Better I watch from the cliff tonight."

"You must take Giles home, Robbie, and you've already made two trips to the cottage today. There is nothing to fear, I promise you." She gazed out over the flat expanse of mud and wet sand, where sunlight danced in the rippled pools left by the ebb tide. "I mean to go into Lancaster tomorrow," she said. "Surely by now there is a letter for me at the Anchor Inn."

She spoke with more assurance than she felt. Miss Wetherwood, headmistress at the Wetherwood Academy for Young

Ladies, had been planning to retire while Lucy was a student there. Her health had worsened by the time Lucy left to take up her post as a governess in Dorset, but she was still at the academy two years later when Diana completed her studies. Perhaps she was there yet. In any case, she was their only hope.

"Lancaster is a far way to go for a letter that mightna be there, lass."

"Yes. But so long as I am in the city, I also mean to consult a solicitor."

"I dinna trust lawyers," Robbie said gruffly.

"Nor do I, although I've never actually met one, but we require legal counsel. Until now I thought it too great a risk, but as things have turned out, we have little choice. I only hope I stumble upon a solicitor who is both honest and competent, for I've no idea where to apply. And tonight I must invent a story that will draw from him the information I require without arousing his suspicions."

Robbie shuffled his feet. "I've not wanted to tell you, but there was a notice in the Carnforth newspaper two days ago. And Carnforth being not much of a town, I expect the notice has appeared from Lancaster to Kendal and beyond. A reward of five hundred pounds is offered to whoever discovers the whereabouts of Miss Diana Whitney. There was a description of her, too. A full description," he added unhappily.

Lucy's stomach coiled into a knot. "Dear heavens. Such a fortune! Everyone and his brother will be on the hunt."

Robbie opened his massive arms. "Come here, lassie."

After a moment she threw herself against his broad chest and permitted him to hold her. The blows had been coming so rapidly that she feared she could no longer withstand them on her own. She was terrified of making a wrong move, of doing the wrong thing. "What would we do without you, Robbie?" she murmured, her face pressed to his rough leather waistcoat. "How can we ever repay you?"

"Ach, never you mind about me. Miss Diana is the age my daughter would be hadna the cholera taken her. Give me one

51

of your smiles now, lass, and let's have no more talk about payment."

Lucy couldn't remember the last time she had smiled and meant it. But she stepped back, carved her lips into what probably looked like a grimace, and blinked back the tears that had gathered in her eyes. It was purely luck, or perhaps divine providence, that she had met Robert MacNab when first she arrived in Lancashire. If it was the Lord who had put Robbie in her path, perhaps He was watching out for Diana after all.

On the other hand, it was surely the devil who had sent Kit to plague them. "I expect Giles has about finished with his patient," she said, brushing her hands against her trousers. "Shall we unload the supplies?"

"I mislike you going to Lancaster," Robbie muttered as they descended the sloping hill. "But if you willna change your mind, I'll come back in the morning with the wagon and carry you to the posthouse."

"Thank you, but it's only a few miles, and I intend to catch the coach that comes by at six of the morning. With Kit snoring away in the cottage, I doubt I'll sleep well anyway."

"You'll be Mrs. Preston?"

"Of course." She frowned as new complications rose up to assault her. "Which means that Diana will have to spend the entire day in the cave, since I cannot be back here before late afternoon. And Kit will be alone in the cottage. Drat. There's no telling what he'll get up to. Can you come by and keep watch over him?"

"Aye. I've a job to do in Beetham, but I'll take care of it first thing and come here directly after."

They reached the wagon, and Lucy gathered an armful of folded blankets, towels, and a pillow while Robbie grabbed a heavy bundle of firewood. Three trips were required before they had carried all the supplies into the cottage, where Giles was closing his medicine case and issuing quiet orders to his patient.

Kit, his arm in the sling and a saintly smile on his face, nodded as if he meant to obey them all.

Not likely, Lucy thought as she walked with Robbie and Giles back to the wagon. "Be careful tomorrow, Robbie. He'll try to quiz you, but tell him nothing. Thus far he knows only that my name is Luke, and he believes that Mrs. Preston is mute. Should he inquire where we have gone, say only that we shall return before nightfall. Giles, can he get about on his own?"

"Impossible to say, Miss Lucy. I don't know what to make of the gentleman. But I slipped a bit of laudanum in the ale I gave him to drink, so you'll not be bothered with him for the next few hours."

"Bless you!" she said sincerely. Then she saw Giles place a large leather boot in the wagon. "What is *that*?"

Giles flushed. "He asked me to get him a pair of boots, what with one of his own being cut to ribbons. I'm taking this along for sizing."

"You'll do no such thing! He'll get into less trouble barefooted. Robbie can bring sandals for him tomorrow, but we'll hide them until he's well enough to leave."

"Very well, ma'am. I never meant to hurry the cobbler, you may be sure. And the gentleman was insistent, so I took the boot rather than quarrel with him."

She patted his hand. "I should learn tact from you, sir. Thank you."

When the wagon was on its way along the narrow track, Lucy went to the rock where she had concealed her cape the previous night. Was it such a short time ago? Twelve or thirteen hours only since she saw the lanterns on the bay? It seemed a lifetime.

She shook out her witch's garb, soaking wet from the rainstorm, and laid it out on the grass to begin drying. Once Kit was asleep, she would take the cape and wig inside and stretch them in front of the fireplace.

She gave some thought to bringing the horse up from the cave and tethering him where he could graze. This was an excellent opportunity to do so, what with the tide out and another hour or two remaining before sunset. But she simply didn't feel up to the task. She'd have to lead him nearly a mile down the beach to where the cliff gave way to a slope he could ascend, and another mile back to the cottage.

Besides, Kit might find him in the morning before Robbie arrived to stand guard. Better the horse remain where he was for now. He was in good hands, that was certain. Diana had taken her scissors to Cow's Mouth Inlet and clipped fresh grass for him to eat, and he would be company for her tomorrow in the cave.

She must be frantic to know what was happening, though. With a sigh, Lucy began the steep descent down a rocky path that any intelligent goat would balk at, marveling that Kit had managed to climb it in spite of his injuries.

A man to be reckoned with, that one. She must never under-estimate what he was capable of doing, or permit herself to trust him for a single moment.

Kit woke, disoriented, sometime in the middle of the night. Except for the crackle of the dying fire, the room was eerily silent. Carefully he raised himself on one elbow and looked over at the pallet alongside the hearth.

The blankets lay flat.

He was almost certain he'd awakened earlier, and had a vague recollection of seeing Luke curled up with those blankets mounded over her. He had wanted to speak to her then, but couldn't get his mouth to move. Even now it felt full of cotton wadding.

That bloody apothecary must have put laundanum into the cup of ale. Lucifer! Next time he would be more careful, but dammit, he had *liked* Giles Handa. And for his sins, he forgot that Handa was in league with a pernicious female who seemed to like Kit Valliant best when he was unconscious.

Well, he was wide awake now. So where was *she*?

Probably she had only stepped outside for a few moments, females being subject to calls of nature, too. He lay back to await her return, resolving to try again to discover who she was

and what the devil she was up to. Time was running out. She'd
not been fooled by his display of weakness, he knew, although
it was not wholly feigned. Almost certainly she would send
him on his way tomorrow, unless he found some way to persuade her otherwise.

He lay quietly for a few minutes, watching the play of firelight on the low ceiling, considering how best to approach her.
If all else failed, he would be forced to identify himself and
place the considerable resources of his family at her disposal.
But he hoped that would not be necessary. He much preferred
to rescue her on his own, assuming she required rescuing, and
his instincts told him that she did. He fancied the opportunity
to prove himself a knight in shining armor, even if he hadn't so
much as a pair of shoes to put on his feet at the moment.

The soft wool of the shawl that held his arm immobile tickled
his neck. He sniffed at it, detecting the faint scent of lavender
that he noticed whenever Luke leaned close to him. It must be
hers, the shawl. He wondered if she had other female garb
stashed away in that mysterious back room.

Looking over, he saw that the door was closed. Perhaps she
was in there with Mrs. Preston. He listened intently for the sound
of voices, hearing only the crackle of the fire and the rustle of
coals and ashes dropping through the grate.

She'd been gone a devilish long time, and that was only counting the time since he woke up. No telling when she'd left the
room. Losing patience, he swung his legs over the side of the
cot and sat upright, pleased when there was no trace of dizzi-
ness. His head was relatively clear, the pain in his shoulder had
settled to a low throb, and a check of his ankle confirmed that
the swelling had gone down considerably. All in all, he felt in
fine fettle and certainly well enough to go exploring.

Giles had placed the walking stick where he could easily
reach it. After coming to his feet, he limped to the door that led
to the back room and pressed his ear against the rough wood.
Hearing nothing, he gently raised the latch and pushed, but the
door remained firmly sealed. It must be barred from within.

After a mental debate, he gave up the idea of knocking for admittance and went to the black-curtained window farthest from the hearth. With one finger, he made a crack between the curtains and peered outside. The night was clear and dark, with the merest sliver of a moon suspended just above the place where woodland gave way to the sweep of grassy hill that led to the limestone cliff.

Robbie had stuffed him into his breeches, but he remained barefoot, shirtless, and had minimal use of half his supply of limbs. Good sense demanded that he wait until she came back, he acknowledged, thoroughly disgruntled. In his usual state of excellent health, he'd have tracked her down if it took the rest of the night.

Well, so long as he was up, he might as well pay a visit to the tree. A widemouthed jar had been shoved under the cot in lieu of a chamber pot, but he misliked putting it to use with two ladies in residence. Stepping outside, he paused to enjoy the cool breeze sifting through his hair and the smell of salt in the cold air. Overhead, stars winked against a black velvet sky. With a sailor's eye, he immediately picked out the North Star and traced the position of the constellations in the October sky. It was close to three of the morning, he would guess from the lie of Orion and Pegasus.

He made his way to the corner of the cottage, relieved himself, and had just buttoned his trouser flap when he caught sight of a greenish white light on the hillside. What the devil? Plastering himself against the tree trunk, he gazed past the gnarled bark at a startling apparition.

It was moving parallel with the top of the hill a considerable distance away, but then it turned and began to descend. At first the shape, somewhat triangular, seemed to be floating several inches above the ground. But as it came nearer he discerned the outline of a glowing hooded cape.

Fascinated, he saw it angle slightly away from him, heading toward the cleft in the limestone crag where Luke had brought him up from the sands last night. Or that was his guess, from the direction it had taken.

Kit put no credit in ghosts and hobgoblins. That was a flesh-and-blood creature stalking the hills, to what purpose he could not imagine, and he'd bet a pony it was Luke's lithe body under the cape.

A moment later he changed his mind. A play of wind lifted the hood from her head, and instead of Luke's boyish cap of hair, he saw long tresses flowing behind her like a bridal veil. If left to fall down her back, the hair would reach to the woman's waist.

So it wasn't Luke after all. Mrs. Preston, perhaps? The long mane of hair could well have been concealed under her hat and veil when last he saw her. The two ladies must be sisters, he decided. He'd known a good many women in his life, many of them intimately, but had never before seen hair of that unusual moonlight color. It must be peculiar to Luke's family.

The revelation, such as it was, explained nothing of any use. So what that the women were sisters? That did not account for their several disguises, especially this particularly bizarre one. As he watched, the caped figure appeared to sink into the bowels of the earth.

It occurred to him that anyone unacquainted with the mysterious goings-on at the cottage would likely take fright at what he had just seen. The figure had been walking along the cliff, he would guess, precisely to terrify anyone who might be out on the sands. Had he not known about the rugged path, the one he had climbed with such effort, he might have been spooked into giving credit to otherworldly apparitions.

What were they hiding?

He had nearly reached the front door when a whirring sound caused him to spin around. A small shape whizzed past his head, arced a turn, and swooped toward him.

"Bloody hell!" He regarded the owl with displeasure. "You scared the devil out of me."

The owl flew past and circled again.

"Want inside, do you?" Kit opened the door. "Well, come on then."

Fidgets flew into the room and dropped something small and brown at Kit's feet.

"What's this?" In the dim firelight, it was hard to tell. A small rodent of some sort, he guessed, poking it gently with the walking stick. A deceased rodent.

The owl, now perched on the coat peg, began making those familiar snoring noises. She looked, Kit thought, rather pleased with herself.

"If this is a gift," Kit advised her kindly, "you really shouldn't have. And here I didn't get you anything. Tell you what, Fidgets. It's the thought that counts. Why don't you take this luscious morsel outside and have yourself a snack?"

The owl tilted her head, regarding him from shiny eyes.

There was no help for it. Kit wasn't churlish enough to refuse the offering, so he lifted the limp creature on the tip of the walking stick and placed it on a saucer. "Yum. I'll have it for breakfast. How very thoughtful of you." He wondered if Fidgets meant to perch there watching him until he ate the thing. "But trust me, bird, I cannot fertilize your eggs, or however it is you owls make more owls. Besides, I'm a ramshackle fellow. All the ladies will tell you so. I'd only break your heart."

He set the saucer on the table, not sure how to proceed. He certainly didn't relish the thought of two round eyes fixed on him for the next several hours. "It's a lovely night," he said firmly, pointing to the open door. "A pretty young thing like you should be out kicking up your claws."

To his surprise, the owl flew out of the cottage.

Before she could change her mind, he hurried to close the door. For a moment he considered opening it long enough to toss the rodent outside, where it could make a meal for some other creature. But what if Fidgets found out what he'd done?

He must be out of his wits to worry about offending a bird's sensibilities. What next? he wondered, stirring the fire with a poker. A would-be witch stalking the headlands and a besotted owl delivering love tokens to the reluctant object of her affections.

Well, he had wanted one last adventure before coming to grips with his future. At nine-and-twenty, a man ought to have chosen a profession and made himself useful. Or so his brother pointed out rather too often. Of late, and without pleasure, Kit had begun to agree. But he enjoyed useless activities, so long as they were exciting, and every profession considered suitable for the son of an earl struck him as crushingly boring.

He had once thought of enlisting in the Royal Navy, but James wouldn't hear of it. One brother in the military would suffice, he had decreed, and Alex was by then a captain in the 44th Foot. Besides, James had reminded him, taking orders and adhering to strict discipline was not in his nature. Kit had no argument for that.

In fact, the only thing he had ever truly wanted was an enormous family—a dozen kids at the least—and a house near the water so that he could sail. Given that much, he would gladly dig ditches or quarry shale to put food on the table.

He placed two more logs on the grate. It would not come to manual labor, he knew. There was money—how much, he'd no idea—willed him by his mother and held in trust by his brother, to be released at the earl's discretion. So far James had not parted with a groat of it, preferring to keep the funds invested until Kit showed signs of settling down.

Just as well. Had James signed over the inheritance, he'd likely have squandered the whole on gifts for the ladies whose favors he enjoyed or rounds of drinks in the taprooms where he spent many of his evenings. Money streamed through his fingers like water. Kit knew better than to ask his brother to release what was rightfully his because it would be needed later, for his children.

Meantime there was the mystery of Luke and Mrs. Preston to unriddle. Surely one of them would return to the cottage before very much longer. He went to the cot, slipped between the rough blankets, and adjusted his arm in the sling. Except for a low, steady throbbing, his shoulder scarcely hurt at all. By tomorrow, he should be able to get around without difficulty, although Luke would toss him out on his ear if she knew it.

He meant to tell her, though, as soon as she came back. Show her, if necessary. It was past time they both started to give over the truth.

But no one came in through the front door, or through the door that was barred, and his eyelids began to feel like lead weights.

He tried to stay awake by reviewing what he had learned about the pearly-haired sisters. Very little, he had to admit, and every new detail left him more puzzled than before. If that had been Mrs. Preston walking on the hillside, where was Luke? And where was it Mrs. Preston was headed when she vanished? Was there something of interest at the bottom of the cliff?

After a while his thoughts began tripping over one another until they were hopelessly entangled. He wondered why Mrs. Preston wore that black veil over her face. He wondered if he was really falling in love with Luke, as he suspected, or merely indulging himself in a pleasurable fantasy. How came it that an owl had chosen him as its mate? He recalled the rodent in the saucer and wondered if he ought to get up and do something about it.

Somewhere along the way, lavender-scented and relentless, sleep washed over him like the tide in Morecambe Bay.

Chapter 6

The sound of groaning hinges prodded Kit awake. Cracking his lids the barest fraction, he saw Mrs. Preston sweep in from the back room carrying a lantern, an umbrella, and a small satchel. As before, she wore a severe black dress, long-sleeved and cut high at the neck, concealing every inch of her skin. Her hair and face were covered by the veiled hat.

She had also, he noted with interest, grown nearly two inches taller.

After placing the lantern near the hearth and the satchel and umbrella by the front door, she gathered dishes from the shelf where they were stowed and carried them over to the table. Then she froze.

Ah yes. The rodent. Kit decided that this was not a good time to pretend to be asleep. "Good morning," he said cheerfully.

The veil lifted slightly as she swung her head in his direction, offering him a glimpse of Luke's firm chin. "I expect you are wondering about the chap in the saucer," he said. "Fidgets brought it in last night. A love offering, unless I am very much mistaken, and no doubt I am expected to swallow it whole. Thus far, I've been unable to bring myself to do so."

With deliberation she set down the dishes and flatware, picked up the saucer, went to the door, and threw the rodent unceremoniously outside. She sent the saucer flying, too.

"So much for love," Kit said mournfully as she returned to the shelf and grabbed a half loaf of bread, a hunk of smoked ham, and a wedge of cheese. She flung them onto a platter with a decided *thunk*.

"Is that our breakfast?" he inquired, sitting up.

Ignoring him, she filled a battered metal tankard with ale from a large pitcher and set it with the food.

One tankard. "Are you going out, ma'am?"

She slammed a knife and fork on the table.

"May I ask where?" he persisted, solely to annoy her. She'd no intention of telling him, he was certain.

Shaking her head, she went to the door. Then she turned back and approached the cot with clear reluctance, pointing to his shoulder.

"Are you inquiring about my health?" he asked, amused. "Indeed, I am precisely at the mark where I require no further medical assistance but cannot leave here in the foreseeable future without doing severe damage to my constitution."

He was fairly certain she muttered an oath behind that heavy veil.

"I'll be gone in a week or so," he assured her with a grin. "Probably to post the banns, if Fidgets has her way with me. Shall I presume that Luke is lurking about in case I need her— er, him—while you are away?"

Tossing her hands in the air in a gesture of disgust, she flounced across the room, grabbed the umbrella and satchel, and departed in a huff.

Temper, temper, he thought, laughing aloud. But where could she be off to in such a rush? It was still pitch-dark outside, he'd observed when she opened the door.

The dirt floor was cool under his feet when he stood to test his bruised ankle. Although painful, it felt sound enough that he decided to do without the cane for the time being. He wrapped a blanket around his shoulders against the chilly predawn air, limped to the table, and tucked into his breakfast. After so many meals of bread and soup, he'd a wolf in his stomach. It was as well the ladies were not present to see him demolish every morsel without resorting to civilized manners.

There had been no sound from the other room, and he wondered if the long-haired sister was in there. When he'd finished his ale, he went to the door and listened as he had done the previous night, hearing nothing. "Hullo?" He rapped on the door. "Anyone there?"

No reply, which was as he'd expected.

"I require help, please." He put a quaver in his voice. "Quickly. I've torn open my wound and it is bleeding in a gush."

Either she didn't believe him or she didn't care. The door remained firmly closed.

Lucifer! These females were hard as standing stones. Without much hope, he tried the latch and was astonished when the door swung open to reveal a windowless cubicle no larger than a stable stall.

Feeling foolish, Kit went back to retrieve the lantern and set about examining the few items stored in the room. There was a three-legged stool, a good-size portmanteau, a wicker cage, and a long wooden box. He raised the lid and sifted through the contents, finding blankets, towels, candles, and at the very bottom, his leather saddle pack. He took it out and unclasped the buckles.

Someone had sorted through the contents, he could tell. The two shirts and half-dozen handkerchiefs were folded more neatly than he'd ever folded anything in his life. Nothing appeared to be missing, though. The searcher must have been disappointed to find so little, but on his adventures he never carried anything that might serve to identify him.

Returning the lid to the box, he seated himself atop it and considered whether it would be worth the effort to try to pull on a shirt. Unlike most females of his acquaintance, Luke seemed singularly unimpressed by the sight of his manly torso, which left him no good reason to continue leaving it bare. And even the soft thin wool of his shirt would offer protection from the cold when he went outside to explore, as he fully intended to do.

He discovered almost immediately that trying to dress himself had been a bad idea, but once started, he was determined to finish the job. A long painful time later, punctuated by searing oaths and any number of pauses to rest, he finally succeeded in stuffing both arms through the sleeves and tugging the shirt over his head.

Fresh blood—not enough to signify, he hoped—seeped through the bandage and spotted the shirt. He waited awhile to see if he'd done himself injury, still sitting on the box and looking carefully around the room in case he had missed anything.

A carpet of sorts, made of tightly woven straw and about four feet square, lay under the portmanteau. Nothing odd about that, to be sure, but his gaze kept straying back to it. There was something about its position that felt wrong. The box, cage, and stool were neatly set against the wall, but the portmanteau rested nearly dead center in the room.

Curious, he went over to it and lifted it off the carpet. His instincts were abuzz, raising the hair on his arms and driving the blood through his veins in a pounding awareness he had long since learned to trust. Setting the portmanteau on the dirt floor, he bent over and raised one corner of the straw mat, not over-surprised to see a hinged trapdoor.

One mystery solved, he thought, folding the carpet over itself to give him access. There was a slim piece of rope wrapped around one of the wooden boards, but he left it long enough to go back and wrestle his arm into the makeshift sling. The bleeding had stopped, fortunately, and the few drops of blood on his shirt were already drying to a rusty brown.

He brought the lantern closer, set it beside the trapdoor, and gingerly pulled the rope. The door lifted soundlessly on well-oiled hinges. He folded it all the way back and peered down, but even when he lifted the lantern directly over the opening, he could see no more than two or three stairs that had been hewn into the limestone. Beyond was darkness, although he scented salty air and the musty smell of rotting seaweed.

Familiar odors, they were. He had set foot in more than one seacoast cave during his desultory career as a smuggler, and several had boasted tunnels leading to concealed exits.

Kit lowered himself to the floor and swung his feet into the opening. Since his one good arm was occupied with holding the lantern, he could manage only a slow, awkward descent down the steep, moisture-slick stairs. For once, he chose to be cautious. The steps were narrow, and should he lose his footing, there was no telling how far he would fall.

At last he reached the bottom, finding himself in a small grotto. A ragged slice of pale light came through an opening directly ahead, just wide enough to slip through if he went sideways. He set down the lantern on the bottom stair, noticing that several pieces of luggage had been stowed in the darkest curve of the grotto. They were of excellent quality, much finer than the shabby portmanteau in the cottage. Jason's saddle was draped over the largest of them.

Blood pulsed in his ears. He thrived on adventure, always had, and this one was a cracker. Tiptoeing to the break in the limestone grotto, he peered out.

Another cave, perhaps thirty feet long and exceptionally high and wide until it narrowed to a smaller entrance, opened onto Morecambe Bay. Jason was tethered to one of the water-worn boulders that littered the floor of the cave, nibbling at a stack of new-cut grass. Small pink crabs scuttled over the sand and rocks, taking strict care to keep well distant from the horse.

As he stood there a fresh sea breeze lifted his hair and billowed the sleeves of his shirt. And the same breeze, stronger at the entrance of the cave, played with the long, curly auburn hair of the woman who was seated on a flat rock with her back to him, looking out into the dawn.

The other Mrs. Preston, no doubt. This time she was clad in a long-sleeved dress of hunter green. She sat motionless, her back straight, unaware that she had been discovered.

Something about her, perhaps her grave stillness, held him in place. He was reluctant to startle her or, worse, to alarm her, and an uneasy sensation tingled at his spine. He felt pain and longing resonating in his body and, most particularly, in the region of his heart. All his protective instincts went on fire. Whoever she was, she needed help.

It finally dawned on him that she did *not* possess the long, straight, pearly hair he had been expecting. This woman could not have been the specter he'd seen walking the cliffs last night, and Luke was already ruled out because her hair, while the right color, was even shorter than his own. Could there be three women instead of two hiding out in this remote cottage?

While he was considering the best way to approach her, Jason took the matter out of his hands. Kit was standing downwind, but the sea breeze had filtered through the splice in the rocks, bounced off the grotto walls behind him, and carried his odor back to the horse. Scenting a longtime friend, the bay lifted his muzzle and whickered.

The woman turned her head then, and he got the barest glimpse of a beautiful profile before she jumped to her feet. Keeping her back to him, she gestured him frantically to go away.

"It's only the gimpy lodger," he said, taking a few steps in her direction. "I was wondering where you'd gotten to."

Her gestures grew wilder.

He stopped. "You wish me to leave, I take it."

She nodded vigorously.

"My apologies, ma'am, but I'm afraid I cannot oblige you on this occasion. One of you must explain to me what is going on here, and the other young ladies are nowhere to be found."

Again she turned, showing him that splendid profile as she put a finger to her lips. Then she used it to make a negative gesture.

"Ah. I had forgot. You cannot speak."

She nodded even more forcefully and repeated her go-away sign.

"The thing is, my dear, I would bet a pony that you have a perfectly good voice. What I cannot reckon is why you are pretending otherwise. It's all some part of these mysterious goings-on, to be sure, but singularly useless when directed at me. I am not your enemy, my dear."

Suddenly she bolted forward in the direction of the sands, but she halted almost immediately, her shoulders slumping in a gesture of unmistakable resignation.

He moved slowly toward her. "I would be unable to catch you if you chose to run, you know." When he was only a few feet away, she turned slightly. He saw a tear streak down her smooth cheek. *Lucifer!* Did she imagine he would do her harm?

"I can speak," she said quietly. "But I will tell you nothing."

"Not even how I can be of service to you?"

She brushed away a second tear. "That is simple enough. Leave us, and forget that you ever met us."

"I cannot do that, butterfly. You are in some sort of trouble, and I wish to help. Actually, I insist on helping."

"How can a smuggler be of any use? The last thing we require is a hunted criminal on the premises."

"Oh, my. You begin to sound exactly like Luke, or whatever her name is."

"We don't know your name either," she pointed out.

"Christopher Etheridge," he said easily. "Call me Kit. And you are . . . ?"

"I am being sought by people who must not be allowed to find me," she said in a bleak voice.

"Then we shall see to it they do not. I *will* help you, you may rely on it, and I would die before betraying you. As Luke never fails to remind me, I owe you my life. Consider that even a smuggler may have some claim to honor."

She turned her back to him again, arms clasped around her waist as if she were holding herself together by force of will.

He remained where he was, giving her time. She was no more than eighteen or nineteen, he would guess, but he sensed enormous strength in her. At length, she came to a decision. Her spine went arrow straight, she lifted her chin, and without a word she wheeled to face him directly.

Dear God! With effort, he showed no reaction when he saw her right cheek, the one she had so carefully kept from his view until now. He looked at it, of course. He could not help himself.

Marked out in angry red ridges, the scar covered most of her cheek. It resembled a piece of mirror glass struck hard by a pebble. There was a small round scar at the center with narrow lines radiating from it that were sometimes connected by other lines, much like a spiderweb.

The injury could not have happened very long ago, a few weeks perhaps. It was healing cleanly, and he supposed that much of the redness would fade over time. But the scar would remain with her forever.

He lifted his gaze to her eyes, which were shimmering with tears as she awaited his judgment. She expected revulsion, he knew. Perhaps worse. He felt nothing of the like, but for once his glib tongue failed him. How could there be words?

He was enraged at what had been done to her. And he wanted to weep for her, but she would surely mistake his compassion for pity. In the end, not knowing what else to do, he slipped his arm from the sling, moved to her, and drew her into an embrace.

She stiffened, resisting his sympathy, but he rubbed her back with one hand and combed through her hair with the other. Her unscarred cheek was pressed against his chest. He held her for a long time, rocking her gently, and at last she went limp against his body.

Then the tears came. They soaked into his shirt as she wept soundlessly, the minutes passing one after the other while he could do nothing but hold her and wait.

"Oh, dear," she finally mumbled against his shoulder. "Forgive me. Truly, I have sworn n-never to be a watering pot when there is anyone to see me."

"Except perhaps this once," he said mildly. "Tears heal a wounded heart, or so I believe."

"You are much mistaken, sir. I have cried buckets of them, and they serve only to swell up my eyes."

He tilted her chin with his thumb and gazed at her red-rimmed hazel eyes and the long dark lashes, spiky and clumped together with salty tears. "Not this time, I promise you."

"A safe enough promise," she declared with a return of spirit, "since I cannot prove you wrong. You may be sure that I keep well away from mirrors since my . . . since the accident."

He released her, except for the one hand he put gently on her shoulder to hold the connection between them. "Will you tell me what happened, my dear?"

She sighed. "I suppose I must, since you have already found us out. But it is a long and unpleasant tale, sir. You are certain to find it tedious."

"That is most unlikely. I wish to hear every detail, or at least the ones that will direct me to how I can best be of service. But my sore ankle has begun to make its presence felt. Will that fine-looking rock seat us both, do you think?"

When he was settled on one side of the flat stone, she stepped back and regarded him thoughtfully. "The sling is tangled every which way, sir. Shall I remove it and undo the knots?"

"By all means." She required a few moments to regain her composure and order her thoughts, he understood, bending his neck so that she could lift the shawl over his head. "May I know your name?"

"Diana Evangeline Whitney," she replied, sitting beside him with the shawl in her lap. "Under the circumstances, formality would be pointless. Please call me Diana. And my friend—there is only one, by the way—is Lucinda Jennet Preston."

His heart plunged to his feet. She was married! "There really is a Mrs. Preston then," he said tightly.

"A Miss Preston," Diana corrected, working at the knot. "When it is called for, Lucy disguises herself as a widow. Unfortunately, she is compelled to use her own name when dealing with bankers and the like. But as no one knows her here in the north, it is probably safe enough."

Now it was Kit's turn to regain his composure. The brief seconds he had thought Lucy beyond his reach had all but unmanned him.

The significance of what had just happened struck him

forcibly. So there it was. So now he knew without question. He was in love with her.

Indeed, he had suspected as much. His generally reliable instincts had shouted the news when first he saw her, he realized on looking back at the scene. But at the time he'd been half-buried in the sand with blood pouring out of him, and so much had happened since to distract him that he had never decided if his strong attraction to her might be a good deal more than that.

Well, at least *one* problem had been put to rest. Love it was. Convincing her to feel likewise about him was another matter entirely, but he could not get about his wooing right away. Diana's problems, whatever they might be, were clearly more urgent. "If she is playing the part of the widow when she isn't playing Luke," he said, "then who was it masquerading as that luminescent creature I saw last night?"

"Oh, that was Lucy, too." She glanced over at him. "You have been nosing about rather energetically for a man we thought not so very long ago to be knocking at death's door."

He grinned. "Masquerades are not reserved for females, you know. But if that was Lucy on the cliff, how came she by the long hair?"

"It's a wig, of course, but—" She pressed her lips together.

"But what?"

"If you wish to know more, sir, you must ask her to explain. I am willing to tell you about myself and what Lucy has done on my behalf, but I'll not speak of matters which relate to her in a personal way. She will be more than displeased to learn I have spoken with you at all."

He had no doubt of that. "Very well. I'll not intrude, and if I forget myself, cut me off. Is it permitted to tell me why she was stalking the cliffs? Granted she was quite terrifying at first sight, and I presume she means to discourage company from dropping by. But this strikes me as a peculiar way to go about being unneighborly."

"I have never approved of the hauntings," Diana said, "although Lucy is convinced they are effective. She may well be correct. While it is no secret that a reclusive widow has taken up residence in the cottage, no one has dared to pay a friendly call. Do you reside in the area, sir?"

"These days I come and go, but I grew up within two hours' ride of here."

"Then perhaps you are familiar with the story of the Lancashire Witches." She finally succeeded in undoing the troublesome knot and stood to shake out the fringed shawl.

"Never heard of them. Westmoreland runs more to sheep than witches."

"As does Lancashire these days. But two hundred years ago, over by Pendle Hill, a number of women were tried for the practice of witchcraft. It was all nonsense, to be sure, but they were condemned and hanged nonetheless. Most every Lancashire child grows up hearing the stories. Their parents, who were told the same stories when they were children, believe that the witches still walk these hills, casting spells and doing wicked things to anyone who comes within reach."

"I see. Lucy is exploiting a local superstition to keep people away. Devilish clever of her."

"Foolhardy, in my opinion." Diana draped the shawl around his neck and moved behind him. "But she won't be stopped. Once Lucy gets something into her head, she is more stubborn than a Lancashire farmer, which is saying a great deal. Until a few weeks ago she had never set foot in Lancashire, but she soon heard the legends because there is no escaping them. And by purest coincidence, one of the poor women hanged was named Jennet Preston. That's how she got the notion, and I'm sorry to say that she found someone—the apothecary who tended to you yesterday—who could show her how to make her cloak shine in the dark. He gave her an ointment that turns the trick, and off she went to strike terror into the hearts of poor cocklers and fishermen. Truth be told, I think she rather enjoys being the Lancashire Witch."

Kit burst out laughing.

"It's not in the least amusing, sir. One of these nights, someone who doesn't believe in supernatural creatures will accost her to prove himself right."

Still chuckling, he allowed Diana to encase his arm in the sling and adjust the length. "I'm sure you are correct," he said, trying to sound sincere. But oh, how he admired his witch for conceiving of the idea in the first place. And he wouldn't object in the least to a night of haunting in company with Lucy. It was just the sort of adventure he most relished.

"Is that comfortable?" Diana asked, holding the corners of the shawl behind his neck.

"Perfectly. Tie it off, madam. And while you are about it, tell me about Miss Preston. Does she make a habit of wearing trousers?"

"She has found it convenient from time to time, especially when she was meeting with me at my parents' "—her voice faltered—"at my uncle's estate. She masqueraded as a gardener's assistant then. And I think she sometimes wears trousers in her usual position, but you must ask her about that."

For all his compelling wish to learn more about Lucy, he knew he must stop prodding Diana for information. He felt her hands trembling against his nape as she secured the knot. "Perhaps I will one day. But the moment has come, I believe, for you to tell me your own story."

Without responding, she returned to her place on the rock and sat with her fingers tightly laced together.

He was content to give her as much time as she required. It was early morning yet, barely an hour since dawn. The tide had moved in quickly since first he entered the cave, slowing when it reached the sloping rise that let to the cliffs. No more than twenty yards away, fluttery waves lapped at the sands. With shrill cries, a flock of sandpipers swept in and began to bustle about on whisker-thin legs.

She released a long sigh. "So much has occurred that I can scarcely think how to tell you. It began last year, when my parents died of the typhus. Father was the fifteenth Baron Whitney of Willow Manor, which is located to the east of Lancaster, and the title passed to his brother, who is now my guardian. I met him once or twice when I was a child, but he had not called on us this last decade or more. Father would surely have made other provision for me, had he known what manner of man his brother has become since then. My uncle was livid to discover that his inheritance is confined to the title and the entailed portion of the estate. The Whitney fortune came to me, and is being held in trust until I turn one-and-twenty. He cannot touch a penny of it."

"What sort of man is he then?" Kit asked, although to be sure, her scar fairly well told the tale.

She considered for a few moments. "A prodigiously foolish one, at bottom. When he took up residence at Willow Manor three months ago, it was primarily to escape his London creditors. I am guessing only, because he certainly does not confide in me, but it's likely that he celebrated his inheritance rather lavishly, without understanding its limitations. Now he is deeply in debt, and he has already sold a number of paintings that rightly belong to me. He daren't touch the valuable ones, of course, but he reckons that a mere female won't notice a bit of pilfering."

"You should inform your trustees, Diana. Or the solicitor who managed your father's affairs."

"Perhaps. I know little of such matters. My education was confined to the learning and accomplishments deemed suitable for a young lady who is expected only to marry well. Indeed, I have been pampered my entire life—until just recently—with no aspirations beyond a London Season and a bevy of handsome suitors from which to make my selection." Her hands twisted in her lap. "The loss of a few trivial possessions means nothing to me, sir. I loved my parents and was plunged into grief when they died. My uncle could have sold everything with my blessings, so long as he left me in peace to mourn them. But he did not."

"Have you no other relations to stay with?"

"None whatever, I'm afraid. Mama's brother and his wife went out to India, where they died some years ago, and their only son was killed in the Peninsular War. Perhaps there are distant connections somewhere, but I know nothing of them."

"My own family is much the same," he said by way of distraction when she wiped away a tear. "Nary an aunt or an uncle, no cousins, and my parents died in a snowstorm when I was a nipper. But I have two older brothers, and things are looking up because one has already produced a fine pair of sons."

She gave him a smile that caught at his heart. "I'm not altogether alone, you know. I have Lucy. But I must explain how that came about, for it is a great wonder to me. She was one of the teachers when I arrived at Miss Wetherwood's academy, terrified and shy because I had never before been among strangers. Lucy took me under her wing the first two years, and then she left the school to accept another position. Something happened to drive her away, but she will not say what it was. A few of the teachers envied her because she was popular with the students, and I expect they created difficulties for her.

"In any case, we set up a correspondence, although why she bothered with me is a mystery. I never had the slightest thing of interest to say in my letters, being totally absorbed with fashion and schoolgirl crushes on the dance master and the riding instructor. She always replied, though, even after I left school and wrote her infrequently. She had not heard of my parents' death until two months ago, when I sent a letter begging for her help. There was no one else to ask, you see. And without any questions, she came immediately."

Kit nodded, unsurprised. Lucy would do no less for a friend. However little he knew of her, practically speaking, he had already seen evidence of her courage and her loyalty, two virtues he profoundly respected. But much as he longed to hear more about the woman he intended to marry, Diana had not yet come to the heart of her own story. "What led you to call on her, my dear? The brutality of your uncle?"

"He isn't a brute, Kit. He is stupid and greedy, yes, and so excessively superstitious that he consults fortune-tellers and astrologers before making the slightest decision. I suspect that one of them advised him to marry me off to his own advantage, for nothing else could account for his insistence that I wed the man he has chosen. His name is Sir Basil Crawley, and where my uncle found him I know not, but apparently they have come to an agreement that includes a large settlement. Why Sir Basil is so determined to take me to wife is equally unclear. The arrangement was made before ever we were introduced."

"And when you were," Kit said, "you took him in dislike."

"Loathing would be the better word. I cannot explain exactly why. He is not ill-looking, although he is at least twice my age, and he was polite enough in a distant way. But I had the distinct impression that he was wholly indifferent to me. Gentlemen, the few I have met, were always drawn to my—" She waved a hand. "This is difficult. Before the injury to my face, I'm afraid that I was quite vain about my appearance. I was accustomed to being much admired and had come to expect it. But Sir Basil did not seem to *see* me, if that makes any sense."

"Perhaps he did not wish you to think he wanted to marry you only for your beauty, even if that were the truth of it. Have you considered that he might have observed you from a distance at an earlier time, been enchanted by you, and applied to your guardian for your hand?"

"I'm not an idiot, sir!"

Kit realized that he had offended her, although he was not certain why his innocuous observation made her so angry. He thought his suggestion quite reasonable, even if it proved to be inaccurate. But there was fire in her eyes when she stood to face him and fury in her voice.

"I may have wished for flattery and admiring glances from a suitor, but Sir Basil's failure to give them to me is nothing to the point. Had he composed sonnets to my beauty and gone on bended knee to profess his adoration, it would not have swayed me in the slightest. Under no circumstances would I agree to marry such a repellent man. He has eyes like a lizard's, sir, and ice where his heart should be. Had I not good reason to escape him, would I be hiding in a *cave*, for pity's sake?"

Taken aback, Kit lifted his good arm in a gesture of defense. "I did not mean to—"

"Perhaps not. But you were making excuses for him, like one man defending another in some sort of male brotherhood. You were not *listening* to me. He never admired me. He set out to buy me for purposes of his own. They must have been compelling, for when I was no longer beautiful, he persisted in his suit. Don't think it was because he could look past this disfigurement and love me for what I am. Even I do not know what that is. I used to be a spoiled child, relying on my beauty and good breeding and large fortune to carry me through life. Now I am nothing."

Heat scalded his face. She was exactly right, until the last sentence she spoke. He had leaped to Sir Basil's defense for no reason whatsoever, except that he knew men often behaved foolishly when they tumbled unexpectedly into love. His brother had been a prime example, nearly losing the woman who was now his greatest joy. And Kit was feeling none too certain about his own prospects with Lucy after the poor start they had made together, although he was fairly sure he'd be able to turn things around.

The fact remained that he was a man, which meant he thought like a man, and he definitely relied overmuch on his success at winning over most every female who caught his eye. He was too confident. He assumed he understood women when that was patently impossible. But one reason he adored them was their very complexity, and he was currently being given a hard lesson about the danger of jumping to conclusions. About being smug and patronizing, which he hadn't known he was being until Diana took him to task in no uncertain terms.

Were he not already in love with Lucy, he could very easily fall in love with Miss Diana Whitney.

"Have you nothing to say?" she demanded.

He gazed steadily into her eyes. "A litany of apologies, if

you wish to hear it. I assure you that I would mean every word from my heart. But what I most want to say is that you are splendid, Diana. I well understand why Lucy chose you as her friend."

"Don't be that way, Kit. I shall cry again if you are."

"Very well. I think I understand, but most probably I don't."

She sank back onto the rock beside him, making no objection when he wrapped his arm across her back. "I wish Lucy had been here to see this display of temper," Diana said. "She tells me I am passive and weepy and despairing, which is all true. Since writing her the letter that brought her here, which seems to have used up the last of my courage, I have left her to do everything while I float behind her like a leaf on a strong current."

He nearly assured her that that wasn't the case, but stopped just in time. What did he know of it, after all? And in his experience, Lucy took charge and snapped out orders like a field marshal. It would take a strong will to match hers under any circumstances. "You haven't told me how you were injured, butterfly," he said softly. "Have we come to that point in your story?"

"Near enough. I keep thinking of small things that added up to big ones, but there is no explaining them. And always I am guessing at my uncle's motives, not to mention Sir Basil's. He has some hold on the new Lord Whitney, that is certain. The last time he came to call, I declined his offer and made it clear I would not change my mind. Then they were closeted together for nearly half an hour before Sir Basil took his leave. I watched him go from the window of my bedchamber. A few minutes later Lord Whitney barreled into the room. He had been drinking, and he stormed around knocking things off my dressing table and the other furniture while he shouted at me."

She rested her head against Kit's shoulder. "I had to marry Sir Basil, he said, or he would be ruined. I told him I'd sooner die. Then he struck me, hard across the face. It was the first time anyone had ever raised a hand to me, and the blow took me off guard. I remember the stunned look in his eyes just before I fell. By ill fortune, my cheek landed against a fragile bit of ornamental glass, a small flat piece that failed to break when he knocked it onto the carpet. It shattered well enough when I landed directly atop it, though, and the doctor was a long time picking the splinters from my face."

They sat quietly. Kit stretched out his legs and examined his bare feet, knowing he must not push for answers to his many questions until Diana was ready to proceed.

She ought to have reported the incident to the magistrate, of course. Evidence of physical injury would be grounds for petitioning the court to remove her from her uncle's guardianship. But even if she were aware of that, which he doubted, she could not have been thinking clearly at the time. He wondered what explanation Lord Whitney had given the doctor who tended her.

"A few days later, when I learned that Sir Basil was persisting in his suit, I wrote to Lucy. My uncle had long since dismissed most of the household staff, including my maid, but the gardener smuggled the letter out and acted as a go-between when Lucy arrived. I was in the habit of walking on the grounds, so it was a simple matter to arrange meetings where we would not be seen. Each time I wore several layers of clothing under my cloak and carried a few possessions in a picnic basket for Lucy to take away with her. She was also searching for a place to hide me, and when she located this cottage, I contrived to escape."

She sighed. "There was a great deal more to it, you may be sure. The entire process required the better part of a month, and even I don't know the half of what Lucy was up to during that time. Until she met Robbie MacNab, who encountered her walking along the road and offered her a ride in his wagon, she was proceeding entirely on her own."

"And she found you an excellent refuge, I must say. But you cannot be comfortable here for any extended period of time."

"No. The cottage is too near my uncle's estate, for one thing, and I know he is looking for me. Indeed, he has posted a considerable reward for my return. Eventually someone will think to look here. We must leave as soon as may be, but we've nowhere to go and very little money to sustain us. I have no access to my inheritance, and Lucy has already spent most of her savings to bring us this far. She has written to Miss Wetherwood, the headmistress at the school where we met, and we have some hope that she will assist us. I can pay her back when I come of age, and she was always fond of me."

Kit had no great liking for this uncertain solution to their problems. He could do far better. But now was not the time to say so. "Where did Mrs. Preston run off to this morning, by the by?"

"Lancaster. Miss Wetherwood was asked to send her reply to the inn where Lucy stayed when she first arrived. We had no idea where we'd wind up, you see. Perhaps we'll have an answer today. And she has other business there, but I think she would not approve if I spoke of it."

Diana gave a short laugh. "As if she won't be furious enough when she returns to find that you have discovered the cave. And me."

"You mustn't worry, butterfly. I can handle Lucy." He managed to say that with a straight face. "Need I tell you again that you may safely trust me, or have you begun to believe it?"

She twined her fingers through his. "In fact, sir, I am convinced of it. Persuading Lucy will not be easy, but we are two against one. We must take care not to offend her, though. She has—"

"I understand completely," he said, squeezing Diana's hand. "Leave her to me. Meantime you are growing goose bumps, m'dear, and I rather expect you haven't had your breakfast. Shall we go upstairs, build ourselves a fire, and get better acquainted?"

Her eyes widened. "I nearly forgot, Kit. Robbie is coming here this morning."

"Ah. To make certain that I keep out of trouble, no doubt." He stood, still holding her hand, and drew her up.

"Too late for that!" she said with the first real smile he'd seen from her. "He will be vastly surprised to find us together."

Kit led her in the direction of his horse. "Jason looks to be in fine fettle, if a trifle bored." He rubbed the muzzle that pushed at his shoulder. "Don't care for being tethered in a cave, do you? I can't blame you a bit."

"I've gone out to cut grass for him with my scissors," Diana said, "and Robbie brought a sack of oats. Those must be parceled out, though. Oats are too rich for him to eat a great many at any one time without becoming ill."

"You know about horses, I take it."

"A little. I do love them. More than anything else I have left behind, I miss Sparkles. She's a pretty chestnut mare with lots of spirit. I do hope my uncle doesn't sell her off."

"If he does, we'll see you get her back." He resolved to make sure of it. Diana had little enough to cling to, after all.

When they came to the stairs that led up to the cottage, Kit sent her ahead of him and took time to study the trapdoor and what lay below it. If he had found the entrance to the cave, so could anyone else.

Something must be done about that.

Chapter 7

Lucy was unsurprised when the Lancaster-to-Lakeland coach turned up at the posthouse already chock-full of passengers. The entire day had been one disappointment after another.

A light rain had begun to fall, and she had left her umbrella at the solicitor's office. She realized that she had forgot it when she was only a short distance away, but wild horses could not have dragged her back to reclaim it.

"You'll have to ride up here," the driver told her impatiently. "Hurry it up, ma'am. We are running late as 'tis."

"I'll help you mount," the postilion said. "How far will you be going?"

"Warton." She gave him the coins she had already counted out and let herself be pushed from below and pulled from above until she was balanced precariously atop the Lakeland Flyer. Scrambling to a spot between two large portmanteaus tied to the coach with ropes, she had barely settled herself when the horses sprang forward.

Two men in rustic garb were seated at the rear, passing a bottle back and forth. One caught her eye and held the bottle in her direction. "A tot of whisky, ma'am? It'll warm your innards on this cold afternoon."

For a moment she was tempted. A little oblivion would be welcome right about now. But it was a long walk from Warton to the cottage, and the merest swallow of hard spirits invariably rendered her tipsy. She smiled at him. "Thank you, sir, but no. I appreciate your kindness."

And she did. Of late, what with Kit and the smugglers and the repellent solicitor, she was grateful for the slightest favor. Almost as unwelcome as Kit's presence in the cottage was the crumpled letter in her satchel. It had been waiting for her at the Anchor Inn that morning, a few lines of terrible news that multiplied the problems she already confronted.

The new headmistress at the Wetherwood Academy apologized for opening Miss Preston's letter, but she was unable to forward it. Miss Wetherwood had died a few months earlier, and since her fellow teachers served as her only family, they had taken it upon themselves to respond to any correspondence directed to her. Naturally they were sorry for their former student's plight. Miss Whitney's uncle had already made inquiries regarding her current location, and the headmistress promised to say nothing about Miss Preston's letter if approached with further questions. She conveyed her best wishes and her regrets that she could be of no help finding a safe place for Miss Whitney to reside.

It had been a mistake, Lucy reflected, placing all her hopes on Miss Wetherwood—God rest her soul. But who else was there? She could leave her employment, of course, and find a place far from Lancashire to hide out with Diana. For a few months they could scrape by in frugal lodgings, but then her savings would run out. More than half had already been spent to get them where they now were.

But the cottage at Cow's Mouth was no longer secure. She had purchased a copy of the Lancaster newspaper, and sure enough it carried a notice of a reward being offered for the missing heiress. That notice would continue to run, she would wager, until someone tracked Diana down and claimed the five hundred pounds.

The steady rain, little more than a drizzle, seeped through her black kerseymere dress. Beneath the felt bonnet and veil, her brown wig was already sodden.

When Diana wrote of her troubles, Lucy had thought herself capable of handling the situation. Indeed, she had felt an uncommon surge of anticipation at the prospect of a genuine adventure. Were the stakes not so high, she might have enjoyed the challenge and the chance to escape her humdrum existence for a short time. Indeed, she thought with a pang of remorse, there was a brief period in the beginning when she had actually enjoyed putting her imagination and wits to the test. She had felt positively exhilarated at her successes.

But in the end she had failed. Or was so near to failing that it made no difference.

The two men who shared the top of the coach with her had turned their backs, dangling their legs over the side and occasionally swigging from the bottle. While they were paying her no attention she raised the veil and tilted her head to the oyster-colored sky, letting the rain cool her face.

It was Diana who would pay the price for her failure. Why had she been so sure of herself? What might she have done that she failed to do?

Well, it never paid to look back, she supposed. Regrets could suck all the life and hope from a body. And it wasn't as if she could give up, call it a day, and retreat to Dorset. She had taken responsibility for Diana. She was stuck with that decision for the next two years. And she'd make the same decision if she had it to do again, so what was the point of gnashing her teeth about it?

She leaned back against a portmanteau, closed her eyes, and prayed wordlessly for divine help.

"Warton!" the driver called, jolting her from a restless half sleep.

Lucy rubbed rainwater from her lashes and peered through the heavy drizzle. Good heavens, was that Robbie standing beside the coach, his arms raised to help her alight? But why in blazes was he here? He was supposed to be at the cottage, standing watch over Kit.

"Whatever has happened?" she asked as he set her on her feet.

"The cat's from the bag," he replied laconically. "Come along, lass. The wagon's in the stable. I'll tell you the rest when we're on our way."

Knowing that he would speak when he'd a mind to and not before, she waited until he had steered the pony onto the muddy road before plucking at his sleeve. "I cannot endure this a moment longer, Robbie."

"Aye. Well, 'tis a brief tale. Your smuggler found the trapdoor this morning. Miss Whitney has told him the whole, or enough so as he knows who she is and why she's gone to ground."

And so much for the efficacy of prayer, she thought glumly. "Where is he now?"

"Still to the cottage when I left. He was building something or t'other. Sent me off to Silverdale for planks and hammer and nails. When I got back, he told me to fetch you so as you wouldn't have to walk." Robbie chuckled. "The laddie likes to snap out the orders, he does."

"And you took them like a sheep? By now he may have hauled Diana away and turned her over to the magistrate."

"If I thought he'd a mind to that, I wouldna left him alone with her."

Lucy swallowed her first several reactions and released only a sigh. What was done was done. At length she patted Robbie's hand. "There was a letter at the Anchor Inn, but the news isn't good. The lady I applied to for assistance has gone to her heavenly reward, I'm afraid, so there will be no help from that quarter."

"And from a solicitor?"

"Nothing. It was a disaster from beginning to end. The first three I approached turned me away, because I look poor, I suppose. And the fourth was a horrid little man, with greasy hair sleeked back like paint and dirty fingernails. I disliked him on sight, but he agreed to answer questions for ten minutes at no charge, and I was growing desperate."

She grabbed Robbie's arm as he made the turn onto the rough track that led to the cottage. "I made up a story, of course, to explain why I was in search of information about the rights of a legal guardian over his ward. The solicitor appeared to know little of such matters. Practically nothing, in fact. Instead of giving me answers, he kept asking more questions about my mythical younger brother. Specifically, he wanted to know where my brother lived and prodded me to bring him to the office so that he could take up his case. By then I knew he was useless, if not dangerous, and took my leave."

"Well, lassie, it's been a busy day all 'round. Now we've your smuggler to deal with. You want me to take him into Silverdale?"

"I must speak with him, of course. But when he learns about the reward, he will almost certainly try to claim the money. We dare not risk turning him loose until Diana and I are gone. Could you hold him at the cottage for perhaps twenty-four hours? That will give us time to catch a mail coach and be miles away before he finds a constable."

"Away to where?"

"It doesn't matter. The point is, we must leave here immediately."

Robbie frowned. "I can shackle him for a time, but I expect Miss Diana won't like it."

"He has charmed her, I can readily believe. He's a knack for it, and she knows nothing of the world, let alone worldly men."

"I ken she had a hard lesson from her uncle," Robbie said. "As for the smuggler, hauling a load of spirits across the sands don't make him the devil."

"Nonetheless, he is assuredly a thief, a liar, and a lecher. He cannot be trusted. The pattern is unmistakable. When we arrive, please conceal yourself until I give you a signal. He won't be suspicious if he thinks you gone and himself alone with two helpless females."

Robbie subsided into a dour silence.

She'd a fairly good idea what he was thinking, though. For all that she was eight years Diana's senior, she knew little more about men of the world.

To be sure, a number of the men in service at Turnbridge Downs had made advances when first she took up her post, but she made it pointedly clear that none would be accepted. From then on they kept their distance. Otherwise, almost the whole of her experience was confined to males under the age of eleven or twelve. Those she could handle . . . more or less.

Kit put her forcibly in mind of the spoiled, self-indulgent boys she had been governess to these past several years. He had not grown up, and his kind never did. She had observed his like when Lady Turnbridge invited her lovers, which she changed nearly as often as she changed her bonnets, to her frequent house parties. The gentlemen were all cut from the same mold—young, handsome, charming, and unrepentantly immoral.

Exactly like Kit. Well, perhaps without his intelligence and humor, but equally feckless. Kit flirted with her, and there was no mistaking that he did, but he flirted by nature with whatever female was to hand. It meant nothing. When he was gone, she would be no more in his memory than the taste of last night's dinner.

But then, men of that ilk would meet with no success were foolish females not so vulnerable to their smiles and cozening words. She ought to put him from her mind. She *must* put him from her mind.

But there he was, handsome as sin, when she entered the cottage. He was seated across the table from Diana, who was holding up a cracked mirror while he scraped a razor down his lathered cheek.

"How very cozy," Lucy said, dropping her satchel at her feet. "Have you by chance taken leave of your senses, Diana?"

"She has decided to be sensible," Kit advised, "and you are dripping water like a gutter spout. Go change into Luke, will you? No, make it the fearsome Lancashire Witch. I've a fancy to have a closer look at her."

Insufferable! "Come, Diana. I wish to speak with you privately."

Diana followed her into the back room and closed the door. "Robbie told you what happened, of course. Please don't be angry with me, Lucy. I couldn't help that he found me, and I couldn't help speaking with him, either. Nor am I sorry for it. We need his help."

"What we need is to get away from here," Lucy said in a rough whisper. "Speak softly, please. He's probably listening at the door."

"Why would he? I've told him everything. And he expects you to make a fuss about it, too. Indeed, I believe he is rather looking forward to it."

"I daresay." Lucy handed her the veiled hat and started pulling pins from the heavy wet wig. All the trouble she had taken to keep him from finding out, and he had gotten the better of her. She felt like a fool. "He appears in remarkably good health of a sudden."

Diana passed her a towel. "Kit says he is never ill, and that the best cure for a fleabite is to ignore it. This afternoon he—"

"What did he tell you about himself?" she interrupted, wanting as much information as possible before confronting him again.

"Little of significance. His name is Christopher Etheridge and he has two older brothers. Mostly he was asking me questions. When I spoke of my p-parents' death, he said that his own were killed in a snowstorm when he was a child. Otherwise, I learned almost nothing about him that I credit. He has been entertaining me with outrageous stories this last hour, but they are surely invented."

"And what did you tell him of me?" Lucy stripped off the dress and stuffed her legs into Luke's trousers.

"Only those bits that directly related to my own situation. He knows that you were teaching at Miss Wetherwood's academy when we met, and that you left to take another position. I told of writing to ask your advice, and how you have been helping me since. Of course I had to explain Luke and Mrs. Preston and the witch."

There was little else to tell, really, Lucy thought as she pulled on her shirt. The story of her inconspicuous life could be summed up in a few terse sentences. And the one time she had been summoned to do something extraordinary, she had failed to measure up. She had taken responsibility to keep Diana safe for two years, but there was no assurance she could do so for even one more day.

Diana must know it, too. She had already transferred her loyalty to a reprobate smuggler. Lucy decided not to tell her what she and Robbie planned to do. When Kit was safely under guard, she would somehow convince Diana to come away.

She wriggled her feet into Luke's boots and combed her fingers through her damp hair, aware of Diana watching her with a look of apprehension on her face. Lucy cast her a reassuring smile. "We'll come about, I promise you. And do not be overset when Kit and I wind up at daggers drawn. From the first we have disliked each other."

Diana smiled, the first genuine smile Lucy had seen since school days. "Oh, he likes you well enough. And no, he has not said so. But I can tell."

"Goose-wit." Lucy smiled back. "You know even less of men than I do."

"Perhaps that was true a year ago," Diana said softly. "I've since become acquainted with my excessively stupid uncle and the reptile he is determined to foist upon me. I know a good deal about bad men, Lucy. Kit is not one of them."

"I'm keeping an open mind," Lucy said, her hand on the door latch. "Shall we see if he can convince me he is on the side of the angels?"

Chapter 8

Kit was firmly in league with the devil, Lucy saw the very moment she opened the door.

He raised the wine bottle he was holding in a salute. "Come have a drink, Miss Luke. You look as if you need one."

"Where did you get that?" she demanded.

"There's a great lot of it out on the sands, you know. This afternoon I liberated as many bottles as I could carry."

Her heart sank. Anyone could have seen him on the bay at low tide. Had the man no sense whatever?

"Never mind scowling at me," he said. "I knew you wouldn't approve, but I'm fond of good wine and dislike seeing it go to waste. Besides, there was no one out there. I checked with my spyglass."

"As if you could spot a cockler through the fog and drizzle!"

"No more than one could spot me," he replied gently. "And if any such favored this particular area, I expect they'd long since have made off with the wine and brandy. The wagon has already sunk deep into the sand, I'm sorry to say, and the boxes will have disappeared by the next low tide." He crossed to her and pressed a cup into her hand. "Relax, Lucy. Or if you insist, Miss Preston, but I'd rather not."

"Call me what you will," she said indifferently. He would do so in any case. "Diana has told you the whole, I apprehend."

"Enough to explain how you came to be here, and why. In return, I gave her my promise to help. And yes, my dear, I'm well aware you won't permit me to do so without mounting an

89

argument beforehand." He raised his voice. "Come on out, Diana. I require your protection."

Diana slipped through the door, clearly apprehensive.

He guided her to a chair. "It will be safer here," he advised her in a theatrical whisper. "Keep your eyes open, darling, and tell me when to duck."

Lucy glared at him. "This is not a joking matter, sir. Do you take nothing seriously?"

"In my experience, sticking a ramrod up my back never solved a problem." He poured a glass of wine for Diana. "Where is Robbie, by the way? Has he gone back to Silverdale, or is he lurking outside, waiting for the order to clamp me in irons while you scarper?"

So much for keeping one step ahead of him. "I cannot permit you to leave here until we are gone, sir. And you understand very well why that is."

"I understand you think it necessary," he said evenly. "And I mean to change your mind. Shall we invite Robbie to join us? We're going to need his help, once we've settled on a plan of action."

She put down her cup. "I'll hear you out, as if I'd any choice in the matter. But I shall not be easily convinced of your good intentions."

"Somehow I had guessed that." He fixed her with a level gaze. "Remember, Lucy, that it is Diana's future at stake. At the end of the day, she must make the decisions."

"To be sure." And now he was *lecturing* her, for heaven's sake! She stomped to the door and called to Robbie.

He emerged from the heavy drizzle, removing his hat and shaking water from the brim before entering the cottage.

"Oh, do come over to the fire," she said, instantly repentant. "I should not have left you outside in this beastly weather."

"Pay me no mind, lass." He pulled off his gloves. "I'm half m' life in the rain."

Kit handed him the bottle of wine. "This will warm you up, old sod. Finish it off while I broach another."

"Oh, lovely. Precisely what we need here." Lucy watched Robbie drop cross-legged near the fireplace and take a hearty swig from the bottle. "The pair of you foxed."

"Rest easy, Lady Temperance," Kit said. "It would take good Scotch whisky and a lot of it, too, for yon braw laddie to be feeling no pain. And as I've a long ride ahead of me tonight, three or four cupfuls will be my limit." He selected another bottle of wine. "See? You've nothing to worry about."

"Not a thing," she said, throwing up her hands. "And exactly where were you planning to ride, sir?"

"Home." He drew out the cork with the casual ease of experience. "Do you ever mean to close that door, Lucy?"

She did so with a decided slam, feeling outnumbered and overwhelmed. But not overmatched, she told herself bracingly. Should she rule that Kit was not to be trusted, Diana and Robbie would surely back her up. She had already proven herself, after all, while Kit had nothing to recommend him but a honeyed tongue and an undeniable degree of charm.

"Diana told me that you intended to speak with a solicitor today," he said. "Had he anything of use to offer?"

"To the contrary." Lucy released a heavy sigh. "I should not have approached him, knowing nothing of his competence or his character. It was a mistake."

"Seeking counsel from a stranger is generally unwise," he agreed, "but you are correct that Diana's best hope of safety lies with the courts and a legal change of guardianship. Two years is a devilish long time to hide out."

"Eighteen months," Diana amended softly, brushing her scarred cheek with her forefinger. "And I don't mind hiding, you know. I've no wish to go out in public."

"Nor will anyone compel you to do so until you are ready," he assured her. "Still, there is no reason to live in fear of discovery for so long a time. We require a lawyer, the best in the country, and I happen to know how to find him."

Lucy placed little faith in any lawyer Kit was likely to produce. This was not a matter of petty thievery or evading tariffs on imported wine, after all. With effort, she refrained from pointing that out.

He was looking at Diana with a serious expression. "I owe you an apology, my dear. When I introduced myself this morning, I failed to give you the whole of my name. Forgive me, but it didn't seem relevant at the time. I had not heard your story, and because I generally take care not to entangle the family in my more unsavory pastimes, I told a half lie. The Christopher Etheridge part is true, but my surname is Valliant. Which probably means nothing to you," he added with a smile, "since you grew up in Lancashire and our estate is in Westmoreland."

"Pardon me," Lucy cut in, "but what has your name to do with anything? May we return to the point?"

"Patience, moonbeam. I'm getting there. You think me singularly useless, I know, but perhaps you will put a bit of credit in my brother, the Earl of Kendal. He served with the Foreign Office during the war and is acquainted with nearly everyone of importance. I mean to place Diana under his protection, and you may be sure that she could not be in safer hands."

"If you imagine I'll let you take her away and pass her over to a brother who may or may not exist, you are very much mistaken." She advanced on him in a fury. "This is purely nonsense. Another of your lies. You mean to return her to her guardian and pocket the reward."

"Had I such a plan in mind," he said calmly, "we would have been long gone before you returned from Lancaster."

"I know something of the Earl of Kendal," Robbie said. "My wife, God rest her, was cousin to Angus Macafee."

"The gatekeeper at Candale," Kit explained. "That's the family estate, and Angus has worked there since I was in short pants."

Struggling to compose herself, Lucy picked up her neglected cup and took a long drink. The wine felt smooth on her tongue and warm sliding down her throat.

So Kit the smuggler had turned out to be the son of an earl. Well, she could hardly be surprised. He possessed enough self-confidence for ten aristocrats, and he was certainly accustomed to taking charge and issuing orders. But his rank won him nothing from her. She'd no great liking for the spoiled sons of a privileged class, especially those who thought it a lark to box the watch or smuggle wine when they could well afford to buy it from a reputable merchant. And his sort too often assumed that any female luckless enough to cross their path, a governess, for example, was a prime target for seduction. She had stuck a long hat pin into more than one aristocratic hand that wandered where it was not welcome.

"What does it matter that your brother is an earl?" she asked stubbornly, digging her heels into what she knew was shaky ground. "Why would he help Diana? She is nothing to him. And would he not be breaking the law to conceal her from her legal guardian?"

"Bending it, perhaps. He won't mind. And the moment he is acquainted with Diana's circumstances, he will insist on taking her under his wing. I know him, Lucy. And when you meet him, you will trust him as I do."

"But I haven't met him. I've only met you. Need I go into detail about my misgivings?"

"I believe you have made yourself clear on more than one occasion," he said, grinning. "But Diana wishes me to proceed— don't you, butterfly?—so we may as well come to the sticking point. Unless you wish to prolong this row?"

She did, if only for pride's sake, but that was not reason enough. Lucy had been long in service. She knew her own unimportance, and she recognized defeat. "What will you do then?"

Kit regarded her with a look of surprise. "Well, to begin with, I mean to set out for Candale tonight and put my brother to work. He'll know better than I what must happen next, and because he is lamentably methodical, we must assume that nothing will happen quickly. Meantime Diana requires some other refuge than this. I take it that you no longer consider this cottage secure?"

"Not since you arrived," she fired back. "And if smugglers have begun operating in this vicinity, I fear one of them will learn of the cave and make use of it. We never meant to stay here for very long in any case. It is too close to Diana's home."

"She should be removed to another county, I expect, where the Lancashire magistrate has no authority. Candale, most like, but perhaps somewhere else in Westmoreland. We'll see what my brother has to say. In the interim, Lucy, while I am gone, can I trust you not to run off?"

Trust? The word never failed to set demons dancing in her head. She trusted no one, not even herself. But that was not the question, she realized when the demons had retired to the shadows again. Kit wanted to know if she kept her promises, not that she'd given him any, and she didn't know how to answer.

She would deceive him if she thought it necessary. She lied when lies were called for. Truth and trust were ideals, after all. Chimeras. Whom did she know who had kept faith with her? Diana didn't count. Diana had given her faith because she had nowhere else to turn. And by doing so, she had led Lucy to assume false identities and tell one lie after another until she could scarcely keep track of them all.

"How long is an *interim*?" she finally asked.

"Another day," Kit replied. "Two at the most, depending on what my brother advises. And since Diana will most likely be transferred elsewhere, I suggest that Robbie start taking away as many of her possessions as she can do without until she is settled again. There is a considerable amount of luggage in the cave, I couldn't help but notice."

Robbie shuffled to his feet. "If you mean to be going, I'll see to saddling the horse. And I'll carry the cases up here so the lassie can sort through them by the fire."

"Diana?" Lucy crossed to her. "Think carefully. Is this what you wish?"

Head bowed, Diana studied her folded hands. "Not if you mislike it," she said in a meek voice.

Lucy shot a look at Kit. You see how it is? she wanted to exclaim. Diana could make no decision on her own. Or she *would* not. Since writing the letter and pleading for assistance, her one positive action, she had left everything in Lucy's hands.

Kit lowered one hip on the table. "It occurs to me," he said mildly, "that she is torn between her gratitude to you and what she now considers the right course of action. And you *are* asking her to choose sides, you know."

Lucy felt heat rise up her neck. "Is that true, Diana? Do you feel obligated to agree with me against your own true opinion?"

She gave a barely perceptible nod.

Oh, damn. There was only one thing to say then, and it was the last thing Lucy wished to say while Kit was present to hear it. But he would not be dislodged, so she swallowed the frayed remnants of her pride and produced a reassuring smile. "You have mistaken me, Diana. I am quite in agreement with Mr. Valliant's plan, which far surpasses any I could devise under the circumstances. We are fortunate indeed that he has elected to take up our cause. So what do you say? Shall we seize this opportunity while it is ours?"

"Oh, yes," Diana replied immediately. "I'm so glad you think it best."

To Lucy's surprise, Kit refrained from gloating. He contented himself with a nod—of approval, she imagined—in her direction before turning to Diana. "Select only the few items you can carry with you, butterfly. Robbie will bring the rest soon enough. With luck I shall return by noon tomorrow and escort you to your next temporary home. Have you any questions before I set out?"

Diana raised trusting eyes to his face. "No, sir. But surely you will not leave while it is still raining?"

"If I wait, I'll be forced to travel in the dark." He drank the last of his wine and set the cup on the table. "Besides, the sooner I am gone, the sooner I'll be back again."

Robbie came into the room carrying three pieces of luggage. "The beastie is saddled, and I ken he's aching for a hard run."

"Well, so am I," Kit said cheerfully. "Neither of us can bear being cooped up for any amount of time. Have you a place, Robbie, to secure Miss Diana's possessions for a day or two?"

"Aye. There's storage in the rooms above the apothecary shop."

"Excellent!" Kit stood. "When I need to make contact, I'll leave word for you there."

"That's best. I'll stay close to ground, there or here. Ye'll have no trouble finding me."

"In that case, it's time for me to go. Miss Lucy, will you come along with me to the cave? I'll need directions how to proceed from there." He paused by Diana's chair and brushed a kiss on her scarred cheek. "Take courage, butterfly. All will be well."

Heart racing, Lucy went ahead of him down the stairs into the shadowy cave. A heavy mist hovered in the air, and the limestone walls streamed with condensed moisture. The horse was a dark, restless presence, digging at the ground with his hooves and sensing, she supposed, that he was soon to be free of his prison. She stayed well clear of him.

"That galled you, admitting that I was right," Kit said as he came up beside her. "Did it not?"

"I've no idea what you are referring to," she replied acerbically. "We should have asked Robbie to come down and help you mount."

He chuckled. "Confess, Lucy. It's good for the soul. You were practically chewing iron nails when you told Diana that you approved my plan."

"Oh, I did tell her so." Lucy waved a hand. "But I *admitted* nothing. You take my meaning, I am sure."

"A more bullheaded female never walked the earth," he said, ruffling her hair. "But you did the right thing, moonbeam. I'll not tease you for it."

"Thank you for patronizing me, sir. Above all things, I enjoy being treated like a nitwit."

He was standing so close to her back that she could feel the rumble in his chest when he laughed. And feel the heat of his breath against her nape, and then the hand that slipped around her waist and drew her against his body. Wings fluttered against her skin, inside her chest, everywhere that he was not touching her already. She could not account for how she felt, and it terrified her to experience such total—what? Longing? Weakness? Curiosity? She'd no idea. He snatched away every coherent thought and all but the last shreds of her will.

Unable to speak, unable to move, she simply stood where she had no right to be, in the embrace of a man who found it amusing to flirt with her. He held her lightly, his hand resting beneath her breasts, taking no other liberties. She wondered if she would permit them if he tried. She wondered if she wanted him to try.

"Diana will be perfectly fine," he said quietly. "She's a plucky little thing, and once the shock has passed, she will come about."

The sudden change of subject, the very arrogance of his words, snapped her free of his spell. She seized his hand, removed it forcibly from her waist, and turned to confront him. "How can you be so ignorant? You have no idea—none at all—what she has endured and what she will endure for years to come. Wherever she goes, people will stare at her. Some will remark on the scar, some will turn away, and always she will know what they are thinking."

"That is a most cynical view of life, I must say. The next time you are in a crowd, moonbeam, look around you. Do you flinch at the sight of a face pocked from a bout of smallpox, or take disgust when you see a man shorn of a leg or an arm? Some folks are cruel, others thoughtless, but not everyone passes instant judgment based on appearances alone."

"It's not the same thing," she protested. "Diana was meant to have a glorious London Season and marry well. It was what she was bred and educated to do. She knows nothing else. You are of her class, sir. What do you suppose would happen if she appeared at a fashionable ball? Would she even receive an invitation from a hostess who had actually seen her face?"

He looked unaccustomedly serious. "Should she attempt to make her come-out, she would not take. I cannot deny that. But London is not the world, Lucy. There are any number of men who would count themselves fortunate to win her affections."

"Because of her considerable wealth, I daresay. The gleam of golden guineas will blind them to all else. There is little doubt she can wed a fortune hunter, if she so chooses, but is there any hope of marrying for love?" Lucy was in full cry now, and could no more have held her tongue than flown to the moon. "I expect—no, I am sure—that you have enjoyed the favors of a great many women. Was any one of them less than beautiful?"

Color rose on his cheeks. "Must I answer that?"

"You have already done so." She gave him an icy glare of satisfaction.

He met her gaze steadily. "Like most men, I am attracted to beautiful females. I'll not deny it. As for my 'great many women,' you are not far off the mark. There have been more than a few. Were they all beautiful? I'm not certain if others would account them so. I am also drawn to women of wit and intelligence and courage. Women of passion. In some cases— perhaps *most* cases, although I cannot swear to it—they would not be regarded as Incomparables. But I assure you, they were beautiful to me."

The wind fell out of her sails with such a rush that she nearly toppled. And then she remembered that Kit was nothing if not silver-tongued. He could talk the bark off a tree. "Well argued, sir. So tell me this. If Diana were without a fortune, would you ever consider taking her to wife? Could you fall in love with her in spite of her scar?"

His clear blue-eyed gaze never wavered. "I expect so. Indeed, I am certain of it. She is precisely the sort of woman I most admire—gallant and honorable and loyal—Lucifer! I could list the virtues I sense in her for another hour or more. Yes, I could love her and wed her, were she the one who captured my heart. But by the time I discovered Diana skulking in this cave and came to know and admire her, I was already head over ears in love with someone else."

"Oh." Lucy felt small and foolish. Also devastated, although she could not have said why. His romantic attachments were none of her concern. "I beg your pardon, sir. I was speaking theoretically, of course. To be sure you could not wed Diana if your attentions are otherwise directed."

"And so they are. But I take your lesson to heart, moonbeam. You know better than I about Diana's state of mind, and any man who tries to guess what a woman is feeling has attics to let. Shall we cry peace?"

A prickly lump clogged her throat. It was one thing to know she could never have his love and something else altogether to know that another woman already had it. She felt as if she'd just awakened from a dream she couldn't remember. "Sh-should you not be on your way?" she asked in a murmur.

"Yes." He untethered his horse. "Is there a way out of here other than across the sands? I'm not of a mind to play another game of tag with the bore tide."

"Turn to the left," she directed, "and ride alongside the cliff. It ends about a mile down, and if you follow the track from there, you can pick up the road about two miles inland."

"I'll find it. And Lucy, stay to ground until I return. No more—what did Diana call them? Ah, yes. No more *hauntings*. Where did you come by that long wig, by the way? From a distance, it looked exactly like your own hair."

"That's because it is. Did not Diana tell you that I am a governess?"

"Lucifer!" He laughed heartily. "No, she did not tell me, although I should have guessed it. But what has that to do with your hair?" He turned to her, his expression suddenly serious. "Never tell me your employer ordered you to cut it off?"

"She would not dare. I assure you, my employer does everything possible to retain my services against all but impossible odds. Before I came, no governess had survived longer than a fortnight, and I am paid exceedingly well to put up with five boys hell-bent on ridding themselves of all authority. For the most part, I have managed to keep the upper hand these last few years."

Lucy forced what she hoped sounded like nonchalance into her voice. "One night the oldest took a notion to rid me of my hair. He was ever on the lookout for my weaknesses, and must have concluded that I was vain about my appearance. So while I was asleep in my room he crept in with a pair of scissors, took hold of a sizable handful of hair, and sheared it off. I woke immediately, but not before the damage was done. There was little choice at that point but to cut off all the rest, and so I did. When I presented the remains to my employer, along with a list of demands, she gave me another rise in salary and dispatched my hair to Ede and Ravenscroft in London to have a wig made up. At the time I never imagined the use it would be put to, nor did I have occasion to wear it until I began playing the Lancashire Witch."

He was regarding her with a look she could not begin to decipher. "I see," he said, dropping the reins he'd been holding. "Stay, Jason."

Before she guessed what he was about, she was in his arms and he was kissing her. *Kissing her!* And thoroughly, too, in ways she'd never imagined that kisses could be. Time stopped, moons and planets ground to a halt, and her mind spun away, leaving the rest of her to revel in her first taste of bliss.

When he finally let her go and stepped away, she could only gaze blankly at him. Bewildered, bedazzled, she saw him swing onto his horse and look back at her with a smile on the lips she wished were still pressed to hers.

And then he was gone.

She stood for a long time, wondering what had just happened, amazed that she had let it happen. But eventually, she came back to earth. For him, it was only a routine kiss, the kind he gave to any female who raised no objections. To her shame, it had never occurred to her to object. And however soul-shaking and body-melting his kisses, she knew better than to refine too much on them.

This incident had never happened. She would not think on it ever again.

Chapter 9

The rain ceased not long after Kit rode away from the cave, and he was relatively dry by the time he arrived at Candale several hours later.

The butler greeted him with a smile that immediately collapsed into a worried frown. "Er, welcome home, Mr. Christopher. I shall have a fire built in your room immediately. Would you care for a late supper?"

"Hullo, Geeson. You are looking well. I, of course, look like hell, but I assure you that I am perfectly fine. Sorry to barge in without advance warning. I'd welcome a meal about two hours from now, after I'm done consulting with my brother. Where is he to be found?"

"Lord and Lady Kendal are in the upstairs parlor, sir."

He headed for the staircase. "Thank you, Geeson. I'll spring on them unannounced."

When Kit sauntered into the room, the earl was seated at a *secrétaire* with a pen in his hand and Celia was half-reclined on a sofa by the fireplace. "How utterly picturesque," he drawled. "A veritable portrait of domestic bliss."

"Kit!" Celia tossed her knitting aside and jumped up to embrace him. "What a lovely surprise. But what on earth has happened to you?"

He arched his brows. "Why, Celia, I cannot think what you mean."

"Oh." She fingered the fringe on his sling. "Well, then, forget that I asked."

His sister-in-law, bless her, always knew when to let him be. "Where's the infant?"

"Sleeping, I'm afraid."

"And as it required two hours to achieve this miracle," Kendal put in, "asleep he will stay. May I inquire why you are limping?"

"Am I indeed?" Kit made a show of examining his sandaled feet. "Which leg would that be?"

"Ah. I take it, then, that questions regarding the somewhat flamboyant shawl you are wearing would be unwelcome."

"Of course they would," Celia said. "Didn't he just tell us so quite plainly? We're very glad to see you, Kit, and I hope you mean to stay a long while this time. By the way, there are three letters from Charley on the dressing table in your room. He is doing exceedingly well at Harrow, despite the incident with the snake. I only wish the terms were not so long. We miss him enormously."

"I'll nip over for a visit one of these days," Kit promised. "Always a good idea to stay on good terms with the heir in case I need to borrow money." Charley was Kendal's son by his first wife, rising ten years old now, and Kit was especially pleased to hear news of a snake. There was a time the boy wouldn't say boo to a goose, let alone get up to normal schoolboy pranks.

Kendal steepled his hands under his chin. "That means, I presume, that you have dropped by to beg a loan. Or is it that the constable is hard on your heels?"

"Alas, Jimmie, you always think the worst of me. But as it happens, you are right on both counts. Well, I am by no means certain the constables have twigged they *ought* to be chasing me, so perhaps they are not. At least it is the Lancashire officials I have run afoul of this time. Westmoreland has been spared my latest crime spree."

"You relieve my mind," Kendal said dryly. "How much is this going to cost me?"

"I wish I knew. What is the going rate for rescuing damsels in distress?"

"I beg your pardon?"

Satisfied that he had managed to flap his generally unflappable brother, Kit went to the sideboard and lifted the stopper from a crystal decanter. After one sniff, he put it back again. "Hog swill. You may know your brandy, old sod, but you've no respect for good wine. I need the money for the ladies, by the way. My services are free. And, I should add, unwelcome."

"They don't wish to be rescued?" Celia asked, her dark eyes wide with curiosity. "But who are they, Kit? Must you play these games? Do tell us what is going on."

"A more ungrateful pair of wenches you've never met. One of them, anyway. She would sooner see me hang than accept my help." Kit gave the bellpull a hearty tug. "She is also the woman I mean to marry."

Celia emitted a squeal of delight.

"Don't believe a word of it," Kendal advised her coolly. "Kit's love affairs have the endurance of a snowflake on a griddle."

"My *affairs*, perhaps. But when, Jimmie old lad, have you ever heard me say that I was in love?"

"Never," Kendal replied after some thought. "I grant you that. So why is this different?"

"I've no idea. How did you know you were in love with Celia?"

"I believe that you pointed it out to me."

"So I did. Good of you to admit it after all this time." He bowed. "Obviously I am able to recognize the symptoms of true love, and at the moment I've got most all of them. Oh, not the ones which had you behaving like a jackass, for I have been a perfect darling from the first. But Lucy persists in thinking me a villain, and I'll not make any progress changing her mind until the other damsel is free of her dragon uncle."

"And thereby hangs a tale." Kendal went to the sofa to sit beside his wife. "May I hope you will get to it in some comprehensible fashion before young Christopher Alexander starts howling for his next meal?"

"Sorry. I'm partial to melodrama." Kit gave himself a mental kick on the backside for even mentioning his personal interest in Lucy, which would only distract everyone from the immediate problem. Were she present, his beloved would inform him in no uncertain terms that he was being self-indulgent and more concerned with impressing—or shocking—his family than achieving his goals. Which was one of the reasons he so admired her, no doubt. It pleased him that she knew his flaws and weaknesses, of which there were a great many.

Even though she had yet to notice them, he'd been gifted with a few good qualities, too. Splendid looks, or so he had often been told by more forthcoming ladies. Charm. Energy. Humor. A quick mind. Compassion. An ability to mingle in any company, high or low. Considerable talent in the bedchamber. It was true that he'd put his gifts to waste or to no good purpose—not counting his skill as a lover—but he was yet young.

"Sir!"

The gaunt presence just inside the doorway sounded a trifle impatient, and Kit reckoned the butler had been trying to catch his attention for some time. "Sorry, Geeson. I was woolgathering." He flashed one of his sure-to-disarm smiles. "Bring up the best bottle of wine in the cellar, will you?"

With a groan, the earl signaled approval.

When Geeson had withdrawn, Kit dropped onto a chair across from Kendal and Celia. "Fact is, Jimmie, I need your help. A young woman, not the one I mean to wed, is in considerable trouble. There are lots of missing pieces to the story, you will quickly divine, but I shall tell you as much as I know."

He was well into his tale, carefully censored to omit an accounting of the events on Morecambe Bay, by the time Geeson returned with a decanted bottle of wine. Accepting a glass of claret, Kit nodded thanks and took a long, necessary drink. He had just finished describing Diana's scar and how she came by it, and his throat was painfully dry. It didn't help that tears were streaming down Celia's cheeks.

Kendal gave her his handkerchief and wrapped an arm around her shoulders. "Go on, Kit. I assume we've heard the worst, and I'm beginning to understand where you are leading."

He charged through the rest, knowing his brother would wrench order into his disorganized presentation of Diana's situation. "There is reason to believe she is no longer safe at the cottage where she has been hiding," he finished. "If I found her, others could do the same."

"You wish to bring her here then?"

"Will you have her?"

"Certainly, so long as you intend only for us to conceal her. But if you mean for me to undertake legal action against her uncle, which I expect that you do, Candale will be the first place he will look."

"So what if he does? You'd not hand her over."

"I could be forced to by legal means. Miss Whitney is subject to her guardian, however unworthy he may be. Should he elect to exercise his rights over her and pursue the matter diligently, I would have no choice but to, as you say, *hand her over*."

"Whyever not? Whitney cannot mount an army and storm the gates. Who could compel you even to admit she is here?"

Kendal released an exasperated sigh. "Kit, you have danced on the other side of the law for so long that you've forgot where the boundaries are set. I'm a civilized man, not a warlord. We'll do better to employ stealth than common deceit, let alone outright defiance."

"However much he might wish to," Celia remarked, "James will never swear to an untruth. And as you know, I have no gift whatever for deception. If Miss Whitney is here, even the most inept of magistrates would be able to read it on my face."

"There is Alex's house at Coniston Water," Kendal said thoughtfully. "We have not leased it out since the previous tenants moved away. And your own cottage in Hawkshead remains vacant, I believe."

Celia gathered up her knitting. "I have decided that I do not wish to know how you resolve this, gentlemen. I make a poor conspirator, given my lamentable habit of blurting the truth at the most inopportune times. And," she added, brushing a kiss on her husband's cheek, "men always speak more freely without a lady in the room."

Kit opened the door for her. "You're a trump, Countess. Now I won't be forced to mind my language."

"When have you ever done?" She sniffed at him and wrinkled her nose. "Mercy me, Kit. I shall have a tub brought to your room and instruct the kitchen staff to heat a lake's worth of water. Pray advise the servants when you are ready for your bath."

"Lucifer's privates!" Kit swore when she was gone. "How is it, Jimmie, that we have both fallen in love with managing females?"

"Is there any other kind?"

"None willing to put up with the likes of us, I suspect." Kit flopped onto the chair again and stretched his legs to the fire. "Sorry for any unpleasant odors wafting from my direction, by the way. The cottage where I spent the last few days didn't have provisions for bathing. Odd thing is, the ladies always smelled of fresh air and spring flowers. I've no idea how they managed it."

"And this is relevant in what way to the point at hand?"

"Right. Back to business. As you say, any property owned by the family will be a natural target for a search when our involvement becomes known. But is that inevitable? Our name cannot be kept out of it?"

"Not if I file a petition to remove Lord Whitney as the young lady's guardian and replace him with myself, which seems the next logical step. Mind you, I'm no expert on these matters. We require professional counsel before taking legal action of any kind."

"There's a chance you can be appointed her guardian? That would be the ideal solution!" Kit's enthusiasm quickly ran up against a wall. His brother had a family of his own, a large estate to manage, and scores of civic responsibilities Kit knew nothing about. What was more, the Earl of Kendal had never even met Diana Whitney. "Are you willing to take on such an obligation, Jimmie? I always assumed you would act on her behalf, but I reckoned that would involve no more than bringing her to Candale and hiring a solicitor. I never meant you should take personal charge of her."

Kendal draped his arm over the back of the sofa. "I am perfectly agreeable, so long as Celia has no objections. I cannot imagine that she will, but of course I must ask her before committing myself."

"Is that how things are done when one is married? Will I be required to ask Lucy's permission every time I want to buy a horse or . . . or brush my teeth?"

Laughing, Kendal shook his head. "I have pronounced myself willing to take on a ward I've never met and fight her case through the courts if need be, but damned if I mean to start passing out marital advice. When you are leg-shackled, Kit, you can bloody well stumble along the way the rest of us do."

"Sorry again. But the thing is, it's all tangled up together, my passion for Lucy and this mess with Diana. I can't think straight. What are we supposed to be talking about?"

"When we left off, we were discussing where to deposit Miss Whitney while I extricate her from the clutches of her uncle."

Kit adjusted his arm in the sling. "I'd figured on bringing her here, but clearly that won't do. Tell you what, Jimmie. I'm no good with the legal ins and outs, so you take charge of those. I'll put my mind to finding her a place to stay."

"Very well. But I require a good deal more information from you before I can be of service. What level of opposition are we facing?"

"Hard to tell. As I understand it, the new Lord Whitney has been living off his expectations for several years, is up to his eyebrows in debt, and stands to gain by marrying off his ward to Sir Basil Crawley. That's a considerable incentive to fight us for control."

"And what do you know of Crawley?"

"Other than the fact Diana won't have him, nothing. By her account, her uncle is a nincompoop and Crawley makes her skin crawl. He's the one pulling the strings, I have no doubt."

Kendal rubbed his chin. "I've heard his name, or read it, not too very long ago. Let me think on this a moment."

Kit used the opportunity to refill his wineglass and sort out his thoughts. It would be a wonder if his brother could make sense of the bits and pieces he had thrown at him thus far. But then again, who was better qualified? James had slithered through the courts of a dozen countries while Europe was at war, sifting solid information from the chaff of rumors and disinformation, manipulating kings and czars and ministers of state on behalf of England's foreign policy. Such as it was. He often said that England was its own worst enemy, and that he'd rather deal with Napoleon's Imperial Guard than a squabbling Parliament.

"I have it! Or I think I do." Kendal rose. "Come with me."

Kit followed his brother downstairs and into the study where he had been summoned far too many times, never willingly, to hear a lecture on proper behavior or to be punished for his latest offense. The room still made him bloody uncomfortable.

Kendal went to his desk and rummaged through the orderly stacks of paper that covered it end to end. "Yes, this is it. Have a look."

Kit took the folded card and saw his own name inscribed with those of Lord and Lady Kendal and Colonel Alexander Valliant. "He's invited us to a *ball*? Good Lord. Will you accept?"

"Under no circumstances. He has not been presented to me, and I was frankly astounded to receive this card. One only, mind you, addressed to all of us and sent by way of common post at that. I would have immediately declined, but unimportant matters are awaiting the return of my secretary, who is visiting his family in Carlisle."

"Hold off awhile longer, will you? I may decide to make an appearance."

"Is that wise?" Kendal sat behind the desk and steepled his hands. "It will draw unnecessary attention to the family before we are prepared to make our move."

"Know thine enemy, or something of the sort. Besides, I'm devilish curious to meet the fellow."

"If you must. But think on it before making a decision, will you? It won't help our case to put him on his guard."

Kit chuckled. "You never fail to underestimate me, Jimmie. I'll pop in at the ball, do a bit of reconnaissance, and pop out again, leaving Crawley none the wiser. Besides, you can hardly expect me to sit around doing nothing while you and the lawyers are huddled over your books."

"I certainly don't wish to have you hovering about and making a nuisance of yourself. But you must know it will be some time before we begin . . . er, huddling. The solicitor I have in mind to supervise the case resides in London."

"What's wrong with Carruthers? He could set to work immediately."

"To what purpose? He is well qualified to handle my affairs, but Miss Whitney's situation is quite out of the ordinary. There can be little precedent for what we mean to attempt, Kit. I have no connection to her family, nor even a long-standing acquaintance. Convincing the court to overturn her father's will, remove her from her uncle's custody, and declare her my legal ward will not be a simple matter. Indeed, I expect it to be impossible. But a battery of superb lawyers can tie this up in Chancery until Miss Whitney comes of age."

Kit mauled the back of his neck with taut fingers. "What would happen if Lord Whitney failed to contest the petition?"

"That would be altogether different." Kendal raised a brow. "Is there reason to think he will not?"

"Not a one that I know of. Just asking." Kit stood and began to pace, his mind churning with half-formed ideas. None of which he meant to reveal to his brother, of course, even when he had settled on a likely plan. "So what comes next?"

"I shall send a letter by tomorrow's post requesting that Mr. Bilbottom make the journey to Candale, and it will be well if I give him as much information as possible from the start. Tonight, I want you to write down what you have already told me, along with anything else that comes to mind. The injury done to Miss

Whitney's face is of particular importance, being evidence of her guardian's unsuitability. Pray describe it in detail."

"It happens I can do better. She allowed me to make sketches of her, although to convince her to do so, I had to half promise that no one would inspect her person directly."

"The sketches will certainly help, and I'll enclose them with your written report. But you must know that should all else fail, Miss Whitney could be summoned to testify."

"It won't come to that, I assure you."

Kendal looked displeased. "Do you mean to run wild behind my back?"

"Do you really want to know?"

"I suppose not. Just see that we are never acting at cross-purposes, and hold in mind that a young woman's future is at stake."

"I am well aware of that. Good Lord, Jimmie, I'm practically an old man. Knocking at thirty. Credit me with a particle of sense."

"One at most. But I'll spare you another of my traditional lectures, since you pay them no heed in any case." Kendal smiled. "Toddle off to your bath, ancient one. Write up your report and get some sleep. We'll meet again over breakfast."

"How the blue blazes does Celia put up with you?" Kit grumbled, slouching to the door.

"She is a woman of singular endurance, to my great good fortune. And on the subject of long-suffering females, when do I meet the one who may be required to put up with *you*?"

"Not *may*, sir. *Will*, sir. Consider, Jimmie, that if a smug, overbearing tyrant has won himself a wife like Celia, a dashing young cavalier such as myself cannot help but nab an equally remarkable bride. Mind you, if she is to have me, she must first beat out a rival for my affections."

Kendal's smile went cold. "You speak of Miss Whitney?"

"How you *do* leap to conclusions." Kit turned with his hand on the door latch. "I speak of Miss Fidgets, who happens to be an owl."

Well pleased with the astonished look on his brother's face, Kit made his way upstairs. The Honorable Christopher Alexander Valliant had been twelve days old when last he saw him, and two months had passed since then. Fortunately the infant was awake, to judge by the piercing screeches emanating from the room at the end of the passageway.

Celia looked up with obvious relief when he let himself into the nursery. "Come see if you can calm him down, Kit. I've been walking the room with him for an hour, but he won't stop crying."

"He's probably bored with the scenery, love. Try taking him out and about." He settled the infant in the curve of his good arm. "C'mon, rascal. I'll tell you a story about two maidens in distress and how your brave, resourceful uncle saved them from the wicked old dragon."

Celia shook her head when Christopher immediately stopped crying. "How do you *do* that?"

"Ineffable charm," he said, gazing down into a pair of wide blue eyes. "When are you going to grow some hair, young man? You put me in mind of a billiard ball. You're a beauty, though. When you've filled out some, you'll be almost as good-looking a fellow as your uncle Kit."

"I'm sorry to hear that," Celia said. "James tells me that Alex is far and away the handsomest of the Valliant brothers."

"Pay her no mind," he told the babe. "She's never seen him. I bet he'd come home, though, if he knew you were here. Has there been any word, Celia?"

"Not since the letter from Lima, and you've read that one. James replied immediately, but correspondence requires months to pass between England and South America, and Alex rarely stays in one place for very long."

"Take heed, Christopher. Everyone accuses *me* of being a here-and-thereian, but Uncle Alex is the true culprit. And I have excellent news for you tonight. By Michaelmas next, you are likely to have your very first cousin. I'm hoping she'll be a girl, though. Too many males in this family as it is."

"You are serious about this young woman you've met?" Celia asked.

"Absolutely." He glanced up. "If you've no objection, I mean to bring her here within the next few days."

"She is welcome, of course, for as long as she wishes to stay. But won't she prefer to go wherever it is you plan to put Miss Whitney?"

"I expect so. But if the lady I have in mind to ask does agree to take Diana, you may be sure I cannot send Lucy along. We are friends now, but there was a time we were a trifle more than that." Unaccountably, he felt heat rise up the back of his neck. "If you take my meaning."

"How could I not?" she said, laughing. "But will she be a suitable companion for a young girl like Miss Whitney?"

"You used not to be such a prude. Jimmie has corrupted you."

"I have corrupted him," she corrected, "and he has enjoyed every minute of it. But you must know that he can't help watching over you like a fussy hen. I know he gets on your nerves, but he practically raised you from an egg. He feels responsible for you."

"And I've not given him much to boast of since flying the nest." Kit nuzzled the infant's warm cheek, loving the milky smell of his breath and the tiny bubble that had formed at the corner of his mouth. "Your papa will be devilish surprised when I settle peaceably with my moonbeam. I'm going to hand you back to your mama now, and you are to treat her kindly. Agreed?"

The babe gurgled cheerfully, settling into Celia's arms without protest. "You will make a prodigiously fine father," she told Kit in a whisper.

"So I have always believed. And if Lucy gives me the chance, I shall also make a prodigiously fine husband."

Chapter 10

Late the next morning, Lucy took Kit's spyglass and went into the woods to look for Fidgets.

This would be their last day at Cow's Mouth cottage, assuming that all went as Kit had said it would. Diana was prepared to depart, the few possessions she meant to take with her wrapped in a woolen pelisse and tied up with string. She seemed calm, as if she had handed herself over to Kit and need no longer be concerned about her future.

With Fidgets disinclined to respond to her calls, Lucy left the trees and ascended the grassy hill to the limestone headland. The day was cool and clear, with a few clouds hanging in the sky like dandelion fluff and a fresh breeze blowing in from the ocean. She extended the spyglass and looked out over the sparkling bay. Near the shore, shallow water flowing over its long legs, a gray heron stood motionless, waiting for a meal to swim by. Leisurely, she enjoyed the view of Cartmel peninsula across the bay and the Lakeland fells rising in the distance.

At length she turned in the direction of the track that led to the cottage, amazed at how far she could see with the aid of the spyglass. All the way to the Warton road, in fact, although the road itself was invisible behind a screen of trees. She gazed over the rolling hills beyond the road and then back again, just in time to see two horsemen emerge from a break in the trees. They were moving slowly, but quite evidently had set themselves on the track to the cottage. She couldn't make out their faces, but one man was too barrel-shaped to be Kit and the other was far too small.

Wheeling, she sprinted down the hill and dashed into the cottage. "Cave!" she told a startled Diana, grabbing Mrs. Preston's dress from the hearthside where it had been left to dry. They had rehearsed what to do if a stranger suddenly appeared, so Diana went immediately to the trapdoor. Lucy closed it behind her, covered it with the thatched straw carpet, and tugged her portmanteau atop it.

A knock sounded as she was adjusting the wig. Quickly donning her bonnet, she lowered the veil, drew in a deep breath, and went to the door.

"Beggin' your pardon for the disturbance, ma'am," said a burly man with a large nose and red cheeks. "M'name is Ralph Planter, and I be constable for this parish. This here is Mr. Bartholomew Pugg come north from Bow Street, him bein' a Runner. We are come to inquire concernin' a young lady what's gone missing."

"Are you alone here?" Pugg asked, looking past her into the cottage with dark, intelligent eyes.

"Yes, certainly." She stepped aside. "Do come in, gentlemen. I would offer you refreshment, but as you see, nearly everything has been packed up for my journey."

Pugg prowled the room, examining the nearly bare shelves and the sparse furnishings. He paused to examine the spyglass, which she had dropped on the table in her rush. "This is a fine piece of work, madam."

"It belonged to my l-late husband. He died at Waterloo."

The constable regarded her solicitously. "My condolences, ma'am. Them was brave men. I lost a brother there, and another at Vittoria."

Recognizing a potential ally, she slipped her hand into her pocket and withdrew a painted miniature in a gilt frame. She had bought it at a secondhand shop in Lancaster, along with the black dress and the veiled mourning hat. The shop had been filled with items sold off by impoverished war widows, and

Lucy felt sad every time she looked at the face of the dark-haired young man, so solemn and proud as he sat for the artist.

"This is my Henry," she said, remembering to sniffle as she handed the miniature to the constable. "He sent it to me from Brussels, and it arrived a week after I had news of his death. I carry it always."

Pugg was at the window, lifting one of the heavy curtains to look outside. "An out-of-the-way place, I am thinking, for a female to be living alone."

"Oh, I have been here only a short time. Until a few weeks ago I resided with Henry's family. But they had disapproved our marriage, and resented keeping me after he was gone. Finally they decided that they had done their Christian duty by me and proceeded to toss me out."

"With nowhere to go?" Scowling, the constable gave her back the miniature. "That ain't Christian, to my way of thinkin'."

"They believed charity ought more properly to be dispensed by those of my own blood, and to be sure, I was most unhappy in their home. My sister and her husband have agreed to take in the poor relation, reckoning that I can be of help tending to their seven children." She tried to sound martyrish. "Unhappily, Henry and I had none of our own."

"That don't explain what you are doing *here*," Pugg said, turning with his hands clasped behind his narrow back.

Even through the heavy veil, she felt the force of his sharp gaze. No fool, Mr. Pugg, and singularly unimpressed with her tale of woe. But she went on with it, head bowed, for the constable's benefit. "A capricious fancy, I'm afraid, which struck me on the long journey from Devon. You see, since learning of Henry's death, I have never been alone to grieve for him. His parents are cold by nature and disliked any show of sensibility, and when I move in with my sister, there will be little chance for solitude amid so large a family. I suddenly longed to bid him farewell in my own way, near the seaside Henry and I so loved."

She made a distracted gesture. "A tedious story, I know. You must pardon me. I decided to seize a few weeks for myself before proceeding to York, so I turned west, to the coast. This cottage was available, and my savings reached to a month's rent. Does that answer your question, sir?"

He shrugged, and she could read nothing from his expression. "Seems odd for someone sez she likes the out-of-doors to keep the curtains closed. And I can't help but wonder why you are wearing that veil."

"My eyes," she said. "They can tolerate no more than a brief exposure to bright light, especially sunlight. I was born with the ailment, and it has proved a vast inconvenience, you may be sure. 'Tis a wonder Henry married me in spite of it, but he always took the greatest care to protect me. Naturally I do not wear the veil indoors when the curtains are closed, but you arrived just as I was preparing to go out for a walk." She lifted the veil and gave him a shy smile. "I am so used to having it on that I did not think to do this beforehand."

He scrutinized her cheek, and she knew that he had suspected it was Diana Whitney hiding herself under the veil. She only hoped he failed to notice that the brown wig was still damp. Pugg was an acute observer, though. Ought she to tell him she had washed her hair that morning?

No. Coming from nowhere, that would only make him more suspicious. An innocent woman is calm, she reminded herself, and curious why two officials had shown up on her doorstep. "I have told you why I took up residence in the isolated cottage, Mr. Pugg, but you've not explained why you are here."

"We are in search of a missing girl," he said shortly. "Reddish brown hair, hazel eyes, a scar on her right cheek. Seen anyone matching that description?"

"I have not, but I see almost no one save the blacksmith who brings supplies as he makes his rounds. I've been into Silverdale a time or two, but cannot recall encountering anyone with a scarred face. Is that all you wished to know?"

"Indulge me a few minutes longer," he said coolly. "If I am not mistaken, you were in Lancaster yesterday."

She gave him a look of surprise. "However did you know *that*? Good heavens. I had heard that Bow Street Runners were enormously skilled, but never imagined one might be keeping track of my inconsequential journeys. Yes, I went into Lancaster to run a few errands. How does it signify?"

"I'm not certain that it does," Pugg admitted. "A gentleman has employed me to trace Miss Diana Whitney, and yesterday a solicitor brought information regarding a veiled woman who made certain inquiries that raised his suspicions. A few routine questions at posthouses and like places directed me to you."

"Indeed? I did in fact call briefly on a solicitor and asked a few questions relating to my sister's unhappy situation. Her husband is something of a brute, and she . . . well, I shall explain the whole if you think it necessary, but I cannot see how it will help you. The solicitor struck me as something less than competent, and I confess to taking him in dislike from the first. After only a few minutes I took my leave." She wondered if Pugg could hear the blood pulsing in her ears. "Did he imagine it was the missing lady who had been in his offices, wearing a veil to conceal her scar?"

"Like as not. There is a reward for information leading to her whereabouts, and all manner of folk are turning up with claims of having seen her, most of them spurious. I followed up on this one because I'd been nosing about in the vicinity earlier in the week and heard reports of odd happenings near to this cottage."

Lucy held herself straight and forced an expression of mild interest to her face. "What sort of happenings? I have observed nothing unusual, but to be sure I generally remain indoors during daylight hours."

"It's an apparition of some sort, which appears only at night. Cocklers and mussel diggers have seen it walking along the cliff. Glows in the dark, it does."

"Some believe it's one of the Lancashire Witches," the constable put in, "come back to punish the descendants of them what hanged her."

"My word! But I must confess that I put no credit in the existence of witches."

The constable scuffed his booted toe on the dirt floor. "Most folk in these parts know the story. Down around Clitheroe, near Pendle Hill, there was some ladies charged with witchcraft and put to the gallows. This was mebbe two hunert years ago, but when I was a lad, there was tales of a witch what lived in this cottage until the landlord tried to evict her. She ran to the cliff and jumped, and he swore that he saw her fly away."

Lucy shuddered. "It's true that I'm not in the least superstitious, but by no means would I have leased this cottage if I'd known it was reputed to be haunted."

"One of the witches," Pugg said, "the leader of the coven, I believe, had the name of Preston. Same as you."

"My. That *is* an odd coincidence, sir. But I am most certainly not a witch. I do, however, occasionally take long walks at night, when I can be outside without wearing the veil. Do you suppose the cocklers saw moonlight reflecting off my clothing and let their imaginations run wild?"

Pugg rubbed at his chin with skinny fingers. "Happen they did. In my job, half the time is spent chasing rumors and following trails that lead to nowhere. But so long as we've come this far, madam, you won't object if we search the cottage?"

Her heart raced. She could think of no good reason to protest, and knew that any hesitation on her part would only increase his suspicions. So she put a smile on her face and made a sweeping gesture. "By all means, sir. There is only this room and the one through that door."

She didn't follow the men into the other room, fearing they would hear her heart thumping in her chest. There was little to see in there, so perhaps they would not remain very long. Moving to the doorway, she saw Pugg lift the portmanteau as if checking its weight. Did he imagine the missing girl was encased within it?

The constable appeared a trifle embarrassed. "Nothin' in here, sir."

"Evidently not." Pugg put down the portmanteau and examined the walls. "This bit was added on after the cottage was built. I wonder there's no window."

"Windows be taxed from time to time," the constable observed.

With horror, Lucy watched Pugg's gaze shift to the thatched carpet. Then he shrugged and started toward the door. She barely had time to exhale with relief before he abruptly went back, grabbed hold of a fraying corner, and pulled the carpet to one side.

She closed her eyes, unable to watch what was coming next.

"Eh, what's this?" The trapdoor creaked slightly as he pulled it open.

Forcing herself to look up, she saw both men bent over the square opening. Surprised that Mr. Pugg did not immediately make a move to descend the stairs, she drew closer and looked over his shoulder.

She gasped. "Dear me. I had no idea this was here." They were the only true words she had uttered since the men arrived. Instead of the shadowy cave and stone steps, there was only a wooden box about eight inches deep, the rough-hewn planks unevenly nailed together. Cobwebs matted the corners, and scattered in the sifting of dust covering the bottom were, unless she was very much mistaken, several of the shiny pellets Fidgets sometimes regurgitated. "Whatever can it be?"

Pugg lowered the trapdoor. "A hiding place for valuables, most like, dug out from the ground and lined with wood. This one's crude, but I doubt the people who constructed it had much to conceal. Any other buildings on the property, Mrs. Preston?"

"No." She followed him into the other room, the scalloped edges of the miniature she was still holding digging into her palm. "Is there anything else you wish to know, sir?"

"The location of the nearest pub house," he replied with a self-mocking laugh. "I owe Planter a pint. He told me this would be a wasted errand, and so it has proved to be. Save for the pleasure of making your acquaintance, ma'am." To her astonishment, he gave her a courtly bow.

She might have curtsied in return, but she feared her jellied knees would not lift her up again. "I am unfamiliar with the local watering places, but I expect Mr. Planter knows the best ones."

"Oh, aye," the constable said. "Sorry to have troubled you, ma'am. We'll take ourselves off now so that you can get on with your walk."

Remembering to lower her veil beforehand, she opened the door and led them outside. "I do hope you find the missing girl," she said.

"You may be sure of it." Pugg mounted his horse. "God grant you a safe journey to York, Mrs. Preston."

Lucy managed a friendly wave as they rode away and waited until the curving track took them around the woodlands and out of her sight. Careful not to appear in a hurry, she returned to the cottage and raised the trapdoor a few inches. "Diana?"

"I'm here." Her voice sounded hollow. "What is happening?"

"All's well, but stay where you are for now. I'll explain everything later."

She disliked leaving Diana alone to fret, but since the men expected her to take a walk, she had better do so. The tenacious Mr. Pugg might decide to swing past the cottage again, hoping to catch her by surprise. Taking the spyglass with her, she strolled up the long hill leading to the cliff and gazed out over the bay.

The tide had begun to retreat, and above the water she could discern the very tops of the boxes on the wagon. She'd never have spotted them if she hadn't known precisely where to look. Raising the spyglass, she pointed it in the opposite direction to the one the men had taken and slowly made a half circle. A few moments later she saw them, tiny figures rounding a small hill and, glory be, making the turn to Warton. They were soon out of sight, but caution sent her walking along the cliff for nearly a mile, checking constantly for any sign of them. If they circled back through the thick woods, she wouldn't know it until they were nearly upon her.

As she walked, disconnected thoughts tumbled over one another in her head. When first she saw the men, she'd been certain that Kit had dispatched them here. But when they did not immediately go to the trapdoor, she realized her mistake.

It had been that reptilian solicitor after all. She longed to wring his scrawny neck with her bare hands.

Kit must have nailed that box together. She had to grant he was clever, if nothing else. Well, also intelligent, witty, and leagues too handsome for his own good, she would be forced to admit if she allowed herself to think on it, which she was careful not to do.

Taking care did not always turn the trick, though. It had no effect whatsoever when she tried not to think about his kiss. That proved as impossible as not thinking about an elephant when told not to think about an elephant, after which one could think of nothing *but* elephants.

His kiss had been an elephant stomping back and forth through her thoughts ever since it happened.

Summoning all her willpower, she wrenched her concentration to Pugg. Runners were for hire, she knew, and Sir Basil Crawley must have paid him a pretty penny to come so far north. It was he who posted the reward, no doubt, since Diana's uncle hadn't two sixpence to scratch together.

Sir Basil knew about Diana's scarred face, although he'd not seen it, but it appeared he was still determined to wed her. It was a good investment on his part, Lucy supposed. Diana was a great heiress and her family had held the barony for centuries.

She wondered what it was about Sir Basil that Diana so detested. By her account he was a well-looking man, somewhat rough about the edges by the standards of old aristocratic families but impeccably dressed and well-spoken. To be sure, any man of forty probably seemed ancient to a girl half his age. In any case, Diana had found him repellent when first they met, and she undoubtedly feared him. "Even thinking about him makes him somehow present," she had once said. "I only want him *gone*."

Lucy respected Diana's feminine instincts. She only wished she had a few of her own. Pragmatism and experience had been her guides as she steered through a bramblebush life, subject to the whims and dictates of those who paid her wages and put a roof over her head.

She took another long look through the spyglass, seeing no sign of Pugg and the constable. Diana must be in agony by now, wondering what had occurred. Lucy headed down the hill, choosing the track that skirted the woodland on her way back to the cottage. Her senses were at knife edge. She expected Pugg to leap out from behind every tree she passed. But she heard only the soft sifting of the afternoon breeze through the woodlands, and birdsong, and the crunch of her boots on fallen leaves.

She ought to be making plans, she thought as the cottage came into view. But her mind felt swaddled in wool, and she could not think beyond the next footfall.

"Pssst!"

A scream jumped to her throat. Forcing it back, Lucy swung her gaze past the thick undergrowth and saw Kit leaning against the trunk of an oak, grinning at her.

She had never in her life been so happy to see anyone. And she wanted to throttle him for scaring the stuffing out of her. She threaded through the bushes to a small clearing where Kit's horse was nibbling grass.

"You arrived just in time," Kit informed her. "I'm in serious danger of being ravished."

Following his gesture, she looked up to a branch directly over his head where Fidgets was perched, staring at him with owlish concentration.

"While I've been waiting for your guests to leave and you to return, my suitor—or ought that be suitress?—has supplied a picnic lunch." He pointed to the limp figure of a vole stretched inches from his boot. "Mind you, I've always longed to be

123

wooed. It's deuced unfair, don't you think, that men have to do all the work of seducing while females have only to flutter their lashes and flirt?"

"I never flirt," Lucy snapped. In truth, she'd no idea how to go about it. And how came they to be chattering nonsense in the midst of a crisis? "Not that you seem to care, but a constable and a Bow Street Runner were here not an hour ago, looking for Diana."

"A Runner?" Kit frowned. "Bad news, Runners. In my experience the local constabulary is a pack of well-meaning fools, but Runners are smart and relentless. They never give up until the mission is accomplished."

"You may well believe it. I told more clankers in the last hour than I've told in all the rest of my life, and I'm not sure if he credited a single one of them. They certainly did not dissuade him from searching the cottage." She shuddered to remember what had happened next. "He found the trapdoor."

"But not the cave, I take it. Feel free to praise me for divining a way to conceal it. An inspired notion, wouldn't you say?"

"I *might* say, had you not anticipated me." She gave him an exasperated look. "No wonder that poor Fidgets is enamored of you, what with you displaying like the vainest peacock in all creation. He thinks you to be some sort of oversize bird."

"*She,* please." He whistled softly, and Fidgets swooped down to perch on his shoulder. "We've been practicing this for the past hour," he told her when she gaped at him. "Come along, Lady Lucy. We have much to discuss, but Diana should be present for all the important bits."

She took the arm he offered her, keenly aware of its solid strength under the obviously expensive sleeve of a bottle-green riding coat. His left arm was still encased in the sling made from her Norwich shawl, and he limped slightly as they made their way to the cottage, but otherwise it was hard to remember that he had ever been injured.

"Tell me about the box," she said. "How is it affixed?"

"Stop that, you impertinent wench!"

Startled, she looked over to see Fidgets grooming his hair with a sharp V-shaped beak.

Kit grinned at her, rolling his eyes. "She thinks you her mother and me her mate. Would that make you my mother-in-law?"

His *mother-in-law*? Was that how he saw her? The elephant stampeded through her skull.

"I'm no carpenter, as you can tell from a close look at the box. It's propped up with sticks of wood cut to the distance between the box and the first two steps leading down to the cave, and I imagine it would collapse if given a good hard push from above. The important thing was making it simple for Diana to manage, and she practiced until she could install it in a hurry."

"It was a superb notion," she conceded. "It assuredly saved us this afternoon, sir, and I am most grateful to you."

"Hear that, Fidgets? Your mama approves of me for a change." Letting go of Lucy's arm, he opened the cottage door, but before she could enter, he leaned over to whisper in her ear, "My inamorata won't like it, I expect, but if you hope to take her with you when you leave, Fidgets ought to be confined now."

The owl was none too pleased about it, but Lucy managed to secure her in the wicker traveling cage.

"Who were those men?" Diana demanded as Kit helped her ascend from the cave.

"I'll tell you later," he replied, carrying the three-legged stool to the table. "There's no immediate urgency, sweetheart, but I'd like us to be on our way within the hour. Any questions that can wait probably should. Good work with the box, by the way."

Diana dropped onto a chair. "I was scared out of my wits."

"But you did just as you ought in spite of being afraid, which is precisely what it is to be brave. Things are well in hand now. My brother is assembling a formidable regiment of lawyers, and believes that a good case can be made for overturning your uncle's guardianship. Naturally he will do all in his power—

his *considerable* power—to bring that about, and at the end of the day, you will be perfectly safe."

"What about the first part of the day?" Lucy asked tartly. "What do we do in the meantime?"

He smiled. "I've spoken with a good friend, a widow who lives alone on a small farm not many miles from here. Her husband was killed early in the war, and since then she has made ends meet by raising pigs to sell at the local markets. The farm is isolated and a trifle rank to the nose, which helps to keep people away." He sat on the stool and took hold of Diana's hands. "You'll like her, I promise, and she welcomes both the company and the opportunity to earn a bit extra by taking in a lodger. I'll tell you more about her on the way there."

"Lodger?" Lucy had not missed his use of the singular noun. "Am I not to go with Diana?"

"One person is more easily concealed than two," he said, "and the house is small. Robbie is on his way there now with her belongings, after which he'll arrange passage for you on a coach headed south. It may not be possible, though, for you to leave until tomorrow morning. Will you mind greatly remaining alone here for the night?"

She waved a hand, unable to speak. He had taken complete charge of Diana's future and drummed Lucy Preston from the ranks as if she were no longer of the slightest use. The Earl of Kendal and his brother had stepped in with all their power and money and male arrogance, and might just as well have said, "Run along, Miss Preston. We'll handle things from here on out."

Tears sprang to her eyes, the first she could remember for many long years. She wished she had not removed the veiled hat. Kit would be even more certain he was right to dismiss her if he saw her weeping. She went to the window and lifted the curtain slightly, gazing outside with burning eyes, seeing nothing. She could not even think how to fight him. What more could she do for Diana, after all?

There was little reason not to return to Dorset and her wearisome job. And really, she had failed Diana at the end. She'd no place to take her, no money to hire a reputable barrister to plead her case in the courts, no excuse to stay. She had done her best, but it wasn't good enough. Diana would be far better off with a powerful earl to champion her cause.

Two warm hands settled on her shoulders. "What's wrong, moonbeam?"

"N-nothing. I'm glad you found somewhere Diana can be safe while the lawyers wrangle. Please thank his lordship on my behalf for his assistance. And I don't mind remaining here until Robbie comes to take me to the posthouse. My employer will be pleased to see me, I've no doubt. I told her I'd be gone a fortnight, but it's well beyond six weeks already. I simply had no idea how long it would take to steal Diana away and—"

"You're babbling, poppet. And crying, too. I suspect. Did you imagine you were to go home?" One hand lifted to stroke her cheek. "As if I'd permit you to escape so easily. You've not heard the other half of my plan, you know."

She could not help leaning into him, despising her own weakness even as she relaxed against his hard chest and savored the feel of his callused fingertip on her cheek. "W-what is the other half?" she murmured.

"Well, as to that, I cannot say. Primarily because I've not yet worked it out, but it promises to be a cracker. We shall put our heads together when you arrive at Candale."

She pulled away from him. "I cannot possibly go to an earl's estate. It's unthinkable. Just look at me."

"Mrs. Preston ought to depart the vicinity, I agree, which is why you'll first take a southbound coach. A carriage will be waiting at one of the posthouses along the way, one where the passengers are given time to have a meal. A room will be reserved for you, and a maid will be waiting there with your next disguise. Lest anyone miss you, she will transform herself into Mrs. Preston, take your place in the coach, and continue on to Liverpool for a visit with her family."

"But Mrs. Preston has to go to York! Mr. Pugg expects her

to." Lucy knew that sounded ridiculous, but she could not let go of the idea that he would verify the story she had given him.

"Should he retain the slightest interest in Mrs. Preston, which I very much doubt, he will do no more than make a few inquiries regarding her departure. If he checks at any of the coach stops, people will recall seeing her, and she must necessarily go south before transferring to a coach heading across the Pennines. He'll not attempt to trace her very far, I assure you, and we are taking excessive precautions as it is."

She supposed so. But he had not met Mr. Pugg, nor experienced the terror she'd felt when he probed her with his sharp, assessing gaze. All the same, she might as well go along with Kit's plan since she had none of her own to propose. "I—perhaps this is an improper question, but I must ask why it is Diana must stay on a stranger's pig farm instead of—"

"If you imagine she is unwelcome at Candale, that is far from the case. But when it becomes known that the earl has taken up her cause, Mr. Pugg and his like will come looking for her there. It's remotely possible that Lord Whitney could secure a warrant to search the estate and the several other properties in the area owned by our family. Better she be stowed safely elsewhere, I am persuaded. Only Robbie and I will know where she is, so that the rest of you can in all honesty deny any knowledge of her location."

"But I *wish* to know. And I am an exceedingly good liar."

"Such an accomplishment!" he chided, grinning. "So am I, as it happens. But the truth is easier to keep track of, and this one time I am heeding Kendal's advice. He is a master of deception— used to be a diplomat, y'know—and he instructed me to tell him absolutely nothing he did not need to know. The same applies to everyone else, including you. Don't quarrel with me on this subject, Lucy. It is for the best."

She slipped around him and went to where Diana was sitting quietly, waiting while other people made decisions on her behalf. In her place, Lucy knew that she'd be furiously demanding to express her own opinions on the subject of her future.

"Are you in agreement, Diana? Will you mind staying with someone you have never met?"

"No. It is precisely what I most wish, a quiet place where I can come to terms with myself. There has been no time for that before now. But I'm glad you are not returning to Dorset just yet, and that you'll be close by." She lifted her gaze to Kit. "Might she send me letters, telling me how things are proceeding?"

"Why not? I'll deliver them when I visit, or she can send them through Robbie. We don't mean to abandon you there, butterfly. This is a temporary arrangement only. I think we should be on our way now, since I mean to take a roundabout way to the farm. Are you ready to go?"

"Nearly." She stood. "Let me fetch my cloak and gloves. They're in Lucy's portmanteau."

"Dig out the witch's cape and wig, will you? I want to take them with me."

"Whatever for?" Lucy asked as Diana went into the other room.

"They may prove useful. I'm not altogether sure how, but as I told you, I'm still thinking about my next plan. Meantime we need to complete the one in progress. Are you clear on what you are to do?"

"I am to wait here for Robbie, who will take me to the coach, probably tomorrow morning. At some point I'll leave the coach and change into clothing provided me by a servant. How am I to know which posthouse is the right one?"

"The driver and the maid will be watching for you. Don't worry about the details, Lucy. Robbie and I are seeing to them. You have only to relax and do your part. By tomorrow evening at the latest, you will be joining the family for supper at Candale."

He could hardly have said anything more likely to rock her on her heels. As it was, she put a trembling hand on the table for support. "Is that necessary? The last thing I wish is to encroach on your family. I would much prefer to remain somewhere out of the way."

"The countess would not hear of it," he said in an amused voice.

Diana returned, wearing her cloak and gloves, Lucy's black cape folded neatly in her arms. "The wig is wrapped inside," she said, handing the bundle to Kit before turning to embrace Lucy. "Thank you so very much for all you have done. I can never repay you as you deserve, but I shall always pray for your happiness. And please don't be concerned for me. I have never seen a pig, you know, but I expect I'll come to like them."

Eyes burning, Lucy could only hug her tightly. She had loved few people in her life, and none who failed to betray her trust. Even Miss Wetherwood had dismissed her from the academy after heeding the lies of another teacher. Although she later discovered the truth, apologized, and offered Lucy her former job with a rise in salary, Lucy had declined. She corresponded with the headmistress during the next few years, but their relationship was never the same.

It was difficult to admit to herself that she loved Diana, and impossible to say so aloud, but she knew that she did. She hoped that Diana, with the fine-tuned instincts Lucy so admired, was aware of it, too.

"Ahem," Kit said from the door. "Not to interrupt, but you'll be seeing each other again sooner than you expect. Detach yourself, Diana, and come along."

Lucy followed them to where the horse was tethered, feeling an unexpected shot of jealousy when Kit helped Diana to mount and swung himself onto the saddle behind her, wrapping one arm around her waist. And all with one arm in a sling, Lucy thought with some amazement.

"Last chance, moonbeam. Any questions?"

Probably a score of them, but she couldn't think of one. "No. I suppose not."

"I'll see you tomorrow then. Give Fidgets my love." With the slightest nudge of his knee, he turned the horse and guided it deeper onto the narrow track.

Lucy suddenly thought of a question. "What disguise?" she called after him. "What sort of costume are you sending me?" She heard him laugh as he disappeared around a curve.

Chapter 11

In other circumstances, Lucy might have enjoyed the luxury of Lord Kendal's elegant crested carriage as it made its way along the turnpike road. Beside her in the wicker cage, Fidgets had long since gone to sleep, leaving her alone with her tumultuous thoughts.

So far, all had transpired exactly as Kit said it would. At a posthouse south of Lancaster, a pretty young girl led her to a room where a change of clothing was laid out for her on the bed. Then the former Mary Fife, now Mrs. Preston for the rest of her own journey, went downstairs to join the other passengers as they reboarded the Lancaster-to-Liverpool Comet. Lucy was to wait, Mary told her, until a footman came to get her.

Alone in the bedchamber, she took the time to examine her appearance in the cheval mirror. In the rush, she'd paid no attention to what she was putting on, but when she had a moment to look, she scarcely recognized herself. The lavender carriage dress had been made over to fit her, she could tell, but she'd never worn a lovelier gown. It was embroidered at the hem and around the neck with violets, and there was a pelisse of darker purple to match.

When had she become so vain? She had never been so before. But she could not help turning her head this way and that, delighting in the French bonnet of tulle and watered silk with lush satin ribbons that framed her face to advantage. Only her black half boots, the ones she had to wear because the lavender kidskin shoes sent along with the dress were far too small, spoiled the image of the otherwise proper lady gazing back at her.

After a few minutes a footman had appeared to lead her to the coach. And now here she was, within a few miles of Candale, shaking like a custard.

It wasn't as if she were unaccustomed to fancy houses and aristocratic families. At Turnbridge Manor, she was sometimes permitted to dine at table when there were no guests of importance, so she knew how to make polite conversation with those above her rank. Primarily, of course, she knew how it felt to be ignored.

Her parents had been too busy deliberately ignoring each other to pay her any mind at all. When she turned nine they had stashed her at Miss Wetherwood's academy and separated, her mother to go off with a man who had a bushy mustache, which was all Lucy knew of him, and her father to bring his mistress to live with him at the small family estate. He ceased to pay tuition for her schooling when she was six-and-ten, and from then on she was left to her own resources.

Neither ever answered the letters she wrote so earnestly for the first few years, until she finally awakened to the fact that they cared nothing for her. So she stopped caring about them, and had not since let herself care overmuch for anyone else.

Thinking on her parents never failed to put her in the dismals, so Lucy unfolded Kit's note and read it for the dozenth time.

The man was addled, really he was. She had now been cast in the role of Miss Lucinda Jennet, since using the name of Preston might call untoward attention from itinerant Bow Street Runners. She was newly come north to meet the family of her betrothed, the Honorable Christopher Valliant, who had met her on his travels and fallen irremediably in love. She was advised to create a suitable background for herself, unless she wished to adopt the one he had thought up. They would discuss it when she arrived, to make sure they got their stories straight.

The next time she saw the reprehensible Kit Valliant, she

would set *him* straight. Fiancée indeed! Under no circumstances would she agree to this infamous deception. What he had told his family she could not bear to imagine, but they would hear only the truth from her. Except the part about her abbreviated name, which suited her well enough. Lucinda Jennet she would be, for the short time she remained where she did not belong.

The coach drew up before a tall set of wrought-iron portals, and a kilted Scotsman hurried from the gatehouse to swing them open. He must be the one related to Robbie's late wife, she thought, smiling when he gave her a friendly wave of welcome.

But her spirits plummeted again when the enormous three-story house came into view a few minutes later. On a low grassy hill, a large square building was set between two wings, forming a block letter *H*, the effect more imposing than graceful. But it was a beautiful house nonetheless, with tall shade trees planted just where they ought to be and an ornamental lake curving around the west wing as if in an embrace. Pale afternoon sunlight glittered off the mullioned windows and turned the massive gray stone walls to silver.

A marble-pillared portico sheltered the wide entrance doors, which swung open just as Lucy was alighting from the coach. A breathtakingly lovely woman with curly golden hair stepped out, a warm smile curving her lips. The countess, Lucy thought, feeling painfully anxious at the prospect of meeting her. She could not bring her feet to move any closer.

Lady Kendal came to her, skirts billowing as she rushed to the coach with her arms open. "Miss Jennet. I am delighted to meet you. Welcome to our home."

Lucy managed an awkward curtsy. "Thank you, ma'am. I shall try not to be any bother."

"Nonsense! We adore bother. Come along and meet Kendal, and then I'll show you to your room and give you a chance to catch your breath. Kit isn't here, I'm afraid. We had no idea what time you would arrive, and he's gone off on one of his errands. It doesn't do to ask him where or what, but he will be back in time for dinner."

Rather sure she'd been caught up in a whirlwind, Lucy accompanied the chattering countess through the marble-tiled entrance hall and down a long passageway.

"Now, I should advise you, if Kit has not already done so, that the earl is not nearly so starched up as he first appears. He spent a great many years in the courts of Europe and acquired a bit too much cosmopolitan polish, but it is beginning to wear off. Don't let him intimidate you, Miss Jennet. It is the last thing he would wish."

Thoroughly intimidated already, Lucy was ushered into an impressive study lined with bookshelves and glass-topped cases. She couldn't see what they contained, her attention riveted by the gentleman seated behind a large mahogany desk. He rose when the ladies entered the room and inclined his head in response to her curtsy.

Her first thought was that Lord Kendal looked nothing like his brother, although they were both tall, slim, and broad-shouldered. But the earl had light brown, close-cropped hair, graceful, long-fingered hands, and a decided air of elegance about him. She thought him handsome, in a quiet way, like sculpted glass. Only his blue eyes put her in mind of Kit, and only for a moment. Kendal's eyes were cool and watchful, not dancing with high spirits and good humor.

His voice was dark velvet when he spoke. "You are most welcome to Candale, Miss Jennet. May I offer you a glass of sherry?"

"Oh, don't be silly," the countess said, taking hold of Lucy's trembling arm. "She has had a long journey hard on the heels of a mighty adventure. I shall sweep her away now, and you will have to wait until dinner to become better acquainted. Come along, my dear, and tell me what you would like to have with your tea as we make our way upstairs. Cook baked apple tarts this morning, and I can testify that they are delicious because I've already devoured three of them."

Lucy stole a glance over her shoulder as Lady Kendal pulled her from the room. The earl was smiling.

"You must pardon me for rabbiting on," the countess said a few minutes later as they sat drinking tea in a beautifully appointed suite of rooms while servants filled a copper bathtub with steaming water. "We receive so little company these days, Miss Jennet, and I've not had another female to coze with since months before Christopher was born. He is ten weeks old now, with a temper he must have gotten from me and a demanding nature inherited from his father. I am trying not to spoil him, but it is difficult to do otherwise. Kit tells me you have been governess to five young boys, so you must know how it is."

"I've little experience with infants," Lucy said, the first words she'd had a chance to say for quite some time. And just as well, since her tongue seemed to be swollen in her mouth. She was overwhelmed by these charming aristocrats and their lavish hospitality. "May I see your son? Only if that would be acceptable, of course."

"Whyever would it *not*? You must run tame at Candale, Miss Jennet. Go where you will and do whatever you like. We do not stand on ceremony here." The countess patted her hand. "I daresay you will feel more comfortable when Kit returns. And now I must leave you to your bath before it grows cold. Have yourself a good nap and use the bellpull if you require anything at all. We keep country hours, so dinner will be at seven."

Moth wings beat inside Lucy's stomach. "Must I join you, Lady Kendal? I've nothing to wear, and—"

"Mercy me! Did I not tell you? More than half the gowns in my wardrobe no longer fit since I began eating like a horse. Nursing a babe makes me voracious, and of course my breasts are swollen like ascent balloons. When Kit told us you were to pay a visit and explained the circumstances, I put a seamstress to work altering a few of my dresses to your size. It's a hurried bit of patchwork, I'm sorry to say, but there are several gowns hanging in that armoire, and the chest of drawers contains whatever else I could think of—night rails, robes, handkerchiefs, and the like. If you require anything I forgot, you have only to ask."

"Th-thank you. I am most grateful."

"Piffle! You can have no idea how pleased I am to have you here." She rose, plucking an almond biscuit from the tea tray. "Young Betsy Slate aspires to be a lady's maid, so I hope you don't mind if she practices on you. She'll come to your room an hour before dinner to help you dress and show you the way to the parlor for a glass of wine before we sit at table. Kit insists on wine before dinner, and we accommodate him whenever he comes home."

Lucy stood, dazed and uncertain what to say or do. The next she knew, she was swept up in a warm embrace.

"May I call you Lucy?" the countess asked when she stepped away. "And will you call me Celia?"

Melting under her smile, Lucy could only nod. She would never be able to address the countess by her Christian name, she was certain, but now was not the time to say so. Lady Kendal blew her a kiss as she left the room, and Lucy stood for a long time staring at the closed door, wondering how on earth she could endure another hour in this house. Every minute she stayed here would make her want more, and it would never do to become accustomed to such luxury.

As they departed the dining room Kit drew Celia aside, leaving his brother to escort Lucy to the drawing room for coffee. Her hand stiff on the earl's arm, Lucy cast him a sulfurous look over her shoulder, the first sign of spirit he'd seen from her all evening.

"What the devil's the matter with her?" Kit asked when Kendal and Lucy were out of earshot. "She pushed food around on her plate all evening and hardly spoke ten words altogether. Have you been beastly to her?"

"Oh, indeed. We imprisoned her in the wine cellar the entire afternoon." Celia gave a delicate shrug. "She is a trifle uncomfortable among strangers, I daresay, although from your description, I had not expected her to be shy."

"Well, she isn't, and I'm not a stranger. I don't think she

looked at me above twice, though. It must be the neckcloth. I knew I shouldn't have worn it." He sliced Celia a grin. "Dire measures are called for, I'm afraid, if I am to get my Lucy back. Methinks a good row will turn the trick."

"Mercy, Kit. You don't mean to pick a fight with the poor girl?"

"That would be ungallant, m'dear, and I am a prince among men. I merely plan to invite her to a ball."

"Oh, dear."

"Precisely. Do me a service, will you, and extricate your husband from the drawing room before the fireworks begin." He took her arm. "*Now* would be an excellent time."

Kit watched with appreciation as Celia tactfully maneuvered Kendal from the room within a few minutes. Lucy tried to follow them, but he intercepted her before she could reach the door. "I take lots of sugar in my coffee," he said, steering her to a chair beside the low table.

Lips set in a rigid line, she dutifully filled a cup with coffee, chipped off a sizable hunk of sugar to sweeten it, and held it out. All without once looking in his direction.

He took a sip. "Perfection. Thank you. Now, do you intend to tell me why you are blue-deviled, or must I drag it from you?"

"You know very well why!"

Well, that didn't take long, Kit thought. There was much to be said for loving a woman with a flashpan temper.

"Men never know *why*, moonbeam. And why is it you females always force us to guess what we've done wrong?"

"Because you ought to know, that's why." She threw up her hands. "You are hopeless, the lot of you. But I shall explain in words even you can understand. *I do not belong here.*"

"If you think that, you are the only one who does."

"I haven't finished. *I am not your fiancée.*"

"A mere bagatelle. Sometimes the facts take a while to catch up with the truth."

"What in blazes does *that* mean? No, don't tell me. I am sure I do not want to hear any more of your moonshine."

She was looking at him now, her gray eyes shooting sparks and sending heat all up and down his body. That's my girl, he thought, readying himself for the next assault.

"Lord and Lady Kendal have been prodigiously kind, and I feel horrid to repay them only with deceit. Masquerades are defensible when there is no other choice, sir, but this one serves no purpose at all."

"Ah, there you are wrong. It is a significant part of my plan, the one I am working on. Not all the pieces are in place, but it's coming together, and meantime we are laying the groundwork. Consider this. When constables and lawyers and Runners start prowling around, how else to explain your presence at Candale?"

"No explanation would be required if I weren't here. And I wish to leave. Tomorrow."

Kit drank the rest of his coffee while he considered how to proceed. Telling her that he understood her feelings—which he did—would probably result in the coffee service being thrown piece by piece at his head. She was in no mood to be soothed, that was clear. For now, he had better concentrate on bending her to his will, which he had learned was best accomplished by confronting her with a challenge.

"You are not a prisoner here, Lucy, but you are very much needed. You are the one Diana trusts. If you abandon her, she will lose all faith in the rest of us."

"I— Do you think so?"

"You must finish what you began, moonbeam. We can none of us consider our own wishes until Diana is free of her uncle and the man who is pulling his strings. Am I right?"

"Aren't you always?" she grumbled, twisting a silver spoon in her hands. "But how am I of any use? What am I to *do*?"

"I'm delighted that you asked." He set his cup and saucer on the tray, using the time to seize a deep breath. "As it happens, Sir Basil Crawley has invited us to a ball."

"What?" She regarded him in disbelief. "How could he? He doesn't know that I exist."

"Well, technically, it's Kendal he hopes to snag. But Kendal won't go, and Celia cannot because she is nursing her son, which leaves it up to us. My name was on the invitation, too, and I would hardly attend a ball without my fiancée, would I?"

He expected her to object ferociously to the whole idea, but she sat back in her chair, brow wrinkled as she considered the possibilities. Or he hoped she was considering. There was no way to tell from her expression.

"I would certainly like to meet the blackguard," she said thoughtfully. "But what is to be gained from making his acquaintance, short of satisfying our curiosity about him?"

In his opinion, that was quite enough reason by itself. But he was a creature of the process, preferring the journey to the destination, while she required definite goals. What a perfect team they were going to make. "I mean to befriend him, if the opportunity arises. No, *befriend* is not the proper word. *Insinuate myself,* perhaps. Someone needs to take his measure, you must admit, and what better chance will we ever have?"

"There are other difficulties to consider. I have nothing to wear, I have not danced since lessons at school, and I may kill him on sight."

Kit burst into laughter. Only Lucy would say such a thing. And mean it, too. "The ball is Friday night, so we have four days to rig you out in style and practice our dancing. As for your homicidal instincts, I am inclined to share them. But we'll keep each other in check."

"You've already sent an acceptance, haven't you?"

Flames darted up his cheeks. "Maybe."

She shook her head. "I may be towed to the gallows for murdering you long before I get my hands on Sir Basil."

At least the fire was in her again. She was Lucy once more, not the pale, nervous creature he'd sat to dinner with two hours earlier. "And no one would blame you for it. I am a great trial to all who know and love me." He grinned. "Have I groveled sufficiently, or must I go on?"

"Oh, I think you must, but at a later time. Let me sleep on this, Kit. I know it's a perfectly stupid idea, attending the ball, but I confess that I am tempted. At least I'd be *doing* something instead of wafting around this enormous house, getting in everyone's way and feeling indebted to strangers, however kind they may be."

He held out his hand. "Come with me, moonbeam. I want to show you something."

The nursery was lit only by a single candle when he led her inside. The young maid keeping watch from a chair near the cradle stood, curtsied, and withdrew to the passageway, closing the door gently behind her.

Holding back, Kit watched Lucy approach the cradle on tiptoe, clearly fascinated and a trifle reluctant. She stopped about two feet away, bending forward to look down at the sleeping infant.

"He's so very *small*," she whispered.

"And so very fierce," he said, moving to stand beside her. "He rules this house and everyone in it. The rest of us can only stand in awe of him. He is a miracle, Lucy. All children are miracles. The world is their inheritance, and we are no more than caretakers. One day he will stand, gazing down on his own son or daughter, and think the same thing as we are thinking now. This is what matters . . . love and family and children. This is what we are born for, and why we live."

She gazed up at him, candlelight dancing over her smooth, flawless cheeks. "I think I don't understand you at all, Kit."

"That's why I brought you here. If ever you wish to know me, past the smuggling and the willfulness and the constant irritation I provide you, remember what I just said." He took her arm and led her to the door. "For now, I mean to sit with the Terror of Candale for a time. I shall see you tomorrow, Lucy, when I've returned from visiting Diana."

Chapter 12

Lucy stood precariously on a footstool while the assistant seamstress draped her with yet another swath of glittering material.

"*Tiens!*" The mantua-maker shook her head. "With hair of such a color, she is most difficult to clothe. And I regret to say she has not enough bosom for the pattern she has chosen."

"Then I shall select another pattern," Lucy said irritably. She could scarcely grow larger breasts in three days. "Any of them will do, Madame Broussard. It matters little how I look."

"I cannot agree. My reputation must be considered, mademoiselle." She turned to the countess, who was observing the proceedings from a sofa. "Will you leave this in my hands, Lady Kendal? In the shops, I shall discover a fabric to suit both the young lady and the gown I have in mind for her."

"What think you, Lucinda? Shall we give Madame Broussard carte blanche?"

"By all means." Lucy jumped down from the stool. "If it means an end to this poking and prodding and measuring, she may outfit me in a burlap sack."

"*Bon.*" The mantua-maker beckoned to her assistant, who began to gather up the lengths of material strewn over the furniture. "On Thursday, the gown will be ready for fitting."

Remembering her manners, Lucy smiled. "Thank you, madame. I am certain to like it enormously."

"*Certainement.* You are a beauty, mademoiselle, and I shall create a gown to bedazzle all the gentlemen." Two hawkish eyes examined Lucy one last time. "Have you any pearls to wear?"

"Yes," said Lady Kendal before Lucy could reply. She stood. "A tray of refreshments will be sent up for you, madame. Lucinda, will you join me in the nursery?"

Lucy suspected that she was in for a well-deserved chiding. "I was terribly rude, wasn't I?" she said on their way upstairs. "But this all seems so . . . frivolous."

"Under the circumstances, I am certain that it does. You may be sure, however, that madame took no offense. She is herself rather plainspoken."

"That is no excuse for my reprehensible conduct. Everyone has been so kind, and all I do is snap and snarl."

Lady Kendal paused outside the nursery door. "You are on edge with worry about your friend, which is perfectly understandable. And somewhat nervous about the ball, yes? But the dance lesson went exceedingly well this morning, Monsieur d'Alacoque informs me, and before Friday you will feel quite confident taking the floor with Kit. He is a splendid dancer."

That was *not* what she needed to hear. "We are going to this ball only to scrutinize Sir Basil Crawley. It will not be necessary to dance."

"That would be a shame, but you must do as you wish. Take care that Kit does not stampede you. The Valliant men, at least the two I have met, are fond of having their own way."

And generally got it, Lucy thought sourly. "I would not mind so much if Kit would cease introducing me as his fiancée. How will it reflect on your family when nothing comes of our supposed engagement?"

"That doesn't signify in the least. We are quite accustomed to Kit's scandals, you know. And compared with a jailing, a mere jilting is of no consequence whatsoever." Lady Kendal smiled. "To be sure, we shall be sorry if you decide not to wed him after all."

"There can be no question of marriage! Did he not make it clear that this betrothal is only another of his games?"

Celia looked evasive. "He said something to that effect, I suppose. You have probably discovered that it is sometimes difficult to tell when he is being serious. May I give you a word of advice?"

"Oh, yes," Lucy replied hastily. "Please do."

"When I was in difficulty, Kit was a rock. You may trust him."

Lucy waited, but that brief pronouncement was the total of Lady Kendal's counsel. And it wasn't very helpful. Lucy was not inclined to trust *anyone*, let alone a highborn scoundrel like Kit Valliant. "Thank you, ma'am. I shall hold in mind what you have said."

"Fustian! You are thinking that my situation cannot compare with your own, but you are quite mistaken. My mother was the daughter of an impoverished baronet and my father . . . well, the less said of him, the better. I was so eager to escape him that I married an elderly man who bred chickens." She shuddered. "But this is a long story, and as I can hear my son squalling for his luncheon, I shall save my tale for another time. Just know that I was not born into Lord Kendal's world, and I well understand how it is to feel an outsider." She opened the nursery door. "You won't mind if I leave you now? While nursing Christopher, I can think of nothing but him."

Unable to speak through the knot of envy in her throat, Lucy waved a hand and turned away. Her breasts, the ones Madame Broussard had dismissed so cavalierly, began to ache as she imagined how it would be to hold a babe in her arms and feel its tiny mouth suckling at her nipple.

The fantasy possessed her all the way to the stable, where she fled for refuge from the imposing house and any possibility of encountering Lord Kendal. He had been kindness itself since her arrival, but he intimidated her nonetheless. She was far more comfortable in the company of Fidgets, who had settled into the stable as if she owned it.

My only child, she thought. *An owl!* Well, one must make do with what one has. And at the moment she desperately craved a bit of affection, whatever the source.

As she stepped inside, a redheaded lad of about nine years looked up from the saddle he was polishing. "C'n I help you, milady?"

"I came to visit Fidgets, if she is anywhere about."

"Right over there." He pointed to a ladder propped against the wall. Fidgets was perched on a middle rung, regarding her sleepily. A moment later the shiny eyes closed.

So much for birdly love. Sighing, Lucy sat on a bale of straw beside the stableboy. With young boys, at least, she always felt at ease. "Will you mind if I keep you company for a little while?"

His freckled face lit up. "I likes company. Mr. Reese sez to tend to the saddles, though, so I gots to keep workin'."

"Do go on. I am Miss Jennet, by the way."

"Oh, I knows that. You is the one what will marry Mr. Christopher. I be Timothy Slate, but everybody calls me Timmy."

Good heavens, even the servants thought her betrothed to Kit! Servants gossiped with the townsfolk, as well she knew, so perhaps this was a necessary lie. But she was growing sick at heart at the deception. There had been too many lies, too many disguises. Sometimes she wondered who she really was, and how she would find herself again when this latest masquerade was concluded.

"Your owl is an uncommon fine 'un," Timmy said. "I've not seen any so friendlylike as 'e is. Most is skeered of people."

"*He?* Are you sure of that? I had thought Fidgets to be female."

"Oh, 'e's a boy all right. The boys be a mite smaller than the girls and they gots whiter feathers in the front."

Lucy stifled a laugh. "Are you absolutely certain?"

"Oh, aye. I knows lots about owls. They looks to be smart, but they mostly be stupid. The same way as some people. Hard to tell about folks just from lookin'."

Profound wisdom from a stableboy. "Well, don't tell anyone

else about Fidgets's gender," she advised him. "It will shatter a number of illusions if you do."

"If you say so," Timmy agreed cheerfully. "What's a 'lusion?"

"Well, it's rather like a dream, or a wish. Something a person wants to think is true even if it isn't." Rather like imagining Kit in love with her.

"They be good then," Timmy piped. "I got lots of 'lusions. Nothin' much else to do when I is workin' but to dream 'bout doin' somethin' else."

"What do you dream of?" she asked curiously. For all her tedious existence, the one she would soon return to, Timmy's prospects were even less promising.

"Mostly I 'magines meself a jockey, me bein' small and good with 'orses. But sometimes I thinks about sailin' boats on the lakes, or mebbe even the ocean. One day I means to do one or t'other."

"I am certain that you will, Timmy." She stood, catching the rough heel of her half boot on the hem of her skirt. She had been measured for new shoes, but they would not be delivered before tomorrow. Meantime she clomped about Candale in her weather-beaten boots, wearing Lady Kendal's made-over dresses, wishing she could be Luke again. Or even Mrs. Preston, cloaked head to toe in black. Anything but a patched-together frump!

Fidgets made a low noise in his throat, and she turned to see him poised for flight. A second later he swooped past her. She heard the sound of hoofbeats then, and guessed that Kit had returned.

Shading her eyes against the afternoon sun, she went outside and saw him rein in, Fidgets perched atop his hat. A misbegotten pair if ever there was one, she thought. Almost as unlikely as the Honorable Christopher Valliant mated with Lucinda Jennet Preston, governess.

Dismounting, Kit opened the saddle pack and removed a parcel tied with string. "I brought Fidgets a present," he said.

"The least I could do, considering the number of voles she's dropped at my feet."

"What of Diana?" she demanded impatiently. "How is she?"

"You may read the news for yourself." He withdrew several folded sheets of paper from his coat pocket. "She sent a letter."

Lucy seized it and quickly scanned the pages, inscribed with a pencil in Diana's elegant handwriting. Then she read it again, more slowly, while Kit was in the stable with Timmy, seeing to the horse.

Fidgets had relocated to his shoulder when Kit returned, examining his beaver hat with a frown. "Look at this," he said, holding it in front of her. "Cost me a pretty penny, this bonnet."

She saw several small holes in the crown where eight talons had knifed in. "Better the hat than your head," she said unsympathetically. "Consider it the price of love."

He gave Fidgets a stern look. "Just for that, milady, I may not give you your present after all."

The owl made a low moaning sound.

"The letter tells me Diana is happy and well, but of course she would say that. You spoke with her, Kit. How is she truly getting on?"

"Far better than I expected. Country life appears to suit her. When I arrived she was mucking out a sty and singing naughty songs to the piglets. Later she introduced me to geese and ducks and cows and goats, each one by name." He regarded her with a pensive expression. "It is well, I believe, that she has work to occupy her time and new experiences to keep her from reflecting overmuch on the old ones."

She nodded. That had often been her thought at the cottage, where Diana had little to do but mope. "Was she making a pretense, do you think, so that we'd not be concerned about her?"

"She would likely have done so, were it called for. But Nell—er, her hostess—confirmed my own impressions. They have already become fast friends and were planning to cook up a batch of jam this afternoon. I am promised several jars for the Candale pantry on my next visit."

Her heart considerably lighter at such an encouraging report, Lucy smiled. "Well then, I shall worry about her only every other minute. And, Kit, I *am* sorry about your hat."

"As you said, the price of love." He tossed it onto a fence post and offered her his arm. "Will you walk with me for a few minutes? There is something I wish to discuss with you."

Her heart sank again. From the glint in his sky-blue eyes, he was up to something she was not going to like. But what could be worse than his last appalling idea—their appearance at Sir Basil Crawley's ball—or the one before it that cast her as his fiancée? Fingers crossed that he had only minor devilry in mind this time, she allowed him to escort her to the hill that rose up behind the paddocks.

As they began the climb a cool breeze tugged at her bonnet and lifted his hair, burnished to gold by the midafternoon sunshine. The hill was mostly bare, sprinkled with scarlet-berried rowans and birches cloaked with gold-brown autumn leaves.

Fidgets picked his way down Kit's other arm and began to peck at the string tied around the parcel in his hand. "Such a greedy wench you are," Kit chided.

"What did you bring hi—her?"

"Chicken feet. Celia won't allow poultry on the premises, so I was forced to import them from the farm."

She eyed the parcel dubiously. "Are owls partial to chicken feet?"

"Devil if I know, but they're a far sight easier to come by than voles. Shall we find out?"

When they reached the top of the hill, Kit placed Fidgets on a tree branch and moved about twenty yards away. The owl immediately flew to his shoulder. "No, no, my dear." He returned Fidgets to the branch. "Be a good girl and stay where I put you."

A few moments later Fidgets was on his shoulder again. Patiently, he repeated the exercise several times, with similar results.

"Whatever are you doing?" Lucy asked as he carried the owl back to the tree once again.

"Trying to get a stubborn female to obey me, which I daresay no man has succeeded in doing since the dawn of time." He stroked Fidgets's head. "Stay, beloved. Please. Do it for *me*."

This time Fidgets remained in place when Kit walked away. Keeping his back to the owl, he opened the parcel and withdrew a gray-pink chicken foot. Then he turned and held it out. "Come, Fidgets. Come and get it!"

The owl tilted its head, regarding him curiously, but stayed where it was.

"You're confusing the poor thing, Kit. First you tell her to stay, and then you insist that she come."

"Precisely. There really is a point to this, moonbeam. All will be made clear. I simply want to discover if Fidgets can be persuaded to come to me when I give her the signal, and apparently a chicken foot fails to turn the trick. It seems I'll be put to hunting down a mousie to tempt her."

"Will that not signify that Fidgets has trained *you*?" she observed tartly.

He chuckled. "I'm doing something wrong here, obviously. What draws an owl to prey? Odor? A rustling sound in the undergrowth?"

"Either would do, I suppose. Owls generally hunt at night, which is about all I know of the matter. They can see creatures moving in the dark, don't you imagine, the way cats do?"

"Lucy, you are positively brilliant. That's it, of course. Watch this!" He waved the chicken foot back and forth in an arcing motion.

With a shrill cry, Fidgets swooped from the branch, plucked the chicken foot from his hand, and settled on the ground to gobble it up.

"Well done," Kit said, "but that beak came a bit too close to m'fingers. I'd as soon not lose any one of them on our next try."

Lucy watched him tie the string that had secured the parcel around a chicken foot and move some distance away. Then he swung the string round and round over his head. In a flash,

Fidgets was onto the target with extended claws, ripping chicken foot and string from Kit's hand and carrying it to the tree branch.

Kit followed, drawing his knife from the sheath to detach the string before Fidgets swallowed it. "That's the secret," he called to Lucy over his shoulder. "She flies to whatever moves, so long as it resembles a meal. By tomorrow, with practice, I'll have her coming and going whenever I wish."

Bully for you, Lucy thought, toes curling inside her half boots. He could not rest until he had seized control of everything and everyone. Even a befuddled, infatuated owl must be trained to obey him.

He placed another chicken foot on the branch for Fidgets, retied the parcel, and approached Lucy with a wide grin on his face. "Let me guess. You are wondering what this is all about."

"Male supremacy, I would presume. A demonstration of how clever you are."

"I am sometimes clever," he said unrepentantly. "But the man who thinks himself supreme is a fool."

"Just so."

"Lucifer! A man could shave with the edge of your tongue. Cry peace, will you, long enough for me to explain?"

Contrition burned in her throat. "I beg your pardon, sir. I have no right to speak to you in such a way. It is—I mean—oh, I don't know what I mean! In future, I shall think twice and then again before—"

"Don't you dare," he said softly. "I mean it, Lucy. Speak your mind with me at all times. Have you ever known me to take offense?"

"N-no. But I always assumed that was because you didn't give a twig what I had to say. Like not taking offense when a dog barks or a frog croaks."

"Ah. I see." He put down the parcel and placed his hands on her shoulders. "I've not made myself clear. Believe me, I do give a twig, Lucy mine, for every word you say and for every expression on your face and for every gesture you make. I give whole forests for each one of your rare, beautiful smiles."

Breathless, she gazed into his clear blue eyes. It would be so easy to lose herself in him.

"Come," he said, releasing her shoulders. "Beyond that cluster of birches is a splendid view of the fells."

When they reached a promontory shaded by a large oak, they stood in silence for several minutes, gazing over the sheep-studded dale to the rugged crags beyond. In the far distance, the fells looked to be made of twilight-blue smoke.

"I have been thinking," he said, "what else can be done for Diana. She is in good hands, of course, but Whitney still holds the trump card. So long as he owns the legal right to demand she be returned to his custody, he can make matters exceedingly difficult. He'll not get hold of her, you may be sure. No one within a hundred miles will defy the Earl of Kendal on this matter. But should Whitney petition the Chancery Court, and I expect he will, things could get slippery."

"How? I know nothing about the courts. Tell me exactly."

He gave her a lopsided smile. "My acquaintance with the law is primarily from the opposite side, Lucy. You must ask Kendal to explain the finer points. I do know that Chancery moves at the speed of a glacier and that there's little chance Lord Eldon will render a final judgment before Diana comes of age, at which point the ruling becomes moot. But she may well be called to give depositions, and there is a remote possibility she'll be summoned to London for questioning."

"We mustn't let that happen," Lucy said instantly. "It would be a frightful experience."

"The more so because she originally said that the injury to her face was the result of a fall, without explaining it was Whitney caused the fall by striking her."

"But she only lied because she fears him. Anyone who sees her face will understand why."

Kit ran his fingers through his hair. "I should never have gone down this track. It has alarmed you and led me away from my point. Diana will not be returned to her guardian under any circumstances, and Kendal will stand her protector so far as the law permits. But should Whitney dig in his heels, she is certain to be subjected to a great deal of unpleasantness before the case is finally resolved in her favor. I wish to spare her that."

"By all means!"

"*Any* and all means," he said. "Keep to that thought while you hear me out. Our problem is simple enough—we must convince Whitney to sign over custody of Diana to my brother without taking the matter to court. We know Basil Crawley has been pulling his strings, but we're not altogether certain why."

"He wants to marry Diana. You already know that. She inherited a considerable fortune."

"But he is, by all accounts, a wealthy man. Possibly a greedy one, which would explain his persistence, but he may have an altogether different motive. Perhaps Kendal's investigation into his business affairs will disclose what it is, although we'll have no answers anytime soon."

"So how can they signify?" She scowled at him. "You are dancing around the point, sir."

"Yes. Sorry. I'll come at it directly, if you promise not to object until I've finished explaining how we shall bring Whitney to heel."

"There is a way to do that?"

"Of course." He grinned widely. "I have a plan."

Oh, dear, she thought, sealing her lips and gesturing him to proceed.

With boyish enthusiasm, he launched into a plot so outrageous that she could not believe her own ears. With growing dismay, which soon ratcheted up to stunned disbelief and went from there to absolute horror, she listened to the most improbable scenario ever devised by a supposedly sane man. By the end, she was practically sputtering.

"So," he said, looking excessively pleased with himself. "What do you think?"

What she thought was easily summarized. "You are deranged."

"That aside, you have to admit it's a devilish ingenious scheme."

"It's sheer lunacy. Who could believe such a thing?"

"No one with a crumb of sense, to be sure, but we are dealing with Lord Whitney. And if you pause to consider, Lucy, playing at witchcraft was your idea in the first place."

She threw up her hands. "That was to keep anyone from venturing too close to the cottage where we were hiding. And yes, mostly to scare Lord Whitney away. When Diana told me he was superstitious, it put me in mind of my name, Jennet Preston, and the Lancashire Witches. But what I did was nothing whatever like what you have proposed."

"Nonetheless, I am convinced it will work. This morning I spoke at length with Diana about her uncle. Did you know that he keeps a pair of scissors under the doormat to prevent witches from entering his house? Don't ask me how scissors could stop a witch, were there any such thing, but he is sure they will. He picks up every bit of metal he sees on the ground—nails, pins, discarded tin cups—lest a witch craft it into a weapon to use against him. Diana says he has filled a trunk with the metal odds and ends he has accumulated. He is forever touching wood and tossing salt over his shoulder and muttering imprecations meant to keep devils at bay."

"Lots of people are more or less superstitious," she cut in. "Their habits are generally harmless."

"But few people are quite so stupid as Lord Whitney. What's more, he feels guilty for what he did to his niece. I must take her word on that, but she said that he has wept and apologized profusely on more than one occasion."

"Crocodile tears. He hoped to use her beauty to his own advantage, and now he has destroyed it."

"I'm not so sure that he is insincere, Lucy. And he's lost nothing, because Crawley still wishes to wed her despite her appearance. Keep in mind our primary goal. If Whitney is spooked into

153

signing a few legal documents, Diana will not be dragged through the courts. Isn't that worth taking a long shot? And consider this. Superstition, stupidity, and guilt make a potent brew. We have only to light a spark and Lord Whitney will go up in flames."

Lucy gave him a penetrating look. "*You* are the one consumed by this farce, sir. You are so caught up in the theatrics of your scheme and the childish notion of running wild on All Hallows' Eve that the end result is inconsequential. May I hope you told Diana nothing of your absurd plan?"

"You may be sure I did not. She has enough on her plate as it is. And I expected you to react in precisely this fashion, Lucy, so don't imagine I'll be talked out of having a go. After leaving the farm, I rode over to Silverdale and spoke with Robbie and Giles Handa. They've agreed to join up, and Giles has all sorts of ideas I'd never have thought of. Apothecaries can do wondrous things with saltpeter and sulfur and charcoal. You will be amazed."

Her heart plunged to the vicinity of her toes. She'd have sworn that stolid, sensible Robbie would have no part of this circus. And serious-minded Giles Handa? But of course, she recalled in some wonder, they had believed in her when she asked their help, asking no questions, trusting her instantly.

She had never brought herself to return their trust. At every moment she expected them to betray her, especially when she learned of the reward posted for Diana's return. But they had remained loyal and generous, with little hope of repayment for all they had done on behalf of two strangers. Tears welled in her eyes to think of it. She turned away so that Kit would not see them.

She felt him move behind her then, sensed the warmth of his body against her back and the brush of his breath against her hair, and nearly fled from the startling intimacy of his closeness. But she couldn't find the strength to move. To her horror, she didn't even try very hard. Nor did Kit touch her, although he sifted through her skin and flesh in a way that made her almost believe in spirits and demonic possession.

"Will you enlist with us, moonbeam?" he asked softly. "You'll be sorry if you don't. I mean to bring Timmy into the plot, and Fidgets, too. Just imagine how it will feel to be left behind, wondering what we are up to and fretting because you aren't there to see it."

It was plain as a pikestaff that she had no choice in the matter. Kit would proceed with or without her, and someone in possession of a full deck of wits had to go along to keep an eye on him. "Oh, very well," she said, turning to face him. "What part will I be playing this time?"

"Why, the witch, of course. And so will I. A copy of your wig is being made for me to wear, and I shall have a lovely new cloak, too. Fidgets will play the Demon Owl from Hades, and I'll think up a ghoulish role for Timmy." He grinned. "Wait until you see the creepy setting I've selected for our drama. I'll take you there tomorrow."

"Thank you." She shook her head in profound disgust. "I can hardly wait."

Chapter 13

"We're almost there," Kit said, reaching for the silver-knobbed walking stick he'd borrowed, along with the crested coach and liveried footmen, from his brother. "Chin up, moonbeam. It won't be as bad as you are imagining. In fact, I expect we'll have ourselves a fine time tonight."

Lucy ceased pleating her skirts between stiff fingers long enough to glare at him.

"None of that when we are inside," he warned. "Remember, you adore me."

"Yes, and I am a twittering imbecile to boot. Fear not, sir. I know my part. But keep to your promise that we won't stay overlong."

"I have already done so, merely by arranging for our late arrival. Be glad of it. We'll not have to walk the gauntlet of a receiving line."

The carriage turned onto a circular drive and drew up in front of the entrance porch. Kit had been a guest at the house on two or three occasions when it still belonged to the Witherspoon family, as it had done for several generations of Witherspoons. But a series of bad harvests quickly plunged them into debt. The mortgages were called, the house was sold at auction, and Sir Basil Crawley had snagged himself a bargain.

A footman let down the steps and Kit jumped out, turning to assist Lucy to the ground. Music floated down from the ballroom, light poured from every window, and a regiment of servants waited in the entrance hall to accept their cloaks and Kit's hat and cane.

"Welcome to Crawley Hall," the butler said archly, gesturing to the sweeping staircase. "Follow me, if you please. Whom shall I announce?"

"Not a soul," Kit responded blithely, taking Lucy's arm. "We prefer to enter quietly, seeing as how we are so late. M'fiancée took a devilish time primping herself out, didn't you, m'dear? But I must say it was worth it."

And so it was, a thousandfold. Her ball dress was not one he'd have chosen for this occasion and the role she was to play, but it suited her to perfection. She might have been clothed in pure moonlight, so pale was the gauzy silk that draped gracefully and unadorned over her slender figure. An invisible thread studded with pearls had been woven through her hair, and three strands of pearls formed a high collar around her long, graceful neck. She wore kidskin gloves that reached above her elbows, pearly satin slippers, and carried a delicate ivory fan.

Were he not already in love with her, he'd have tumbled head over heels at first sight of the elegant beauty who descended the staircase at Candale only a few hours before. She had been more than a little impressed with him as well, although she took care to give no sign of it. But when she thought he wasn't looking, she had cast admiring glances at the fine figure he cut in formal evening wear. It was almost worth enduring the constriction of a high starched collar and elaborately crafted neckcloth to see her regard him with unprecedented approval.

She clutched at his arm as they slipped into the ballroom and took shelter in a quiet corner behind a potted orange tree. The company was thin, Kit saw immediately, no more than sixty or seventy people in a room meant to hold twice that number. A lively country dance was under way.

No expense had been spared in decorating the ballroom, which had been undeniably shabby when last he saw it. Crimson brocade wallpaper and large gilt-framed mirrors adorned the walls, flamboyant chandeliers hung from the ceiling, and the new and intricate parquet floor was waxed to a high sheen. Beside a burbling indoor fountain, the orchestra was ensconced on a satin-draped stage. The overall effect was showy, lavish, and of decidedly inferior taste.

He turned his attention to the others guests, recognizing several wealthy landowners and a few notable parvenus. Not one of Westmoreland's aristocratic families was represented, although they must have received invitations. If Crawley was so bold as to send a card to the Earl of Kendal, he'd not have overlooked peers of lesser distinction.

"I do believe," Kit remarked to Lucy, "that I quite outrank everyone here. And considering how frightfully low on the order of precedence we younger sons of earls are to be found, that is something of an accomplishment."

"How pleased you must be. But is that of any significance?"

Trust her to come directly to the point. "It is to our advantage, I believe. No one with a speck of good breeding will approach us, which I am sure you are delighted to hear. But more consequential is the pronounced smell of ambition in the air. I surmise that Sir Basil has a fancy to climb the social ladder, and a wife of impeccable birth and breeding would give him a great boost up."

"Yes, indeed." Her brow furrowed. "That would explain a good deal, wouldn't it? I wish we knew more about his origins. Diana said only that he used to live in Manchester and that he was granted a knighthood on recommendation of the prince regent."

"Then we may assume he purchased it, at least indirectly. Prinny is in debt up to his several chins. When my brother has sniffed out how Sir Basil came by his money, I'll be very much surprised if he acquired it honestly."

"Where do you suppose he is? I see no one matching the description Diana provided me."

"Nor do I. Not precisely a cordial host, our dear Sir Basil. But perhaps he is disappointed at the turnout and considers the few guests that did show up to be unworthy of his attention."

"Which would make him nearly as toplofty as the highest-ranking gentleman in the room," she observed with a sly smile. "We came here only to meet him, Kit. There can be no reason to stay if he's already toddled off to bed."

"Nice try, moonbeam, but we'll keep our anchor in the water a bit longer. The cotillion is forming, I see. Would you care to dance?"

Her cheeks drained of color. "No, please. I am quite sure I've already forgot the steps."

"Then we shall make a grand circuit, arm in arm. You will gaze insipidly at me while I look down my nose at everyone else." He threaded her arm through his, feeling her tension, keenly attuned to her mood and to the warmth of her body and the faint fragrance of lavender that hovered about her. Ordering his unruly body to behave itself, he led her in procession along the edge of the dance floor, smiling coolly at the people he knew without approaching them and ostentatiously ignoring the others.

Lucy despised the role she was playing this night, he knew, but he was even less at ease. In other circumstances, he'd have greeted old acquaintances instead of shunning them, danced with the prettiest girls and with the wallflowers, too, and flirted with all the dowagers. He was unused to walking high in the instep, as he was doing now, and found it devilish unpleasant.

They were making the turn that would lead them in front of the orchestra's stage when he glanced toward the ballroom door and saw five men enter. One, a large stocky man with spiky black hair, he recognized immediately. It was the man who had shot him.

"What's wrong?" Lucy asked softly, following the question with a fatuous giggle.

Good girl! "Don't be obvious about it, but steal a look at the men who just came into the room. Could any one of them be Crawley?"

"Yes," she whispered after a moment. "He's the tall man with

159

the beaked nose. But we must leave here immediately. Bartholomew Pugg is with him."

Kit seized a flute of champagne from a passing servant and turned to Lucy, shielding her with his body. "Who the devil is Bartholomew Pugg?"

"The Bow Street Runner. The one who came to the cottage. The one who is coming this way right now."

"Damn." Feigning a laugh, he held the glass to her lips. She sipped obediently, pretending to look into his eyes while she watched the Runner. A tiny shrug of her left shoulder told Kit when Pugg was close to them, and on which side. With a move designed to appear casual, he drifted a turn, keeping himself between Lucy and the spot where the Runner had halted. He felt the man's sharp gaze pronging into his back.

"What are we to do?" Lucy mouthed silently.

"Nothing. Go on as you are. Touch my cheek and act besotted."

Her fingers lifted to his face and curled around his jaw. For a moment he nearly forgot the Runner, and why they were there, and everything else on the planet.

She still had hold of her wits, it seemed. "He is bound to know me," she murmured into his neckcloth. "I was Mrs. Preston then, but although he saw my face only in the dim light from the fireplace, he's the sort who could pick me out in a crowd of thousands."

Kit, reckoning he could find her in a crowd of millions, took her certainty to heart. "We'll do best to get it over with then. I am going to steer us in his direction. Take the glass, Lucy, and follow your instincts."

The orchestra's music cooperated, by luck swinging into a bouncy rhythm that practically begged people to dance. Kit swept Lucy into his arms and improvised a jig, aiming himself at the Runner. Seconds later they collided. Lucy sloshed champagne over Pugg before dropping the glass, which shattered on the floor. He staggered backward, champagne streaming down his ill-fitted coat.

Kit regarded what happened next with considerable awe.

Lucy brushed at the Runner's coat with both hands. "Oh my heavens!" she exclaimed in a tone nearly an octave higher than her usual husky alto. "How terribly clumsy of me. I have ruined your coat."

"'Tis nothing, ma'am." Pugg held up a pair of gnarled hands. "I assure you."

"Kittikins says I've no head for champagne, but I do love it so. The bubbles go up through my nostrils and make me quite giddy. Do I know you, sir?"

Her knees bent, and Pugg grabbed her elbow to hold her upright. For what seemed to Kit an infinite time, he studied her face. Then he turned his gaze to Kit for a long moment before looking back at Lucy. "If we had met, I would recall the time and place," he said in a flat voice. "Perhaps I do. Too soon to tell."

As a servant arrived to sweep up the glass, Pugg released her and gave a short bow. "My apologies, madam, for stepping into your path."

"It was my fault entirely," Kit said, taking Lucy's arm. "Come, beloved. We are in the way of the dancers."

"How could you *fling* me at him in such a way?" she demanded when they had seated themselves on one of the padded benches that lined the wall.

"It was effective, was it not? Now we are certain that he failed to recognize you. He has left the room without speaking to Crawley, which he would surely have done if his suspicions were aroused."

"But they are. He *did* recognize me. I saw it in his eyes. I cannot guess why he said it was too soon to tell when he already knew, unless he meant to throw us off our guard."

"Look happy as we converse," Kit reminded her, relaxing his shoulders against the wall and stretching out his legs. "Perhaps he meant precisely what he said—too soon to *tell*. Pugg is a Runner, not one of Crawley's minions, and he needn't report everything he learns."

She smiled at him blissfully, but her voice could have scorched paint from a wall. "He will be snooping about Candale and watching our every move, you may be sure of it. There can be no more visits to Diana, Kit, and your unholy drama will have to be called off."

"We'll see. Meantime, Crawley is looking in our direction." He took her hand and began to play with her fingers. "I suspect he has no great regard for females, so when he comes over to greet us, confirm his opinion by being exceptionally goose-witted. I'm hoping to draw him into a private conversa—"

"You'll not leave me here alone, Kit. I won't have it!"

He looked up and saw fear trembling behind the fire in her eyes. Lucy had just faced down a Bow Street Runner, but the prospect of spending a few minutes among strangers in a ball-room was unbearable to her. Well, so be it. "We are insepa-rable, don't you know? I'll not abandon you, but in turn you must convince him that it is perfectly safe to speak freely in your company."

"Because I have the intelligence of a doorstop. Yes, I do understand."

"Take no insult, moonbeam. He will think much the same of me, if all goes well. Ah, here he comes. This would be a good time to fondle any part of me that takes your fancy."

She chose his knee. And she was making such good work of it when Crawley made his bow that Kit could only gaze blankly at the man he'd taken so much trouble to meet.

"You are most welcome to my home," Crawley intoned in a stiff voice. "I beg your pardon for failing to greet you when you arrived."

Kit detached Lucy's hand from his knee and stood. "You would be Sir Basil then? Pleased to make your acquaintance. I am Christopher Valliant, and the beauty is m'fiancée, Miss Lucinda Jennet. C'mon, puss, up you go! Make a proper curtsy to our host."

She rose, staggering a trifle, and managed a dip before grasp-ing Kit's arm to regain her balance. "I can't think why I am so clumsy of a sudden, sir." She fluttered her lashes. "What did you say your name was?"

"Sir Basil Crawley," he replied, looking pained. "A pleasure to meet you, Miss Jennet."

"She's had a bit too much champagne," Kit confided in a whisper. "Goes right to her head, it does, but she *will* keep tippling. Don't much care for the stuff m'self."

"Might I offer you something more to your taste then? Although I have been in residence here for only a few weeks, I made it a point of urgency to establish a prime cellar, and there is quite a passable vintage decanted in my study. Will you join me, sir? My cousin, Mrs. Milque, will be pleased to introduce Miss Jennet to some of the other guests while we become better acquainted."

Lucy grasped Kit's arm and clung like a limpet. "But I don't *want* to meet these tiresome people," she whined.

Slicing Crawley a man-to-man look, Kit shrugged. "Another time, perhaps. She has already plowed into a gentleman and spilled her drink over him. No telling what she'll get up to next, especially if she thinks I've deserted her. She don't like letting me out of her sight. Isn't that right, puss?"

She hiccuped.

"Bring her along then," Crawley said in a resigned tone. "I quite understand her reluctance to mingle in this company. Take no insult, but Westmoreland society is not at all what I had hoped it to be."

With Lucy teetering alongside him, still clutching his arm, Kit followed Crawley from the ballroom into the passageway. He wondered what had become of the man who had put a bullet in his shoulder. With all that had happened since first he saw him, Kit had lost track of his location. Just as well. If they came face-to-face, he might have been tempted to do something rash. The confrontation with Pugg had been enough of a rumpus for one night, he supposed, and beating his onetime assailant to a pulp would attract far too much attention of the wrong kind.

Reluctantly, Kit consigned his personal grievance to the distant future. At the very least, he had learned this night that Crawley was more than a persistent suitor for Diana's hand. He was in league with the ruffians who had been terrorizing peaceful smugglers in order to stock his wine cellar, and at least one of those thugs had no scruples about killing.

Crawley ushered his guests into a dim room overcrowded with furniture. A large desk was covered with ledgers and stacks of paper, all neatly ordered, showing him to be a man of precise habits. After directing Lucy and Kit to a sofa near the fireplace, he went to an array of crystal decanters on the mahogany sideboard. "I regret that the earl was unable to join us this evening," he said, filling two glasses with wine and reaching for a third.

"None for my puss," Kit advised him. Lucy had rested her head on his shoulder and turned a vacant gaze to the ceiling, her expression so stupefied that it was all he could do to keep from laughing. "As for Kendal, he can't be pried from the house these days. Not since that squalling brat took up residence, although why he wanted another when he's got an heir stashed away at Harrow escapes me. But there it is. He has become quite a bore."

"The countess is his second wife, I understand. No doubt she wanted children of her own."

"Most like. And he is well under her thumb already, I can tell you. It's all very well to be in love with one's wife, but quite another thing to hand over the reins. When Lucinda and I are leg-shackled, I mean to call the shots." He wrapped an arm around her limp body. "There is much to be said for choosing a bride in possession of a large fortune and very few wits."

Crawley handed him a glass of wine. "Will you reside in Westmoreland after you are wed?"

"It is undecided. She fancies a London town house, and for that matter, so do I. But her money will soon run out if I spend it as we both wish, and then where would we be? Her family wants us to settle in Devon, of course, so that they can keep an eye on me." He forced an aggrieved look to his face. "They're in trade, you know. Don't pass that around. M'brother is none too happy about it, but without sixpence to scratch with, it's not as if I could marry within my own class."

"You have an aversion to trade?"

"Always did, until I met my pussycat." Kit glanced at the head resting on his shoulder. "Lord, I think she's gone to sleep. Can't say I'm sorry for it. When she's awake, she chatters like a magpie."

"A considerable distance from here, Devonshire. Are there no eligible young ladies closer to hand?"

"Any number of them, although few have claim to beauty and fortune. One or t'other, but not both."

"Indeed, it is a rare combination." Crawley sipped at his wine. "Did you perchance pay court to a Miss Diana Whitney? I am informed that she is a considerable heiress and exceedingly well favored."

"Never heard of her. No Whitneys in Westmoreland, I'm fairly sure, or none of any consequence. Is she out?"

"The family estate is a little way south of Lancaster, I believe, and her debut was postponed due to the tragic death of her parents."

"There you are then. Stands to reason I'd not have come upon her. And now, of course, I have my Devonshire puss. Couldn't cry off even if I wanted to, not since her father towed me out of the River Tick. Only to throw me into parson's mousetrap, to be sure, but I go willingly. She's a lusty armful when she ain't rattling on."

Crawley rubbed his long nose with a stubby-fingered hand. "We must all marry to advantage one way or another. I find myself in an equally difficult predicament, with a fortune derived from trade and a wish to better myself socially."

"Then you should buy yourself a wife from the aristocracy in the same way my turtledove's family is buying me." Kit held out his glass for a refill. "This is superb, I must say. French?"

"Of course." Crawley settled on a chair across from him.

"Have you considered investing your wife's dowry in a profitable venture? I don't mean to intrude in your private affairs, sir, but it happens I know of several ways to multiply your investments if you are willing to take a few minor risks. Please stop me if you prefer I not continue."

"By all means, do go on. What have you in mind?"

"Naturally, I can offer no particulars until you have the money in hand. Circumstances and opportunities come and go, and what I would recommend today will be unavailable tomorrow. But when you are in a position to act quickly, I shall be honored to be of assistance."

"In exchange for what?" Kit asked bluntly. "A percentage of the initial investment, perhaps, or a slice of the profits?"

"Dear me, no. What little I could amass in such a fashion is scarcely worth my time. But I apprehend that you are a man of the world, sir, with a grasp of—shall we say?—tit for tat. I propose to inform you of business opportunities, the same ones I select for my own speculations, in exchange for a few introductions."

"Well, that's simple enough. But I should warn you that my reputation hereabouts is not altogether without blemish. Fact is, some of the high sticklers won't have me in their drawing rooms, and once I'm leg-shackled to a cit, my credit will sink even lower."

"My word." Crawley's thin lips curved ever so slightly. "One could imagine you to have no interest in our proposed arrangement."

"Oh, but I do. Just wanted you to know how the wind is blowing." Deciding that he'd endured quite enough of Sir Basil for one evening, Kit nudged Lucy with his elbow. "If you are still of a mind to proceed, we'll speak again when the puss's dowry is burning a hole in m'pocket."

"I hope that will be soon. In the meantime, may I trust that you—"

Lucy shot upright with a squeal. Turning a wide-eyed gaze to Crawley, she shook her head as if to clear it. "Who in blazes are *you*?"

Kit wrapped his arm around her. "Wake up, pussycat. You must have been having a bad dream."

She slumped into his embrace. "Oh, there you are, Kittikins. What happened to the ball? Why aren't we dancing?"

"Why not indeed?" He glanced at Crawley and rolled his eyes.

"Rather have s'more champagne. I'm *thirsty*."

"I shall be pleased to escort you to the ballroom," Crawley said, coming to his feet. "Mr. Valliant, you'll not object if I have several bottles of this excellent wine delivered to your carriage as a token of my esteem? And, if I may be so bold, as a seal on the bargain we have struck?"

"Delighted, I'm sure," Kit replied, stifling a laugh. The blackguard was oiling him up with the selfsame wine he'd stolen from him not ten nights before.

When they arrived at the ballroom, it was apparent that a number of guests had already taken their leave. Several couples were rather lackadaisically engaged in a contredanse, and others hovered around the tables where a supper had been laid out.

"You will pardon me if I do not join you," Crawley said with a bow. "I have pressing matters of business to attend to. Honored to make your acquaintance, Miss Jennet. Good night, Mr. Valliant. Do enjoy yourselves for the rest of the evening."

"Thank heavens!" she said when he was finally gone. "What a horrid man. All the time you were speaking with him, I was longing to claw my fingernails down his face."

"Far less than he deserves," Kit agreed, drawing her away from the open doors into a shadowy alcove. "And all the time I was speaking to him, this is what I was longing to do." Before she could object, he wrapped one hand around her waist and the other around her neck and brought his lips to hers.

He meant only to give her a brief embrace, one that revealed nothing of the passion that burned in him, one she might accept without becoming enraged. But to his astonishment she melted against him, her soft breasts pressing against his chest as she put her hands on his shoulders and allowed him to deepen the kiss.

They were both breathing heavily when he finally lifted his head and looked into her stunned eyes. She rallied quickly, though. Too quickly.

"I didn't mean to do that." Stepping back, she straightened her skirts and stiffened her spine. "It was the champagne. Spirits really do render me witless. Pray forget it ever happened."

"As if I could, moonbeam," he said gently. "But I'll not kiss you again unless you ask me to."

"See that you don't! May we leave now, please?"

"Not quite yet. For one thing, we must allow time for the wine Crawley promised me to be stowed in the carriage. And for another, you have expressed a wish to dance. He will expect us to do so." Kit seized her hand. "Come along, puss. I hear the first notes of a waltz."

Her gaze was plastered on his neckcloth as they joined the other couples, only four of them, on the dance floor. But she moved in tune with him, never missing a step, graceful as a willow in a summer breeze, for all her efforts to hold herself stiffly away from him.

"Never again," she said between her teeth, "are you to call me 'puss.'"

"Agreed . . . until the next time I hear 'Kittikins.'"

She unbent long enough to cast him a saucy grin. "It suits you. But truly, Kit, what was the point of coming here? We learned that Sir Basil is a swine, but we already knew that from Diana's report. Or did you not believe her? You have made a deal with him that you've no intention of honoring, which accomplished nothing whatsoever. A Bow Street Runner is now on to our masquerade and will be lurking in the shadows, expecting us to lead him to his quarry. I told you from the first that this was a terrible idea, but you would not listen. You *never* listen."

"Of course I do. Make no mistake, Lucy. I have the highest regard for your intelligence and judgment."

"Which is why you invariably ignore whatever I say and charge ahead, towing everyone else in your wake."

He took a deep breath. Her words had hit home, or near to, and they hurt. But he'd nothing to hide from her. If they spent the rest of their lives together, which was his firm intention, she was bound to uncover every last one of his flaws. "I demand my own way, Lucy, because I am willful, self-indulgent, impulsive, and—until I met you—without purpose."

Her eyes widened. And her mouth opened to speak, but nothing came out.

For once, Kit reflected bleakly, he had managed to silence her. And startle her, too, with a confession he hadn't wanted to make yet. This was scarcely the time and place to bare his soul. With some effort, he relocated the original subject. "You may well be correct that it was a mistake to have come here," he said. "Nevertheless, I have learned a good deal more than you imagine, and I believe that the information will prove of use."

"What could you have discovered that I failed to note? I have been with you the entire time."

Since he'd already resolved not to tell her about recognizing the man who shot him, there was no clear answer to her question. Nor was he thinking at all clearly, what with her so supple in his arms and so infinitely lovely. A magical creature woven of moonlight and pearls, his Lucy—when she wasn't flaying him alive with her tongue. "We have all the long journey back to Candale to discuss the events of this night, Lucy, or to have a row if you prefer. But for now, I cannot be sorry for any circumstance that permits me to hold you in my arms. The waltz will soon come to an end, moonbeam. Until it does, will you simply dance with me?"

Perhaps it was only that he wanted to think so, but it felt as if she drew closer to him. The tension in her body seemed to dissolve. And the waltz played on, far longer than he dared to hope, attuned to his deepest wishes. Imperceptibly the meter slowed. The tone of the violins grew deep and sonorous, vibrating to the passion banked inside him.

She was gazing somewhere beyond his shoulder, or into herself, her eyes dreamy and unfocused.

He nearly always knew what she was thinking before she told him, and she generally left him in no doubt whatever by speaking her mind. But at this moment, bewildered by the expression on her face and the unfathomable mystery in the curve of her lips, the wistful lift of her brows, and the faraway look in her eyes, he felt powerless.

Kit rested his cheek against hers for a moment. "Tell me what you are thinking about, moonbeam."

Her murmured reply was nearly inaudible.

He thought . . . but no. That wasn't it. She could not possibly have said "elephants."

Chapter 14

In the chill October night, Lucy was glad of her heavy cloak and the oilcloth tarp lining the pit, which was a little larger than a grave but not so deep. She was perched on a small footstool with a swath of black serge draped over her cape to conceal its green-white glow.

Time passed slowly in a peat pit. From her position, she could see nothing but the black sky directly overhead, blazing with stars and the gibbous moon. Wind stirred bracken and dry autumn grasses, and in the copses of hazels and oaks, rooks and wood pigeons beat their wings.

The conspirators had been in position for nearly an hour. Timmy was stationed on a hill overlooking the road, ready to give the signal when Robbie and Lord Whitney came into view. Lucy placed no great faith that they would appear at all.

In her opinion, this entire scheme was sheer lunacy. It had held together thus far only because Kit swept away all objections and plowed directly ahead, relying on everyone else to follow. Which they had done, to be sure.

Giles Handa was stationed in a thick spinney with any number of props and implements spread out on a blanket, including a large thin sheet of metal and a drum. Timmy had practiced until he could deliver a spine-chilling howl, which was meant to sound like a wolf baying at the moon. Since none of the conspirators had actually heard a wolf, there was no way to be certain of its accuracy, but during their practice session it had echoed quite effectively off the surrounding hills.

High atop the burned-out ruin of Arnside watchtower, which he had reached with the use of a grappling hook and rope, Kit was crouched behind the battlement with his own supply of props and devices, including an iron bedwarmer filled with hot coals. From her position about a hundred yards away, she could detect no sign of him. The derelict pele tower, with its broken walls, collapsed masonry, and gaping window openings, was a hoary presence looming near the top of a long sloping hill. The first time Kit brought her here she had looked inside, but there remained only the corbels meant to support the burned-away floor and a spiral staircase ending in midair.

As the minutes dragged by and the moon climbed higher, Lucy grew more and more convinced they ought to pack it in. Lord Whitney would surely refuse to set out for a remote destination in the middle of the night. Especially *this* night, All Hallows' Eve.

Kit's confidence had never wavered. He'd rehearsed Robbie for hours, preparing him to deal with every question and objection Whitney might raise. To avoid being recognized when the escapade was over, the Scotsman had even dyed his luxuriant copper-colored beard, padded one shoulder to give him the look of a hunchback, and inserted pebbles in his shoes to remind himself to shuffle.

If Lord Whitney was at home when Robbie arrived, and if he admitted the disreputable creature past the gate, he'd have heard a plain-enough tale. "Old Fergus," an itinerant ne'er-do-well who sought out deserted crofts and barns to sleep in, had come upon a young woman with a scarred face on the previous night. He saw her through the window of an isolated cottage, moved on to seek shelter elsewhere, and thought nothing more of the incident until he spotted a notice about the reward posted in a shop window.

Now they waited to learn if Lord Whitney had fallen for Robbie's story. Kit had advised her to be patient, for it was a long journey to this spot from Willow Manor, and the last several miles had to be navigated on a rough track through marshy land.

A soft whistle, nearly imperceptible, sounded from beyond a fringe of trees to her right. She listened closely. Next came two shorts and a long, the signal that Robbie was approaching in company with another man. Lucy's heart began to pound.

Dropping to her knees, she rigged a makeshift ladder by placing the footstool atop a small wooden box at the spot where she would emerge from the pit. Kit had demonstrated for her one afternoon, and it had truly appeared that he was ascending from the underworld. Clad in the luminescent cape, her long wig glistening in the moonlight, she would be a ghoulish specter indeed.

She had little idea what was supposed to happen before her cue to rise up, and not much better a notion what would transpire afterward. Kit had told her to follow her instincts, because everything depended on Lord Whitney's reaction to what he saw and heard. She arranged the black serge loosely around her so that she could quickly throw it off and picked up a length of twine knotted around the tiny corpse of a white mouse.

They would come from her right, she knew, pass behind her, and from there follow the curved track that wound up the hill. It would take them directly between where she waited and the shadowy watchtower. Soon she heard the slow beat of hooves against the boggy ground and the creak of wagon wheels. Voices floated to her, the words indistinguishable until the men were only a short distance away.

"I don't like this," said one of them in a nervous, high-pitched tone. It had to be Lord Whitney. "This cannot be the way."

"She's well hid, and that's a fact." Robbie spoke in a rough growl. "I recollect the tower, m'lord. Come by it t'other night, I did."

"We don't even know that she's still there," Whitney grumbled.

"Can't say. Happen she moved on. The cottage be mebbe a mile from here. You be wantin' to go back?"

"No, no. We'll have a look. Cannot this nag move any faster?"

"Not while 'e's goin' uphill."

As the wagon lurched past her hiding place, flickering orange light slid over the pit. Lucy huddled lower until the pit was in darkness again, tracking the wagon by sound. It was making the arc that would take it up the hill.

Soon now. She felt perspiration on her forehead and ordered her hands to stop trembling.

A roar of thunder shattered the night. It seemed to be coming from all directions, bouncing off the hills and echoing back again. Then she heard a loud crack. A bright ball of light soared across the sky.

Lifting her head over the edge of the pit, Lucy saw the wagon at a stop about fifty yards in front of her. Two lanterns hung from the side panels, making a small pool of ruddy light. Robbie had gone to take the frightened horse's bridle, and a pudgy man was crouched beneath the wagon, apparently trying to make himself invisible. He jumped noticeably when the thunder sounded again.

There came an unearthly wail from the pele tower, and another fireball sailed overhead.

For a few moments the night went still. Then she saw, atop the battlements, an explosion of light and a cloud of white smoke. In the midst of the smoke appeared a glowing figure, arms upraised. It was clad in a luminous cape. Long white-gold hair streamed out like a banner in the wind. Flames danced at the witch's fingertips.

"Crambe est vinum daemonium!" it bellowed. *"Ergo bibamus!"*

With a shrill cry, Whitney scrambled from under the wagon and broke into a run.

"Halt or die!" Sparks shot from the battlement, cascading down the stone wall like a waterfall of fire.

Whitney stopped immediately and swung around, head uplifted, to face the tower.

"You have offended!" The apparition jabbed a finger in his

direction and sparks flew from the tip. "Hear me now, insect. I pronounce your doom."

"Wh-who are you?"

"Retribution. Malediction. *Damnation!*"

That was her first cue. Lucy raised her arm and swung the mouse over her head. What with all the fire and smoke and thunder, she rather thought Fidgets would have long since flown to cover in the trees. But he swooped from a tower window with an earsplitting screech, passing within inches of Whitney's head on his way to supper. Whitney screamed as the owl flashed by.

Keeping hold of the twine, Lucy drew Fidgets into the pit and whispered an apology as she pulled off the black serge and used it to hide the mouse. "You can have this later," she promised. He cast her a doleful look and began pecking at the serge.

When she looked out again, she saw another flash from the tower and another cloud of smoke. When it cleared, the figure on the battlement had vanished. That marked her second cue.

"Aaaieee!" she cried, getting into the spirit of things. Her hands were coated with phosphorescent ointment, and she waved them overhead as she mounted the footstool and ascended from the pit. "Aaaieeee!"

Whitney spun around.

"A thousand curses fall on your head," she proclaimed, half chanting the words. "May open sores spring up on your putrid flesh. Arise, ye boils and carbuncles. Devour him alive from his skin down to the very marrow of his bones. He has offended all the powers of heaven and hell."

"Nooo! Please!" He backed away, staggering like a drunken sot until his heel caught on a rock and sent him to the ground. He landed on his buttocks with a cry of pain.

Lucy only wished Diana were there to see this. She advanced a few steps, careful not to get too far from the pit, her shimmering forefinger pointed at his head as another roll of thunder echoed off the hills. "Because you have sold your soul for money, I condemn you to the gutters without a penny to buy a crumb of bread. Because you have brought pain, I judge you to feel pain a hundredfold. Because you have destroyed beauty, I rule a film shall coat your eyes with blindness so that you never more know the rising of the sun."

From behind the tower came the mournful howl of a wolf.

When Whitney turned to look, two fires suddenly blazed from the battlement. For a moment Lucy was as astonished as Whitney must have been. Between the fires came another flash and a puff of smoke, and then the witch appeared again.

Hurriedly, Lucy scampered back to her pit and drew the concealing serge over her cape. "Get ready, Fidgets," she whispered, coaxing him onto her wrist. "We've practiced this. Look up there."

He kept looking down at the mouse she'd exposed until she planted her foot atop it. "Up, Fidgets. Watch the tower."

She did not see the motion that drew him away, but when he left her wrist she peeked out in time to see Whitney flatten himself on the ground as the owl whizzed by. Distracted by the motion, Fidgets circled him once before heading on to the battlement. Kit must have put something tasty on his shoulder. Fidgets landed there, white breast feathers glowing in the firelight as he gobbled up his snack.

Her own part done now, Lucy watched from the pit as Kit began the coup de grâce.

"Kneel, wretch!"

Whimpering, the wretch obeyed.

"You have heard your fate, pernicious one. On any other night but this, it would be firmly sealed. But tonight is Allhallows, when graves open and the spirits of the good and the evil stalk the earth."

The wolf howled again.

"On this night, voices cry out to the Powers who rule us all. Petitions may be granted. Have you aught to say in your defense before I pronounce the words that damn you forever?"

"H-how can I defend what I do not know? What is my crime?"

"Dare you mock the Lord of Darkness?" With another flash of light the figure was again wreathed in smoke, but this time it did not disappear. "Diana, my sister in spirit since time began, bears the mark of your brutality. She can no longer fulfill her destiny. And still you seek her, and scheme to sell her to a creature more loathsome than yourself. Do you deny this, worm?"

"But I never meant to hurt her. It was an accident."

"The scarring of her face? I know that. We all know."

Thunder again, and more howling.

Kit was in full cry now, Lucy thought with grudging admiration as he held out his arms, sending the flames to his left and right flaring higher. She'd no idea how he was doing it, but the effect was stunning.

"Wh-what can I do?" Whitney mewled. "Tell me what to do."

"Repent!" Kit's voice sliced through the cold air.

She couldn't help herself. "Repent!" she echoed from the concealment of the pit.

"Repennnnnt," came a voice from the copse.

"Repent!" Timmy piped from behind the tower, following up with a wolf call.

"I *do*," Whitney squealed. "I repent. Give me penance. I'll do anything you ask."

"We ask nothing. We *command*! Free our sister."

"But how can I free her? I can't even *find* her."

"Fool! We have her in our keeping. The Dark Angel holds watch with a sword of fire, and you could sooner catch the wind than seize her from our protection. Come near to her and you will surely perish."

"I'll not come near her. I promise. Tell her she is free of me."

"You lie!"

"You lie!" Lucy called.

"Lie lie lie!" came from the copse.

Timmy howled.

Whitney huddled in a pudgy lump. "On my mother's grave, I swear to free her."

"Do we believe him, sisters?"

"Nooo."

"Nooo."

"Nooo."

Kit turned his face to the owl, as if consulting with his familiar. Then he flung his hands up, and one of them must have tossed a chicken leg over his shoulder because Fidgets swooped away and disappeared behind the tower. "We demand proof," ruled the witch in sepulchral tones.

Whitney lifted his arms in supplication. "But how can I prove what I say? What must I do?"

"A way will be given you. Watch and listen. You will know it when it comes. We have been merciful this night, dog. But heed my warning. Fail to keep your promise, and the wrath of heaven and hell will be visited on you a thousandfold."

"Oh, I will. I mean, I won't. That is, I'll do as you say. Bless you. Thank you for your mercy. I—"

"Enough! Go home. Meditate on your sins." Kit pointed a finger at Robbie. "You bear guilt for your part in this abomination. Take this mound of dung to where you found him and hie yourself across the waters. If you be in England at next quarter moon, we shall come for you."

"I'm g-gone, Your Majesty." Robbie practically threw Lord Whitney onto the back of the wagon and jumped to the driver's bench. "And I ain't comin' back."

Kit sent another shower of sparks off the tower. "Hear me, Sister Timothea. Dissolve now into pure spirit and follow them on the night wind. And you others, daughters of Lucifer, brides of Asmodeus and Astaroth, come with meee. . . ."

In a flash of light and a puff of smoke, he disappeared.

Lucy ducked back into the shelter of the pit as Robbie turned the wagon and guided it swiftly down the slope. *My heavens.* Lord Whitney had fallen into Kit's trap like a witless rabbit. No rational man could possibly credit that demons and witches bothered with the affairs of puny mortals, after all. Surely they had better things to do.

She removed her wig and luminous cloak and wrapped them tightly in the black serge. The chill wind knifed through her shirt. Speedily she drew on the greatcoat Kit had provided her.

She always felt more secure wearing male garb, especially when it was much too large for her body. It became armor of a sort, protecting her from Kit's heated glances and her own undeniable weakness. Her female clothes were waiting at the inn where the witches and wolves had gathered earlier that evening. Kit had planned well, she had to admit. Whenever she imagined a potential difficulty, he had already arranged a solution. There was a room for her at the Downy Duck if she chose to stay the night, and a coach and driver to return her to Candale whenever she wished to go home.

Home? What a thought! Lucy Jennet Preston had never had a home—only places to be at the sufferance of those who allowed her to be there.

She picked up the length of twine and swung the mouse overhead, hoping that Fidgets hadn't gone off on an adventure of his own. He appeared within moments, though, and she snatched the mouse from his talons. Circling, the owl returned and landed near the edge of the pit, regarding her with round accusing eyes.

She held out her right hand. "Come, Fidgets."

He waddled forward and halted just beyond her reach.

"Yes, I'm a wretched tease. But we require Kit's knife to cut through the twine, which I am persuaded would not agree with you."

With a snort, he hopped onto her wrist and allowed her to put him in the wicker cage. Owls were ever so much easier to reason with than little boys—or grown men who behaved like little boys.

Timmy came bounding up the hill, waving his arms. "They be far gone now, sir."

Lucy gathered her bundle, the mouse, and the cage, set them on the ground, and climbed from the steamy, acrid pit. The last few hours had given her a new respect for peat cutters.

When she reached the tower, Giles was crouched inside the door opening, using a tinderbox to light a pair of lanterns.

"Catch, Timmy!" Kit tossed down his cape and the wig, which landed at Lucy's feet.

She'd not seen it close up before now. "What is this made of? It looks like horsehair."

"Mane and tail," Kit said, fixing the prongs of the grappling hook and dropping a thick rope over the side of the tower. "Only place the wigmaker could find hair the like of yours."

How quickly he doused her secret vanity. Turning away, she went to stand in front of the tower door, cutting off the night wind that was making it difficult for Giles to ignite the lanterns. She hadn't liked watching Kit make the dangerous ascent and could not bear to watch him come down. She heard his boots striking stone as he lowered himself, using the tower wall to slow his descent, and finally the dull sound as they hit the ground.

Safe! Her heart returned to its usual spot in her chest.

Two arms wrapped around her from behind. "You were un-utterably splendid, Sister Lucy. Altogether magnificent! When you rose up from that pit, shining in the moonlight like a cold fire, I swear my hair stood on end."

With his warm body pressed against hers, it was impossible to think clearly. "Fidgets wants the mouse," she said.

"And well she deserves it!" Releasing her, he took the cage from her hand and addressed the owl. "A remarkable performance, madam. Flawless. So where is this mouse you covet?"

"Here." Lucy handed him the length of twine. "It needs to be cut free."

While Kit gave Fidgets his reward, she went to Timmy and helped him wrap the horsehair wig in the cape. He was thrumming with excited energy, very much like Kit, and probably disappointed that the adventure was done. "You were a prodigiously fine wolf," she told him. "And how fast you scampered from place to place. I never knew which direction you would howl from next."

"It were so much fun, miss! I got to shoot the flare gun. Did you see?"

"Yes indeed. It quite startled me, I assure you. So did the thunder."

"Mr. Handa made it, with a big piece of steel or somethin'. Next time I wants to make the thunder."

"So you shall," Kit said, joining them and bowing to Timmy. Solemnly, he shook the boy's skinny hand. "Thank you, young man. No one could have done better than you did this night."

"That man wuz cryin' all the time I followed the wagon, sir. He thunk we all be devils."

"Good. Let's hope he keeps thinking that long enough to sign custody of Miss Whitney over to Lord Kendal." Kit turned to Giles, who emerged from the tower with both lanterns lit. "I thank you, too, sir. For all that you've elected to be an apothecary, you have the soul of a pirate."

"I have always thought so," Giles replied calmly. "It was a pleasure to indulge a few of my secret fantasies, although I should not wish to do so on a regular basis. I have the will, but not the imagination."

"Give me leave to doubt that, sir. You surprised me constantly." Kit made a sweeping gesture. "I pronounce us all brilliant, our melodrama a triumph, and rule that we toast our success over wine—lemonade for you, Timmy—at the Downy Duck. Come, sisters, and let us be off."

"But what about the footstool?" Lucy protested.

Three pairs of startled eyes swung in her direction.

"Oh, you know what I mean!" she told Kit sternly. "We cannot leave all this evidence of our trickery behind. And what of the rope and grappling hook? How in heaven's name are you to get it down from the tower?"

"I've no idea," Kit replied with a shrug. "But I'll figure a way when Timmy and I return to gather up the *evidence*. Not that I think for a moment that Lord Whitney would dare set foot here again. You needn't worry, Lucy. When I'm done, there will be no trace of our presence for anyone to find."

She believed him. How could she not? His outrageous plan had come off exactly as he predicted, although she had balked at every step along the way. But he had swept her up with his enthusiasm and confidence, and she'd obeyed his instructions even as she argued with him because she could not help herself. When she was with him, she found herself believing in the impossible.

And that, she reminded herself, could only lead her to disaster. Turning her back on him, she went to retrieve Fidgets's cage.

Kit took up a position beside her as they followed Timmy and Giles along the path that crossed Beetham Fell. Their destination was a trifle less than three miles away. Far too long to be in his company, she thought, knowing her own weakness and the powerful lure of Kit Valliant. "However did you produce such a display of smoke and fire," she asked with false brightness, "from nothing more than a bedwarmer and a few hot coals?"

"Oh, I'd considerably more to work with than that," he informed her with a cocky grin. "In the last few days I made several trips up and down the tower with supplies. Giles helped enormously. Apothecaries make excellent coconspirators, I have discovered. They know how to do such marvelous things. He prepared torches that would blaze up with the slightest application of a glowing coal and showed me how to cascade sparks down the side of the tower. The smoke and flash of light were produced by tossing a wad of gunpowder onto the coals. That was my idea. I used to throw gunpowder onto campfires when I was a boy."

Which you still are, she thought, keeping her gaze focused on the path because she dared not look at him. A handsome boy with the body of a man who delights in playing pranks and flirting with susceptible females. Few of them resisted him, she was certain. She was less certain that she could do so, what with him being all but irresistible, but she meant to try with all her might. Her already unsatisfactory life would be pure misery if she had to live it with a broken heart.

"You were impressive, I must admit." Lucy knew she sounded like a starchy governess, but at the end of the day, that was precisely what she was. "I thought you a trifle overtheatrical at times, but I suppose you could not help yourself."

"No indeed. I was quite caught up in the moment, and Whitney was such delicious prey. He groveled divinely, don't you think? How was my voice? High enough? Did I sound like a female?"

"Not like a *human* female. Timmy produced a better impression of a wolf than you did of a woman. What you said was clever, though," she added grudgingly. "Except for the Latin bit, which made no sense at all."

He took Fidgets's cage from her hand. "I was never any dab hand at Latin. Couldn't see the point of learning it. Practically nobody speaks it these days but tutors and popish clerics, have you noticed? But a few words were drummed into my head at school and I thought I'd try them out. What did I say?"

"Something to the effect that cabbage was the wine of the devil and we should all drink up."

"Cabbage?" He winced. "Well, let's hope Whitney is no more a scholar than I. In any case, I am quite convinced that I belong on the stage. We younger sons require employment, you know. What do you think, moonbeam? Should I tread the boards? Would you come to the greenroom after the play and offer me carte blanche?"

"Certainly not! And Lord Kendal would never permit you to take up such a profession. Have your wits gone begging?"

Chuckling, he wrapped an arm around her waist.

She'd have pulled away from him, but on the narrow path, there was no away to pull to. Hawthorn bushes hedged them in on both sides, Giles and Timmy were directly ahead with the lanterns, and she could not go running back to the tower. "You are impertinent, sir. It is unfair of you to take liberties when I am unable to evade them."

"I do know how to choose my moments," he said unrepentantly. "But you needn't fear that your reputation is being compromised. Giles and Timmy know of our betrothal."

"Oh, infamous! I promised myself I'd remain in charity with you until we reached the inn, but already I am railing at you like a fishwife. Why do you deliberately set yourself to raise my temper? If you release me, we can have a civilized conversation or walk in silence, which I would greatly prefer."

"But I'm quite partial to your temper, Lucy. It gives me hope."

She looked up at him. "I don't understand."

His smile was singularly sweet. "There's a saying I once heard. Perhaps you've heard it, too. 'When the heart's afire, sparks fly from the mouth.' "

Her heart *was* afire. She could not deny it. The blaze consumed her from the inside out. But whatever he imagined, the source was fury. Not love. Never love. She refused to give him the satisfaction of thinking he'd won her over the way he did all the other women he'd flirted with, or more, before discarding them.

"I'm angry, yes," she told him plainly. "Nearly all the time. But that's because you came swanning in and took over everything—me, Diana, our plans, *everything*. You allow me no choices. You expect me always to do your will."

His fingertips pressed at her waist, and even through the heavy greatcoat she felt them burning against her as if they were touching her bare flesh.

"I know how it is, moonbeam," he said gently. "I've been a burr in your side. But stay the course a little longer. We are going somewhere wonderful, you and I."

Chapter 15

Taking a folded newspaper with him, Kit entered the formal parlor, selected an out-of-the-way chair, and settled back to observe the proceedings.

His brother, somewhat to his surprise, had demonstrated a flair for the dramatic while arranging for this afternoon's spectacle. The lord-lieutenant and the justice of the peace had arrived and were accepting glasses of sherry from a footman. Near the fireplace, the half-dozen solicitors who had been in residence at Candale this week were deep in conversation.

Kit couldn't resist a friendly wave at the pair of constables standing off by themselves, looking singularly ill at ease. At one time or another each had held him in custody. He supposed they had been invited to swell the line of infantry meant to throw Lord Whitney on the defensive immediately he stepped into the room. The heavy artillery—among them two viscounts, three barons, and the Earl of Lonsdale—were waiting with the Earl of Kendal in the upstairs salon until time for their grand entrance.

When last he saw them, Lucy and Celia were in the nursery, fuming. Kendal had ruled that no females were to be present at this settlement conference, and both took great exception to his order. "Men conduct business with other men," he had said firmly. "Like it or not, that is the way the world turns."

Kit was inclined to agree with him, although he understood Lucy's indignation. She had well earned the right to see the end of what she had begun. At least they all hoped that today's events would mark the conclusion, but all remained in doubt until Lord Whitney affixed his signature to the documents.

Kendal's battalion of solicitors had descended on Lord Whitney the very morning after his encounter with the Lancaster witches. By all accounts he had been pale, panic-stricken, and willing to sign anything short of his death warrant. Because his servants could attest to his disordered state of mind in the event of a later appeal, the solicitors wisely left a mountain of papers for him to examine, advising him to engage a solicitor to act on his behalf.

No one could be certain what he would do at this meeting. It was possible he'd declare his intention to pursue the matter in the courts, especially if he still retained the financial backing of Sir Basil Crawley. If not, there was little question that he would attempt to renegotiate, in his favor, the terms Kendal's attorneys had offered him. Which would mean a long, tedious afternoon, Kit thought, opening the newspaper and pretending to be absorbed in what he was reading. The pompous lord-lieutenant had begun to sidle in his direction, apparently bent on striking up a conversation.

"Sir Basil Crawley and . . . er, Mr. Bartholomew Pugg," the butler announced from the doorway in a soft voice that shouted his opinion of their worthiness to be there.

No one else paid the slightest attention to their arrival, but Kit immediately went on full alert. Crawley had brought along his pet Runner, which could not be a good sign. He lifted the newspaper so that it covered most of his face and watched as Crawley accepted a glass of wine from the footman. Pugg declined, and then both men headed in his direction.

"Mr. Valliant, it is my pleasure to see you again," Crawley said with a bow as Pugg separated himself far enough for discretion and close enough to hear what was said.

Kit lowered his newspaper but did not rise, a mild insult that Crawley noted with a flash of anger in his steel-gray eyes. But he never lost his polite smile, and Kit gave him points for self-control. "Lud, half the population of north England must have been invited to this party," he said, lounging back on the chair with his legs crossed. "I don't suppose you know what is happening here?"

Crawley looked puzzled.

"No? Well, that makes us a pair. M'brother is up to something, I daresay, but damned if I can make any sense of it. Some sort of legal kafuffle, I suppose, what with a clutch of lawyers infesting the place."

"You are not involved in this matter?" Crawley asked, recovering his stiff poise.

"Lord no. My beloved Lucinda—you met her t'other night—is having one of her moods, and I'm far safer here than elsewhere in the house. The woman can peel the hide from a fellow with her tongue." He shuddered theatrically. "So why have you come? If it's to pay a call on the earl, allow me to advise you this is not the best of times."

"So I apprehend. But as it happens, I have some minor stake in this afternoon's proceedings."

"Well, don't tell me about it." Kit waved a negligent hand. "I mean to drink Kendal's wine, read my paper here in the corner, and maybe have m'self a snooze. But who is that odd chap came in with you? He looks disposed to pilfer the silver."

Crawley gave him a cold smile. "I doubt he will. He's a Bow Street Runner."

"Indeed?" Kit raised the quizzing glass he'd borrowed from Kendal for this occasion and examined Pugg from head to toe. "Never saw one before now. Can't say I'm very much impressed, though he looks smarter than the two constables lurking across the way. What's he doing here?"

"I could ask the same about the constables," Crawley said, dancing to his own evasive tune.

"Lord Whitney," the butler intoned, "and his associates." Geeson stepped aside to admit the guest of dishonor, who was followed by two men wearing badly fitting coats, baggy breeches, and furtive expressions.

"M'brother is keeping sorry company these days," Kit said,

clicking his tongue. "Who is the one looks like a bloated codfish?"

"A fool," Crawley said tersely. "Perhaps a madman. He claims to see witches and demons, and fears that a giant bird will rise up from hell to peck out his eyes. Pray excuse me, but unfortunately I have need to speak with him."

"By all means." Kit turned his attention to Lord Whitney, taking note of his blotched, pasty skin, his bulbous red nose, and the belly sagging over the waistband of his breeches. He had been no great beauty when Kit saw him cowering on the ground at Arnside Tower, but in the three days since, he appeared to have gone entirely to seed.

Were Diana's fate not at stake, Kit might have enjoyed this circus. He would certainly have liked to eavesdrop on what Crawley was saying to Lord Whitney, but the Runner had stationed himself where he could observe everyone in the room. He was sure to notice if Kit showed even a mild interest in Crawley's business.

Unaccustomed to sitting back and allowing someone else to order events, Kit found it devilish hard to maintain his careless pose. He'd passed the reins to Kendal, which was without question the correct thing to do, but that failed to stanch his frustration. Lucy must have felt much the same when Kit Valliant swept onto the scene and immediately took charge.

With a considerable degree of ceremony, Geeson stepped into the parlor and read off a long series of names and titles. One by one, virtually everyone of rank in the county of Westmoreland made a dignified entrance. Lord Kendal was the last to appear, and Kit covered an inordinate desire to laugh by coming to his feet.

The earl, impeccably clad in a pewter coat, darker breeches, and dove-colored stockings, entered his parlor as if it were the court at Versailles. A hush descended and all eyes were focused on him as, supremely aloof, he paused and slowly swung his gaze around the room. When it fell on Lord Whitney, the baron's face turned an alarming shade of purple.

Paying him no special notice, Kendal continued to briefly examine each man in turn until he came to the tall, hook-nosed Sir Basil. With a slight frown, his head slightly tilted, he studied him as he might a bug pinned to a blotter.

Kit decided he could not bear to miss the fireworks. He sauntered across the room, plucking a full glass of wine from a footman as he passed by, and greeted his brother with an elaborate bow. "I thought you'd never get here, my lord earl. Precisely whom are we burying this afternoon?"

Kendal turned his icy gaze in his direction. "This is none of your concern, Christopher. Unless you can identify the two . . . er, gentlemen standing with Lord Whitney. I cannot think what they are doing in my home. Are they perchance friends of yours?"

Crawley moved forward and bowed. "I have a slight acquaintance with your brother, Lord Kendal, but he is in no way responsible for my presence here. Will you do me the honor of allowing him to introduce me?"

"If I must." With a small sigh, Kendal sliced a meaningful look at Lord Lonsdale, who immediately turned to one of his fellows and struck up a conversation. Others took the cue and moved away, leaving the three men to speak privately.

No one, Kit thought admiringly, exercised power with such exquisite finesse as his brother. Careful not to meet his eyes for fear of laughing, he presented Sir Basil Crawley. "Lucinda and I attended a ball at his home near Flookburgh," he added. "Remember? You were invited, too."

"Was I? Then my secretary must have sent my regrets."

Kendal said nothing more, merely gazing with resigned boredom at a place beyond Crawley's shoulder. Kit recognized his brother's strategy, having been its victim on many nasty occasions, and knew that Crawley would soon jump in to fill the uncomfortable silence.

He made the leap within moments. "I hope you will pardon me for the intrusion, Lord Kendal, but it happens that I have considerable interest in whatever decisions are made concerning Miss Diana Whitney."

189

"Indeed? I cannot imagine why. Your name has not appeared on any of the documents relating to her case."

"My interest is personal, sir. Perhaps Lord Whitney failed to mention it, but I have offered for the young lady's hand in marriage."

Kendal raised a brow. "And how did she reply?"

"Unfavorably, I regret to say. But that is entirely my doing, for I approached her at an inappropriate time." Crawley contrived to look bereft and repentant, although neither sentiment reached his eyes. "She was yet grieving for her parents, snatched from her so cruelly, but I was unaware that they had perished only a few months earlier. I am newly come north from Manchester, you see, and had no acquaintance among the local gentry until I chanced to meet Lord Whitney. He introduced me to his niece, and—well, how shall I say this? It will sound altogether foolish from a man of my years, but I was irreparably smitten when first I clapped eyes her. My impressions of her worth were confirmed as I came to value, even more than her beauty, the charm, intelligence, and grace that stole my heart and sealed my fate."

Horse manure! Kit thought, longing to plant him a facer.

Kendal looked profoundly uninterested.

Tiny beads of sweat had formed on Crawley's brow. "The thing is, I rushed my fences. Instead of allowing her time to recover from her loss, I immediately paid my addresses. Quite naturally, she refused my offer."

"Then I continue to wonder why you are here. Does not her rejection of your suit mark an end to your involvement with Miss Whitney and her affairs?"

"Had I courted her when and how I should have done, you would be correct. But I am persuaded that, given time, she will come to see me in a new light." He lifted his arms in a helpless gesture. "Would you have me forsake all hope?"

"Perish the thought," Kendal murmured.

Crawley drew himself up. "Mock me if you will, sir, but my

intentions are both sincere and honorable. And in my defense, I was more precipitate than I might otherwise have been due to her particular circumstances. Lord Whitney is something of a loose screw, and I feared for Miss Whitney's well-being. Alas, my judgment of her guardian's nature was proven correct when she fled him in terror."

Kit growled low in his throat. How his brother could listen to this hogwash without the slightest reaction was beyond his comprehension.

But Kendal had the situation well in hand. "Your concern for Miss Whitney's welfare was well taken, but no longer necessary. You will be pleased to hear that she will shortly be removed from her uncle's guardianship and given over to my protection." He produced a chilly smile. "As for your wish to marry the young lady, I see no reason to object if she expresses a desire to accept you. Naturally you will wait a decent interval, a year at the very least, before approaching her again."

Left with no other choice, Crawley inclined his head. "As you say, Lord Kendal. But before taking my leave, I should like very much to pay my regards to Miss Whitney and assure myself that she is content with the arrangements you have made for her. Have I your permission to speak with her for a few moments?"

"I would naturally grant it, were she here, but Miss Whitney is not in residence at Candale. When the opportunity arises, I shall make certain to convey your good wishes. And now, if you will excuse me, a number of gentlemen are awaiting my attention. Christopher, be so kind as to show Sir Basil out."

Well done, Kit applauded silently before turning his attention to Crawley. He was staring at Kendal's back, color high in his cheeks. His usually blank eyes had gone on fire.

"We have both been dismissed, it seems," Kit said lightly. "Just as well, considering the company in this room. Dull dogs, the lot of 'em. Shall we take ourselves off before my brother has us thrown out on our ears?"

Beckoning to Pugg, Crawley stalked to the door, sneering at the butler who held it open for him to pass.

There was more trouble ahead from that source, Kit was certain. Crawley was the sort of man who nursed a grudge and plotted vengeance. He would make no move anytime soon, fully aware that his adversaries were on their guard, but the Valliant family had not heard the last of him.

While a footman went to see his carriage brought around, Crawley drew the Runner aside and clutched his elbow as he spoke in an urgent whisper.

Knowing better than to intrude, Kit took shade under the portico with his shoulders propped against a marble pillar and sipped at his wine, gazing off into the distance. He pretended to be startled when Crawley approached him again.

"I shall bid you farewell now, Mr. Valliant, and expect that we'll not meet again until after the turn of the year. I have business to put before Parliament regarding a turnpike road between Ulverston and Carnforth, along with proposals for the extension of several canals in this area. Likely these matters will keep me in London for a considerable time."

"I'm sorry to hear it, but perhaps we will meet sooner than you imagine. Lucinda is nagging me to take her to London for the Season. And by then I'll have her dowry in m'pocket," he added, "in case you have ideas how I ought to invest it."

"I haven't forgot," Crawley said, his eyes opaque. "You may be sure I'll stay in touch. Might I ask you one last question, as we are business associates of a kind?"

"Fire away." Kit grinned at him. "I always cooperate with anyone who can help me get rich."

"Is it true that Miss Whitney is not in residence anywhere on Lord Kendal's estate?"

"Well, if she is, I ain't seen her. And I'll tell you something else. Jimmie was born with a javelin up his spine. You know the sort—honor and duty and all that rot. If he said she's not here, she's not here."

"I did wonder. The earl appeared to take me in dislike, and I thought he might be fobbing me off."

"Oh, he takes most everyone in dislike. He don't like *me* above half, and I'm a darling. Think no more of it."

With a stiff bow, Crawley went to the carriage that had just pulled up.

Kit watched with amusement as the man who had shot him opened the paneled doors and let down the steps for Sir Basil. Unfinished business, he thought, but it would have to wait for a suitable opportunity. He couldn't very well call out a *flunky*.

"A moment of your time, sir?"

Turning, Kit saw the Runner approach him from the other direction, leading a saddled horse. "By all means." He produced his sunniest smile. "Mr. Pugg, is it?"

"Pugg will do. Sir Basil has informed you that he is on his way to London?"

"So he did, although I cannot imagine why his whereabouts should interest me. You are in his employ, I believe?"

"At one time, but no longer. I can tell you, sir, that it's a sad day when a Runner elects to leave a job unfinished. But so I have done. Sir Basil will learn that I am off the case when I choose to tell him, which will not be in the near future. Meantime he won't be hiring anybody else, if you take my drift."

"As a matter of fact, I've haven't the foggiest clue what you are blathering about."

Pugg grinned, revealing a set of spiky teeth. "If you say so. My regards to the young ladies, sir."

"Which young ladies would those be?" Kit inquired blandly.

Pugg mounted his horse with considerable grace. "Oh, the one what sometimes call herself Mrs. Preston when she ain't dancing with you at a ball, and the one what are at the pig farm." He lifted his hat and bowed from the saddle. "If ever you be in need of a Runner, sir, you c'n find me at Bow Street."

Well, well, Kit thought as Pugg nudged his horse to a canter and sped away. Who would have guessed it? The Runner had found them out and jumped over to their side.

In a reflective mood, Kit rested his shoulders against the pillar once again and turned the glass of wine in his hand, watching the deep red liquid swirl around. One day he would seek out the honorable Mr. Pugg, invite him to a pub house, and ply him with enough ale to loosen his tongue. If he ever lost guard of it, to be sure. There was a good chance Kit would never discover exactly what Pugg had learned and how he'd come by his information, but he wanted to buy the man a drink anyway.

Ought he to tell the others about this? he wondered. Not Diana, certainly. She should never know how close they had come to disaster. His brother, yes, and Celia, no. As for Lucy, he would have to think on it. From here on out he wanted no more secrets between them, but a few matters might do better to wait until his ring was on her finger.

Meantime he was supposed to be witnessing the events going on in the parlor so that he could give her a full report. Quickly finishing off his wine, Kit returned to the house, steeling himself to endure an hour or two of lawyerly gibberish.

Chapter 16

"I cannot bear this another moment!" Lucy looked again at the clock on the mantelpiece in Lady Kendal's private parlor. The hands appeared to have frozen in place. "Why is it taking so long?"

"One must allow for posturing and long speeches, I expect. You must have observed at table this week that Mr. Bilbottom admires the sound of his own voice. The other solicitors will attempt to match him, if only to justify their fees, but there can be no doubt of the outcome. Kendal has everything well in hand."

Lucy was not so sure, although she couldn't very well say so to his wife. Lady Kendal had not been fighting this battle for nearly two months, on the brink of losing it a hundred times or more. She wouldn't understand how it felt to be excluded from the final confrontation when no one had a greater right to be there.

The countess scowled at whatever it was she had been knitting and began to unravel the yarn. "I simply cannot get the hang of this, Lucy. Whatever I knit grows into a shapeless, unrecognizable *thing*."

"Why do you keep at it then?" Lucy asked indifferently.

"Oh, I don't know. Because I want to see my babies wearing mittens and caps I have made for them with my own hands, I suppose. At least I am able to provide them with blankets, although the blankets all started out to be something else entirely." She glanced up with a smile. "Why not go for a walk while the weather is so fine? It will spare the carpet you are wearing down with your pacing, and if you stay in sight of the house, you will see the carriages come around when the gentlemen are ready to depart."

Realizing that she was making a nuisance of herself, Lucy curtsied and headed for the door. "I shall go to the hill behind the stable," she said. "Please send for me if anything happens that I ought to know about."

She stopped by her bedchamber for gloves and a bonnet before taking the back way out of the house. Carriages, some bearing crests, were lined up in the stable yard, and several of the drivers and postilions were hunkered over a game of dice. Timmy waved at her from atop one of the coaches, where a kindly driver was apparently showing him how to hold the reins.

Life goes on, she thought. How few people in the world knew what was transpiring in Lord Kendal's parlor this afternoon. And when Diana's fate was settled, primarily by men who had never even met her, how few would care what became of her.

No one at all, save Diana, would care what became of Lucy Preston. She would return quietly to Dorset and take up her position at Turnbridge Manor, if Lady Turnbridge had not already hired someone to replace her. Eventually, whatever befell her when the boys were grown and she was turned off, she would dwindle into an old lady who had once experienced a splendid, terrifying adventure.

When she reached her destination, she immediately regretted returning to this spot. Instead of contemplating Diana's situation and her own future, she kept imagining Kit as he had been a few afternoons ago, with a parcel of chicken feet in his hand and Fidgets perched on his shoulder. Which led to thoughts of Kit wearing a horsetail wig and cascading a fall of sparks down the pele tower on All Hallows' Eve. From there she went all the way back to the first time she saw him, trapped in the sands of Morecambe Bay, and began to relive, in vivid detail, each moment they had spent together since then.

There was a stir at the back of the house, and she shaded

her eyes with her hand to better see what was happening. From such a distance, she could make out only that a carriage was in motion, and then another. The gentlemen were leaving. It was over!

Lifting her skirts, she pelted down the hill, her thoughts two steps ahead of the rest of her. What had happened? What if Lord Whitney had refused to set Diana free? From the nursery window she had seen Sir Basil Crawley's arrival and knew that he'd come to make trouble. Had he succeeded? Oh, dear God!

She reached the steepest portion of the hill, where she ought to be watching her step, but by now she was accelerating rapidly. Her feet, with a will of their own, pounded at an alarming rate, and it was all she could do to remain upright. Then a figure loomed directly ahead of her and she lost control. Arms spinning like windmills, she flailed for balance, felt her shoes slip on the grass and out from under her, and next she knew, she was hitting the ground on her backside with a loud *oomph*.

When she regained her breath and her wits, she lifted herself up on her elbows and found herself at eye level with a long pair of broadfine-clad legs. They were Kit's legs, of course. She would have known them anywhere. And it was no more than her usual bad luck to have fallen like a hailstone at his feet.

He dropped to one knee beside her, his brow etched with concern. "Have you hurt yourself, moonbeam?"

"Only in the vicinity of my pride," she said in a strangled voice. "Never mind that. What about Diana?"

"The Earl of Kendal has got himself a ward, signed and sealed. Delivery will have to wait until tomorrow morning, but I'll go first thing and fetch her to Candale."

"But she knows the meeting was to be today," Lucy protested. "You cannot permit her to worry all of tonight about the outcome. You must go immediately and tell her that the news is good!"

"A footman is already on his way with the message I dispatched after Lord Whitney signed the documents. There was another half hour of nattering about hows and whens and wherewithals before the assembly broke up, and then I came after you." He sat beside her, drew up his legs, and folded his arms across his knees. "For all practical purposes, Kendal is her legal guardian until she comes of age. You may as well know—although Diana need not—that Whitney could petition the lord chancellor for reinstatement should he change his mind. But there is no reason to believe that he will."

"Sir Basil Crawley is a reason. You know very well that Lord Whitney was his creature when this nightmare began, and I've no doubt he can bend Whitney to his will yet again."

"Nor do I. But Crawley is on his way to London and will not return until spring, if then. Meantime Kendal will continue to investigate his background and business practices. Should he attempt to make trouble in the future, we shall be better prepared to deal with him. I believe Diana is perfectly safe, but you can be sure we'll not lower our guard until she has reached her majority. Well, not even then. She is part of our family now, you know."

Amid her relief and gratitude, Lucy felt a shot of monstrous envy. But Diana truly *needed* the support of others. Lucinda Jennet Preston had gotten on very well by herself until now and would continue to do so until she'd stuck her spoon in the wall. "What about the . . . the wherewithals?" she asked, plucking spears of grass from the ground one after another.

"Trifles, actually. Kendal has arranged for an immediate evaluation of the contents of Willow Manor, since they belong to Diana by her father's will. Until she has a home of her own to take them to, Lord Whitney will be accountable for every last teaspoon. Whitney has also agreed to vacate the premises for a month, during which time Diana can retrieve her clothing and whatever else she wishes to take with her."

"This all sounds too good to be true, sir. Did not Whitney bargain for anything on his own behalf?"

Kit rested his chin atop his folded arms. "In fact, Whitney's solicitors protested every jot and tittle, whatever a tittle is. And all the while Whitney poured wine down his throat, scarcely attending to what was going on. Not until the question of Diana's injury came up did he assert himself, and then he refused absolutely to accept responsibility. His lawyers produced signed testimonies from a dozen people who heard Diana say it was an accident, and we know well enough that she did. If ever the truth is to be known for the public record, she will have to face down her uncle in a court of law and retract her previous statements."

"She will never do that."

"I know. We would prefer, of course, that Whitney had admitted to striking her, but this will only become an issue if the case is ever dragged into Chancery Court. Should that happen, we shall deal with it. Any other questions before I turn the subject?"

What happens to *me*? she thought instantly. But she already knew the answer. "No more questions, sir." She rose and brushed down her skirts. "I wish to go to Diana now. Her whole life is in the balance and you sent a *footman* to give her the news? That was badly done. She should be brought here straightaway."

Kit was on his feet before she could move past him. "Tomorrow will be soon enough, love. She is reticent about being seen, and at Candale she will be facing a great many strangers. Allow her a little time to prepare herself."

"Yes. I hadn't considered that."

He tilted her chin with his forefinger. "She will do well enough, Lucy. You must cease worrying about her now and begin considering your own future."

Elephants charged through her head. She gazed at him mutely, wishing she were Mrs. Preston again, veiled and not expected to speak. How could she, when he was looking at her the way he was just now, his blue eyes glowing with an inner fire and a smile of uncommon sweetness curving his lips?

"Marry me," he said softly. "Will you, moonbeam? I meant to lead up to this gracefully, but I cannot wait a moment longer. I even prepared a speech, but I can't remember it now. I'll give it to you later, with all the words of love and fidelity you could possibly want, and I'll mean every one of them. Just please, please, Lucy, say that you will marry me."

"No!" she blurted before she said something appallingly stupid, like *yes*. Before she said what she wanted to say, which was also *yes*.

He must have been expecting a refusal, because his confident smile never wavered. If anything, he looked mildly amused. "You don't mean that, beloved. You know that you don't. Tell me why you said it anyway."

She turned her back because it was impossible to face him when she had to tell lies. His eyes, or so she imagined, could see past all her defenses, into her very soul, and even she didn't know what was buried down there. She could not bear the thought that he knew her better than she knew herself.

Above all things, she must be rid of him before either one of them made a terrible, unalterable mistake. "You do me too great an honor, sir," she said in a voice so calm that she was amazed to hear it. "When you have taken time to reflect, you will realize that I am a wholly unsuitable wife for one of your position."

"Balderdash. You were more on the mark when you thought me a ragtag smuggler and far beneath your notice. The accident of my birth into the Valliant clan is nothing to the point, and I've certainly done no credit to the family name. What has my *position* to do with love? Think of Celia. She came from nowhere to marry an earl, and you won't find two happier people in England. Just ask her—"

"What, sir? I am not she, and you are not your brother. *They* fell in love. You and I have done nothing but quarrel since first we met."

"*You* have quarreled, Lucy. I have been a model of patience."

That was so true that it infuriated her to hear him say it. She had been a shrew, no question about it, but how dare he point it out in such a way? Surely a lover, a true lover, would not recount her flaws in the middle of a proposal!

"You have been caught up in an adventure, sir, and think to

prolong it with a wedding. But there is nothing in the least romantical about what we have done, you and I, during this last fortnight. We were merely coconspirators. When you come to your senses, you will accept that the adventure ended when we rescued the fair maiden."

He came around in front of her and seized both her hands in a firm grip. "Whatever are you nattering about now, moonbeam? I am in full possession of my senses. Asking you to be my wife is the most sensible thing I have ever done. It's my heart that has gone missing. I lost it to you early on, perhaps the moment I first saw you, and it will be in your keeping forever. I'm asking only that you take the rest of me, too." He grinned. "Some parts of me, I promise, you'll be glad to have."

Were he not holding on to her, she would surely have dissolved into a buttery puddle. She wanted so much to believe him. To trust him. But Kit Valliant was a charmer of fits and starts and whims who lived only in the present moment. He would change the very next second, and the next, giving all of himself to whatever new adventure and new woman had crossed his path.

And if it happened that she was wrong about him, she was certainly right about herself. No one had ever loved her before. How could *he*?

Not that she was ashamed of what she was. Lucinda Jennet Preston was getting on very well, thank you, and she had actually been of genuine value in one person's life. Not everyone could boast so much, certainly not the likes of Lord Whitney or Sir Basil Crawley, to list the first examples that sprang to her mind. No indeed, she did not underrate herself, nor did she feel sorry for herself. She was simply wise enough to know that golden men did not fall in love with dagger-tongued governesses.

She pulled her hands free and squared her shoulders. "Whatever you believe at this moment, sir, we are not at all suited. It won't be terribly long before you come to agree. When I have returned home—"

"That is out of the question. Your home is with me."

"No, Kit, it is not. You know nothing about me and nothing of my plans." She forced her traitorous body to stand straight and still. "My home will soon be with the man I intend to marry."

Ashen-faced, he gazed at her with a stunned expression.

"I am betrothed to the curate of a church not far from the estate where I am employed. We might already be wed, had not Diana's letter called me north." Lucy picked out her words with care. "So you see, there was never any possibility of my developing a *tendre* for you. I have all this time been promised to another man. And naturally, I must go to him as soon as may be."

She had meant to say more, but her courage had all run out. Not daring to look at Kit, she made a quick curtsy and fled down the hill.

Chapter 17

The next morning, Kit went to the pig farm to collect Diana and escort her to Candale.

Lucy had declined to accompany him, which was not unexpected as she'd spoken scarcely a dozen words to him since refusing his marriage proposal. He had watched her push food around her plate at supper and escape to her room shortly thereafter, pleading a headache. He had not seen her since.

Nor was she waiting with James and Celia in the entrance hall when he led Diana into the house, and he wondered if perhaps she was truly ill.

Celia came forward, arms outstretched. "Welcome, Miss Whitney. We are so pleased that you will be staying with us."

Diana curtsied prettily. "Thank you, Lady Kendal. The house is very lovely."

"Indeed it is not!" Celia protested with a laugh. "Candale was too long in the hands of men, who are more apt to decorate the stables for their horses than replace worn carpets in the drawing room. I am making little progress undoing so very many years of neglect and hope you will be kind enough to assist me."

It was exactly the right thing to say, Kit thought. Diana visibly relaxed, the notion that she could be useful instead of a burden drawing color to her pale cheeks.

"Come meet your new guardian," Celia said, taking her arm. "You must not let him intimidate you, even when he scowls. He's not nearly so formidable as he likes to appear."

"Take no notice of anything she says about me," the earl advised, smiling warmly. "We are both delighted to have you stay with us, and you may be sure that I stand as your guardian for legal purposes only. You needn't fear that I'll interfere with your wishes or attempt to manage your life. Think of Candale as your home, and feel free to ask for anything that will make you more comfortable."

"I am so very grateful to you, Lord Kendal." Diana clutched at her skirts. "I cannot think how I shall ever repay your kindness and generosity."

"Mercy me!" Celia declared. "*Repay?* That word has no meaning here. But you must be wanting to see your room, Diana. May I call you Diana? Go on about your business, gentlemen. We ladies are off to have a cup of tea and a good gossip."

Kendal arched a brow as his wife towed a bewildered Diana up the stairs. "There is much to be said for managing females," he observed dryly. "This one will see that my new ward settles in before nightfall. Join me for a glass of sherry, Kit?"

Vague alarms sounding in his head, Kit followed his brother to the study and held his peace until he'd downed one helping of wine and poured himself another. "Where is Lucy?" he asked, trying to sound casual and failing miserably. "Is she ill?"

Kendal went to the chair behind his desk. "In fact, Kit, she's gone."

A cannonball thudded into his stomach. "Where?"

"She wouldn't say, beyond that it was a journey of several days. Directly after you left this morning, she came downstairs with her portmanteau in hand and a determined look in her eyes. Celia and I tried to hold her here, of course, but she would not be stopped."

"Lucifer! She has a five-hour start on me. How is she traveling?"

"Post chaise. She intended to use the public coaches, but there I drew the line. William Reese is driving for her and will arrange accommodations along the way. She'll be perfectly safe under his protection. Oh, and she insisted on leaving me her written voucher to repay every penny of the costs, including Reese's salary. A headstrong young woman, your Miss Jennet."

"You don't know the first part of it." Knees melting under him, Kit dropped onto the sofa. "And her surname is actually Preston, by the way. Never mind why we told you otherwise. It's a long story."

Kendal steepled his hands. "Do you care to tell me what happened? It's perfectly obvious that she departed in a hurry to avoid seeing you again. Have you quarreled?"

"No more than usual. What set her off was my proposal of marriage, which she speedily rejected. That led to the quarrel, and now she's scarpered. Tell you what, Jimmie. I rarely know what to expect of her, but never once have I conceived of her running away. She stands her ground or she advances, but she never retreats."

"Going where she chooses to be is not an act of cowardice, Christopher. It is a decision. When a lady declines an offer of marriage, it must be accepted with good grace. You cannot compel her to be your wife."

"Don't bet on it. Nothing has changed since yesterday, save that now I must go and fetch her back." He took a drink of wine. "The moonbeam is proving devilish hard to snare."

"And that, I suspect, only whets your appetite for the hunt. Consider her feelings in this matter. Has it crossed your mind that she simply does not love you?"

"I thought of nothing else the whole of last night. It was the worst night of my life. Did you know, Jimmie, that thoughts have claws and fangs? That they can shred a man from the inside out? It was quite the revelation to me."

"I have felt them," Kendal said quietly. "Too often to count. You have been fortunate to have escaped those fangs and claws for so long a time."

"Last night was enough for any man, I assure you. But I wrestled the demons down." He grinned. "Good practice for the next match with my formidable Lucy. I need the use of your curricle, m'lord. And the bays."

Kendal groaned. "Not the *bays*."

"The bays," Kit said firmly, coming to his feet. "And a bit of the ready. Make it a large bit. I've no idea how long this is going to take."

"Dare I point out that you don't even know where to go?"

"Diana knows where she lives. I'll wring the information from her." At the door, he turned back. Kendal wore an expression of weary disapproval, which Kit had seen far too many times over the years. He'd given his brother more than enough reason for concern, God only knew, but this time he was aimed directly on target. "In case you are wondering, Jimmie, I do care about Lucy's feelings. Profoundly. And in this instance, I know better than she does what they are. The moonbeam loves me, that's certain, but she's got it in her head that she can't have me. I mean to convince her that she can't get rid of me."

Kendal shook his head. "Coxcomb."

Laughing, Kit took the stairs two at a time and came upon Celia as she was leaving Diana's room. She put a finger to her lips and drew him down the passageway to a small parlor.

"You are in remarkably good spirits, Kit. I rather expected you to be downcast at the news."

"Being downcast accomplishes nothing, in my experience. I'm going after her, of course, but I need to speak with Diana. Unless you chance to know where Lucy is headed."

"Not precisely. She once mentioned that her employer's estate was in Dorset, if that is of any use. Do please take a chair, Kit, before you knock something over."

"Sorry. I can't stay still. Chafing to be off, actually. Why did you wish to speak with me?"

"To prevent you from speaking with Diana, and you needn't glower. I'm on your side, you know. Don't forget that I pursued your brother quite shamelessly, with no regard to the rules of proper conduct, and I mean to help you as best I can. That does not include placing Diana in a difficult situation, however. She is unable to bear the weight of any more troubles, even if they are not her own."

"How so?" He was genuinely puzzled. "Everything has worked out far better than we had any reason to expect. I'd have thought she would be happy."

"Men! Sometimes I despair of the lot of you. Never mind that she is but ten-and-nine, has endured a terrible ordeal, has been brought to live among strangers, and will wear that scar for the rest of her life. She will be happy one day, please God, but not anytime soon."

Kit rubbed his head. "Lucy told me something of the like. And you are both right, of course. But why cannot I ask her one perfectly simple question?"

"Where Lucy has gone to? I asked that question myself, and I assure you that if she would not tell me, she'll not tell you. Lucy left her a good-bye letter, and apparently it contained a plea to keep her destination strictly secret. Think on it, Kit. Ought we to ask Diana to choose between loyalty to her friend and the sense of obligation she doubtless feels to us?"

He had heard words much like those some weeks ago, but at the time they had come from his own mouth. He'd been advising Lucy not to put Diana in a position similar to the one he'd been about to create by demanding an answer she could not in good conscience provide. "No, Celia. I'll not ask it of her. Forget I ever thought of doing so. But dammit, what am I to do? Call at every house in Dorset in hopes of finding Lucy there?"

"If you must. But I expect you can catch her along the way." She went to the escritoire and drew out paper, pen, and ink. "William Reese has made the journey south a hundred times or more. He knows the best places to change horses, have a decent meal, and spend the night. On the occasions James and I have traveled with him, he invariably stopped at the same posthouses."

"You're a trump, Celia!" He paused to ruffle her curls on the way to the door. "Write them down while I pack. And instruct a footman to put out a ladder and unlock the attic, will you? I mean to rummage through a few trunks."

"Mercy me. Whatever for?"

"Oh, there are all sorts of things up there. My ancestors were hoarders of the first order. Never threw anything away. You should have a look sometime."

Lucy made it through her first day on the road without a tear, but it took every ounce of her failing strength to hold them back until William Reese escorted her to her room at the comfortable posthouse where she was to spend the night.

Then her tears fell in torrents.

But by morning, which dawned cold and clear, she was dry-eyed again and even more firmly resolved to continue on. There had been times, a great many of them during her sleepless night, when she was tempted to turn back and accept whatever Kit could offer her, for however long it lasted. She had even come to the point of being willing to accept the pain when he tired of her and wandered off to another adventure and another woman. Surely a brief, shooting-star love was better than no love at all.

But reason prevailed. She had maneuvered through a life mostly crammed with closed doors by being practical about the few opportunities that opened to her. Beyond doubt her only hope for a secure future lay with Jonathan Stiles.

He no more loved her than she loved him, to be sure, but their circumstances did not permit either of them to be overly particular. A cleric in hopes of securing a parish of his own required a wife, and a governess longing for a home and children required a husband.

Jonathan was kindly, unimaginative, and steadfastly devoted to his duties. He rather feared her, she'd often thought. She was too plainspoken and assertive. He invariably stammered in her presence and rarely looked her directly in the eyes. It must have required an act of courage for him to approach her with an offer of marriage.

In the year that had passed since then, he had not dared to

press her for an answer. Now and again, when they met after services or at a charity event, he referred obliquely to the pending matter of their betrothal. But she always suspected he meant only to remind her that he stood ready to honor the proposal he had made. He certainly showed no great enthusiasm, and he was clearly in no rush to meet her at the altar.

She had done him a disservice, she thought guiltily, by withholding a response. He might have cast about for a more suitable bride had he not felt obligated to her. But he would have her answer shortly, and she would do her very best to make him a good wife.

She was picturing herself taking the vows, wondering how many lies she would be telling when she did so and trying in vain to remember what her future groom looked like, when the carriage suddenly veered to the right and shuddered to a halt.

"Stand and deliver!"

Dear heavens. She leaned forward and looked out the window.

Astride a gargantuan white horse, a spectacular creature brandished a sword in one hand and a pistol in the other. Sprung from a century or two ago, he was clad in midnight-blue brocade, with deep flared cuffs on his sleeves and bucket-topped boots that reached to his knees. Lace billowed at his throat and wrists. Atop a flamboyant black periwig sat a tall-crowned hat festooned with ostrich feathers.

Oh, for pity's sake! Lucy flung open the carriage door, jumped to the ground, stalked directly up to the would-be highwayman, and planted her hands on her hips. "What in all creation do you think you are doing?"

"Why, I'm pillaging and plundering, of course." He boomed his lines as if playing a part in another of his overwrought melodramas. "Surrender your valuables, wench, and be quick about it."

"Don't be ridiculous! And put away that gun before you shoot somebody."

"You quite disarm me, m'dear." He slipped the pistol into his saddle pack. "It isn't loaded, by the way."

"I should think not. The sword, too."

With a dramatic sigh, he slid it into the scabbard at his waist and swung down from the saddle. "Madam, you leave a gentleman of the road no choice but to pluck your treasures with his bare hands."

"Someone has plucked your wits, sir. Of all the fits and starts you have taken, this is the most addlepated yet. Now you get right back on that horse, Kit Valliant, and take yourself away this very instant!"

He laughed. "Is this how you address the unfortunate young fellows in your charge, my terrifying little governess? No wonder they went after your hair with a pair of shears."

Her cheeks burned from that telling blow, but she quickly rallied. "This is *precisely* how I deal with feckless, refractory little boys. And wherever did you come by that foul wig? I just saw a moth fly out of it."

"Lucifer!" He ripped it off and flung it to the ground. "Devilish uncomfortable things, wigs. Good thing I wasn't prowling about when they were all the crack. I rather fancy the lace, though." He waved his belaced wrists in the air. "What do you think? Shall I take up the fashion?"

She was seized with a pernicious desire to laugh. "Kit, do go away and allow me to proceed with my journey. Everything that needed to be said between us has already been said."

"I quite agree." He moved toward her. "Let us proceed directly to the kissing."

She backed up hastily, raising both hands to hold him away. "Don't you dare."

"Come now, sweetheart. We rogues have a reputation to maintain. Just one little kiss, for the road?"

"I am a betrothed woman, sir. And an honorable one. I'll not betray—" She couldn't think of his name! "My betrothed man," she added belatedly.

"Ah. I'm glad you mentioned him. I'd nearly forgot my main purpose for accosting you this fine afternoon. Wanting to kiss you never fails to send my wits scattering to the winds." He made a flourishing gesture. "Oh, look! There they go again."

The laugh rose in her throat, nearly choking her as she fought to hold it in. He truly was the most *impossible* man. "P-purpose," she reminded him.

"Wait." He raised a forefinger to his temple. "Yes. It's coming back to me now. I galloped all the way here to save a hapless cleric from a lifetime of misery."

Suppressed laughter transformed itself to fury. "That is a reprehensible thing to say! I shall make him an excellent wife."

"I'm certain you mean to try. But you will be unhappy, and perforce he will be unhappy. Stands to reason."

"Why should I not be happy? How little you understand, sir. I have wished above all things to have a home of my own to live in, and children of my own to care for."

"And marrying your curate is a means to that end, I presume? One might as well put an advertisement in the newspapers. 'Ferocious young woman requires compliant male to sire children. Must be in possession of a house.' "

"Oh, do stop it!"

" 'He mustn't mind that she is in love with another man, or that her thoughts will be with said other man on her wedding night and every night thereafter.' "

That was so true that she could find no words to throw back at him. And because it was true, she accepted that she could not, *must* not, marry Joshua. Jeremy? The *curate*.

The ground under her feet dissolved. She felt suspended in air. Any moment now she would plunge into a deep dark pit.

Two strong arms wrapped themselves around her. "You have disappointed me, moonbeam. I had not thought it possible you would run away. What became of the daring girl who set aside all else to help a friend? What happened to my brave Lucy, who risked her life to save a smuggler on the sands of Morecambe Bay?"

She drew a steadying breath. "I don't know who she is, Kit.

Someone who is not me. And I don't know who I am either. I don't seem to know anything at all."

"You know that you love me," he said simply.

Her mouth opened to deny it, but this was the one lie that she would never tell. She rested her head against his shoulder and said nothing.

"The trouble is, has *always* been, that you have made up your mind I'll hurt you." His fingers slipped through her hair. "You are afraid to give yourself into my keeping, and take me into yours, because you assume I'll not hold to my vows. Is that a fair thing to say?"

She mumbled a *yes* into the fall of lace at his throat. She could imagine no greater pain than allowing herself to trust him, only to have him betray her.

"Some people believe," he said, "that if you save a life, you become responsible for that life. My life belongs to you, moonbeam. I trust you to care for it the way I mean to care for you. Will you put faith in me, beloved? You may as well, because you'll not rid yourself of me. I'll hound you from here to Dorset and from there to the ends of the earth. Spare us both the chase, I beg you, and say you'll marry me."

Lucy raised her head, looked into his glorious blue eyes, and felt all her doubts and fears go up in flames. Just like that, she thought deliriously. Off they went like ashes in the wind.

"Mmm," he said, bringing his lips to hers. "I heard that *yes* you didn't say."

A long time later, after a great many elephants had thundered by, she gulped a deep breath and produced a firm, heartfelt "Yes."

She saw him close his eyes then, and saw a tear escape one corner to streak down his cheek. He hadn't been so sure of her as he'd made himself out to be, she realized, deeply touched. She held his happiness in her hands as surely as he held hers.

Tears blinded her own eyes for a moment. But when she was able to see him clearly again, a smile that was purely Kit's—

cocksure and dancing with good humor—wreathed his handsome face.

"Brace yourself, Lucy," he said in a mournful tone. "We have one more difficult task ahead of us, and we must confront it together."

Alarm seized her for the barest moment before skittering away. She knew to trust him now. "And what is that, sir?"

He contrived to look serious. "There is another female nearly as besotted with me as you are, I'm afraid. Have you forgot her, moonbeam? Just how are we to break the news of our betrothal, our *real* betrothal, to Miss Fidgets?"

"Trust me, Kit," she said, standing on tiptoe for a kiss. "He won't mind in the least."

*Coming next month, a sensual contemporary
love story you won't want to miss!*

BLUE CLOUDS

by Patricia Rice

Phillipa "Pippa" Cochran has a reputation of
being a regular Pollyanna who smiles her way
through life's tribulations. But when her mother
dies, her nursing career fails, and her fiancé
becomes abusive, Pippa loses her smile. She flees
across the country to live in California and is hired
sight unseen to care for the disabled young son of
Seth Wyatt, a wealthy, handsome, and difficult
recluse.

Unprepared for the altogether-too-attractive hur-
ricane that is Pippa, the troubled Seth and his
lonely son begin to blossom under her care. Then
a series of "accidents" threatens Seth's life as well
as the fragile love that has begun to grow between
Seth and Pippa. Determined to protect the man
she loves, Pippa is drawn into a dangerous game
of cat and mouse that could cost her this precious
new love.

Published by Fawcett Books.
Available wherever books are sold.

Want to know a secret?
It's sexy, informative, fun, and FREE!!!

🌿 PILLOW TALK 🌿

Join Pillow Talk and get advance information and sneak
peeks at the best in romance coming from Ballantine.
All you have to do is fill out the information below!

♥ My top five favorite authors are: _____

_____

_____

_____

_____

♥ Number of books I buy per month: ❏ 0-2 ❏ 3-5 ❏ 6 or more

♥ Preference: ❏ Regency Romance ❏ Historical Romance
       ❏ Contemporary Romance ❏ Other

♥ I read books by new authors: ❏ frequently ❏ sometimes ❏ rarely

Please print clearly:
Name _____

Address_____

City/State/Zip_____

Don't forget to visit us at
www.randomhouse.com/BB/loveletters

regency

*Patricia Veryan,
the reigning queen of Regency romance,
returns with*

THE RIDDLE OF
ALABASTER ROYAL

Captain Jack Vespa, a soldier fresh from battling
Napoleon, is searching for a quiet, peaceful place
to recover from his wounds. To recuperate, he
heads for Alabaster Royal, his country mansion
rumored to be the local "haunted house." What
he does not know is that residing at his new
home is the bewitching Miss Consuela Jones.
Determined to solve a murder, this spirited young
woman believes the old manse is visited by ghosts.
But it is she who will come to haunt Captain
Vespa and bring him to his knees under the spell
of a love too fierce to be denied.

Published by Fawcett Books.
Coming next month to your local bookstore.

Coming next month . . .

THE PIRATE PRINCE

by Gaelen Foley

Taken captive by a fearsome and infuriating pirate captain come to plunder her island home of Ascension, the beautiful Allegra Monteverdi struggles to deny her growing passion for her intriguing captor. Lazar di Fiore is a rogue with no honor and has nothing in common with the man of her dreams—the honorable and courageous crown prince of Ascension, who is presumed murdered with the rest of the royal family by treacherous enemies of the throne.

But Allegra has badly misjudged Lazar, a man with a tragic past and demons that give him no peace. He harbors a secret that could win him Allegra's love and restore freedom and prosperity to Ascension, if his sworn enemies do not destroy him first. And the greatest battle of all must be fought within Lazar's own heart as Allegra tries to prove that, prince or pirate, he is truly the man that she has always dreamed of.

Published by Fawcett Books.
Available wherever books are sold.